The Purple Fence on the Boardwalk

a novel by

Andi Thomas Peters

The Purple Fence on the Boardwalk

ISBN Paperback: 978-1-955032-01-8
ISBN Kindle: 978-1-955032-00-1
ISBN Hardback: 978-1-955032-02-5

www.Andithomaspeters.com

To My Sister Denise,

With love and gratitude for being the consummate cheerleader and reason I attempted to spread my wings...

Part I

Chapter 1

Francie

Every summer, Mom and I would pack the station wagon and move from our home in the Garden District of New Orleans to our home in Blakely Point, Alabama. A little more than a two-hour drive, it seemed to take forever to get there.

I would make sure Becca and Luna were buckled in their seat belts, and we would excitedly start talking about what we would do when we arrived. Becca and Luna were my best friends, and, in fact, my only friends. We loved Blakely Point. We couldn't wait to get there.

Blakely Point was a small town on the Gulf Coast. By the age of seven, I knew that its population of roughly 1,500 people was more my style than New Orleans. It was quiet; it was calm, and it was peaceful. I didn't feel those nervous twitches in my face or stomach there, like I did in NOLA. Blakely Point was a magic wand; it made my anxiety disappear.

Then, I thought all the homeowners in Blakely Point, like us, enjoyed sweeping views of the turquoise water of Mobile Bay. But, the view was only offered to those homes along the boardwalk.

The two-mile boardwalk dissected the Antebellum estates from the long piers extending into Mobile Bay. Picket fences, all the same height, standing like uniformed soldiers, created a border between the flawlessly manicured lawns and the boardwalk. Residents either spent their time on the water fishing, boating, sailing, or sitting on their large porches absorbing the views of the Bay.

Most days, I felt that Becca, Luna and I had the entire Bay to ourselves. We would go on long bike rides and climb the big oak trees that canopied the boardwalk, swim at the pool at the nearby Blakely Bay Inn, build sandcastles on the shore or tell stories while sitting on the dock.

We would be relieved and ecstatic when Mom's station wagon turned onto Scenic Highway 98. It signaled that we were close to our summer destination. It meant that I was close to its magical healing. It also meant we survived the Wallace Tunnel and the Jubilee Parkway.

Luna and I thought it was cool that the tunnel took you under Mobile River. I thought it was like being in a submarine traveling through a tube. Luna thought it was like traveling in a spaceship, with the rows of continuous bright lights running along the domed ceiling.

Both scenarios freaked out Becca. I tried to comfort her that everything would be OK because Mom had the chakra system of energy crystals. I didn't really understand what that meant at the time.

As we would pass through downtown Mobile, before entering the tunnel, Mom would pull out her crystals and place them on the dashboard. She said, "they created cosmic energy flow." Becca never believed in the crystals; she thought it was a "bunch of hooey." She would start singing "Jesus Loves Me" with her eyes clinched shut until the tunnel deposited us along the twin bridges of the Jubilee Parkway.

"Hooey" or not, the crystals never failed to deliver Mom safely through the tunnel and across the river. I always thought that if Mom truly believed in her crystals, why did she sit at the edge of her seat gripping the steering wheel during the entire half-mile underwater passage and the seven-and-half-mile voyage over the viaduct bridge? Her fingers were curled so rigidly around that wheel that I thought they may get stuck that way.

She didn't start relaxing until the exit onto Scenic Highway 98, which meant we would soon be sipping milkshakes from Tutti's Soda Shoppe.

A visit to Tutti's was our reward for stopovers in Fairchild, the quaint little town near Blakely Point and the location of Mom's two favorite stores: Farrah's and Herb's Earth House.

Farrah's was a cool, eclectic artsy shop. Mom would load up on oils for her homemade soaps, incense for her tiki torches, and Kombucha teas for her kettle. Since these supplies could have easily been purchased in New Orleans, a stop at Farrah's unnecessarily prolonged our arrival at Blakely Point.

I realized that the real reason for the stop was to see Farrah, Mom's only friend in Fairchild or Blakely Point, for that matter. Farrah was about as much of a fish out of water in Fairchild as Mom was in Blakely Point, and I was in New Orleans.

Herbert, the proprietor of Herb's Earth House, was Mom's local source for an array of items. In addition to the herbs for her Cajun dishes, she would stuff big flowing ferns, jasmine, and other plants for our backyard into the station wagon. Herbert would be awaiting our arrival because there was a dedicated spot for Mom in the botanical garden area where he set aside his new inventory of torches, chimes, and metal trellises. My favorite things amongst all his selections were the iridescent glass orbs and the variety of pedestal iron bases for the globes.

The stops at Farrah's and Herb's Earth House marked the start of the summer. Tutti's milkshakes were the exclamation point, worthy of a heart, heart, heart emoji, if emojis existed then. I always ordered banana, and Becca, vanilla. Luna was a crapshoot. Her choices varied from Chocolate with gummi worms, Rocky Road with extra marshmallows, or Neapolitan with an extra scoop of strawberry.

July was my favorite month of the summer because that was when my dad, the Honorable Hugh LeBlanc, would join us. July kicked off his three-week vacation. The courthouse closed on the week of July 4th, and my father, a state court judge in the Orleans Parish District Court, tacked on two weeks of personal vacation. When Dad arrived, he would take us all around Mobile Bay in the boat and fish with us off our long pier. One summer, Becca caught the biggest speckled sea trout I had ever seen. Luna thought fishing was boring; she preferred tubing in the Bay where she never fell off like Becca and me. She would yell at my dad, "Faster, faster!"

The best parts were the sleepovers in our boathouse every July 3rd and 4th. The boathouse was perched at the end of our pier, which extended 250 feet into Mobile Bay. Luna said it was like a floating boat, and she loved being on a boat. Becca thought it was more like a treehouse on the water. I thought they both were right.

Our boathouse had a bedroom, a small kitchenette, and a bathroom. Becca and I avoided the toilet at all cost due to the holding tank that required emptying. We thought that was gross. Luna said it was cool. I think she said that because the big house was too far away.

The big house was an antebellum style built in the 1880s. Its three stories had four, large bedrooms (the fifth bedroom was added later). Its massive, wrap-around porch boasted the largest frontage on the boardwalk. Even after I picked up on the reason that we stayed in the boathouse during those two days, I still loved those times. I loved the reflections of the red, white, and blue fireworks on the water, but my dad's history lessons were the best part.

Dad loved American history. Had he not gone to law school, he would have been a teacher. He would have been great at that too. I learned more history from Dad over the years than in any classroom.

Beginning at breakfast every July 3rd, Dad set the scene of the days leading up to the signing of the Declaration of Independence. He emphasized that the authors of the magical document had taken great risks. They knew that if the revolution failed, they would lose their fortunes and their lives. In his rich recount of the era, he always included the words between John Hancock and Benjamin Franklin: "We must be unanimous...we must all hang together," Hancock said. "Yes, we must, indeed, all hang together, or most assuredly, we shall all hang separately," Franklin added.

Though Luna rarely sat still, she was like a knot on a log during Dad's historical tribute. He explained that even after our founding fathers reached consensus on all the words pronouncing freedom from the British, there were still some who were very reluctant to sign the document and others who signed with deep regret. "They were bold and brave," Dad would say before starting the annual recitation of the Preamble of the Declaration:

> When in the Course of human events it becomes necessary for one people to dissolve the political bonds which have connected them with another, and to assume among the powers of the earth, the separate and equal station to which the Laws of Nature and of Nature's God entitle them, a decent respect to the opinions of mankind requires that they should declare the causes which impel them to the separation. ...

By then, we knew the next part by heart and would recite it with my dad:

> We hold these truths to be self-evident that all men are created equal, that they are endowed by their Creator with certain unalienable Rights, that among these are Life, Liberty and the pursuit of Happiness....

My father explained that the bulk of the document highlighted the list of complaints that the colonies asserted against the British, the reasons they sought independence. When I was too little to understand much of this, he didn't elaborate. With each passing year, he began illuminating, little by little, examples of the complaints: taxation without representation, the British cutting off trade and the deprivation of a right to a jury trial.

Becca, Luna and I would sit mesmerized by Dad's account. It was so vivid that we were right there with the Continental

Congress, scared and nervous. With each passing year, there would be more color and more information revealed about the events leading up to July 4, 1776. Luna's favorite part was the ending when the drafters declared their right to become "Free and Independent States and Absolved from all Allegiance to the British Crown."

Luna would stand up and twirl around waving her hands in the air. She would cheer, "Put your hands in the sky and spell V-I-C-T-O-R-Y!"

Afterward, we would light sparklers on the dock, and wait for the fireworks display from the nearby Blakely Bay Inn. Dad's activities distracted me from the real reason that we abandoned the big house for the boathouse on July 3rd and 4th. It was a way to commemorate America's history and avoid any re-opened wounds from Mom's history. I did share the reason with Becca and Luna on the day of my discovery, though I was too old for my imaginary friends then.

Chapter 2

Francie

I was twelve when I learned the reason we spent July 3rd and July 4th in the boathouse. Since I had outgrown Becca and Luna (although, admittedly, I still talked to them from time to time), I wasn't preoccupied with our activities. Now, it was just Mom's. Each summer, I was learning some new revelation—like the Mercury in retrograde.

When Mom's crystals, incense, herbs, and teas failed to ward off the demons inhabiting her brain, she blamed these episodes on Mercury's backward orbit. Initially, this path was responsible for miscommunication, travel woes, or mechanical issues. But, with each passing year, Mercury's reverse course seemed to cast a much larger shadow over our household. During that period, Mom avoided all kinds of activities, except her relaxation devices.

That day for instance, she said that she needed a long soak in the tub with her homemade soaps, Turbinado sugar scrub, and Jojoba oil. Apparently, she also needed some of her "special" herbs that were commingled among her basil, chives, rosemary, and thyme growing in the large terracotta pots in the backyard. When she returned from her "herb garden," on her way up the stairs for her bath, she thought she discreetly slipped one of Grandpa's vintage pipes in the pocket of her bathrobe.

It was a couple of summers ago when I first witnessed the activities of the "Les Trois Mousquetaires," what Mom, Farrah, and Herbert called their posse. The French name certainly sounded more sophisticated than their unsophisticated behavior, so I just referred to them simply as "The Three Musketeers."

I thought that Grandpa Hollingsworth was probably rolling in his grave when Les Trois Mousquetaires began using his pipes for some of the herbs purchased from Herb's Earth House, now growing in Mom's planters. When I first saw Herbert smoking a pipe, I didn't think anything about it. But Farrah and Mom? Now that was something else! I had never seen a woman smoke a pipe, even in New Orleans. It seemed so unladylike. But, what was even more uncouth was the way Mom and Farrah seemed to lose all inhibitions when puffing on those pipes. They would twirl each other around, sing, and laugh. Mom's dignified aura seemed to take flight in the wind, like the bellows of smoke that came out of her mouth and even her nose! Farrah's giggles were sort of cute, but Mom's guffaws were accompanied with unattractive snorts.

Grandpa raised his daughter to know better, and he would have never permitted her hanging out with the likes of Herbert and Farrah. I knew that because even then, I overheard lots of things about the Hollingsworth family. Everything I previously heard was confirmed; and I learned so much more that day.

Because of Mercury in retrograde, Mom couldn't dare tackle cleaning out the crow's nest. This was a problem because the local handyman was scheduled to arrive the next day to replace the warped floors and reglaze the window frames. The bowed window frames had leaked for some time, particularly during the recent tropical storm that blew through Blakely Point. But for the water stain on Daddy's bedroom ceiling, who knows when the extensive damage would have been discovered. Because the stain was in Daddy's room, it wasn't noticed timely.

By then, Dad had advanced beyond the state court and was now sitting on the federal bench as the Chief Judge for the United States District Court for the Eastern District of Louisiana. So, his weekend visits became sporadic, and he could no longer be absent for three weeks in July—only the week of July 4th. Also, by this time, he and Mom slept in separate bedrooms. Mercury in retrograde had something to do with that too.

"Francie, sweetie," Mom said, as she walked up the stairs with one of Grandpa's pipes in the pocket of her robe, "please take the bins from the crow's nest to your father's room. I'll treat you to a new outfit at Aurora's after Mercury gets back on track."

Aurora was added to Mom's circle of friends after Mom's discovery of her funky clothing store in the nearby town of Daphne. When Aurora joined the threesome, they changed their name to Les Quatre Mousquetaires. Though there was a certain ring to it, I stuck with the English version for their clique, the Four Musketeers, and I also rejected Mom's twist on the name for the new addition to the group.

Mom called Aurora, "Aurora from Daphne." When I asked her why, she said that she liked the "ring of it," and Aurora liked it too. Aurora thought it made her sound like royalty, like Princess Anne of Edinburgh.

The offerings in Aurora's shop in Daphne were definitely not appropriate for a royal. At the age of twelve, I was confident that the funky Bohemian styles weren't for me either, though I did love all the different plaits that Aurora expertly interweaved through my hair.

The truth was that I didn't need to be bribed at all, with a new outfit from Aurora's, with a milkshake from Tutti's, or anything else. My previous trepidation in entering the crow's nest was replaced with an irresistible curiosity. Only because Mercury was in retrograde was I permitted to enter the room without Mom's accompaniment, oversight, and rushed exit.

Mom kept the key to the locked door, and our previous visits only lasted long enough to add more plastic bins. So,

I was looking forward to an extended exploration of the room and the sweeping views of the Bay from this vantage point. If Luna was around, she would have rushed right up there with me; Becca would have probably peed in her pants.

The crow's nest was Frankie's bedroom, Mom's only brother, and after whom I was named. During our previous limited visits, Mom didn't let me linger or touch anything, especially Frankie's model airplanes, which were still in perfect alignment on the shelves. In every picture that I could recall of the uncle I never met, he seemed to always have a plane in his hand. Mom said that Frankie was obsessed with planes and had even been a pilot.

When I asked Mom why Uncle Frankie's room was in the crow's nest, she explained that they needed an extra bedroom after their twin sisters were born. And he loved it up there. He felt like he was in the sky.

He and Mom used to spend hours launching his planes out of the windows. I could tell from the limited stories Mom would share that she and Frankie were thick as thieves. They were only twelve months apart, and six years passed before her twin sisters arrived. This meant that during the summer months, Frankie and Mom shared a bedroom, until the "time came for Frankie to have his own room," Mom said, laughing. I never thought it was funny then, but I guess I sort of do now.

When I entered, I didn't touch Uncle Frankie's model airplanes, but I did survey the contents of the bins before hauling them down the stairs. I was surprised at their organization, a trait that Mom did not possess or one that she had lost over the years. I started thinking these bins were the product of Weezie, the grandmother that I never got to meet either.

The green bins contained nativity figurines, ornaments, a tree stand, and other holiday decorations; the contents of the orange bins ranged from pumpkins, bats, and witches to Pilgrims and miniature turkeys; the clear bins held Easter baskets, bunnies, and lots of plastic eggs. None of these holiday decorations were ever displayed in the house. The red bins outnumbered the other colors by far. After opening the first one, I felt a pit in my stomach.

One entire red bin was filled with American flags and red, white, and blue banners. Another red bin contained red checkered tablecloths, patriotic wreaths, garlands, paper plates and napkins, streamers, and anything else you could have imagined for an Independence Day celebration. Mom never used any of these decorations. But, it was the next red bin that was filled with scrapbooks and newspaper clippings that made me weep.

Chapter 3

Francie

July 4, 1989

"A Beechcraft King Air-200 crashed at 8:35 a.m. near Baton Rouge, Louisiana. The ten-seater plane took off from Houston, Texas, for an Independence Day family gathering in Blakely Point, Alabama. The number of passengers has not been confirmed, but all onboard appear to have perished. The National Transportation Safety Board is investigating the cause of the crash."

July 5, 1989

"It has been confirmed there were five passengers aboard the Beechcraft King Air-200 that crashed yesterday in the Mississippi River near Baton Rouge, Louisiana. None survived.

The King Air-200 was owned by Arthur Francis Hollingsworth, III (Art) and piloted by his son, Arthur Francis Hollingsworth, IV (Frankie).

Art's wife, Louise LeJeune Emerson Hollingsworth, and his twin daughters, Vivian Louise and Charlotte Emerson, were also aboard the plane. The Hollingsworth family was en route to their vacation home in Blakely Point, Alabama to celebrate Independence Day. The family reportedly attended a Debutante Gala on July 2. The family delayed their scheduled departure on July 3 due to Tropical Storm Maureen. When the family departed Texas in the early morning on July 4th, the weather was clear, but as they approached Louisiana, the National Weather Service issued a severe fog advisory. Weather is believed to have been a factor in the accident.

LeJeune (Junie) Hollingsworth LeBlanc, the oldest daughter and a resident of New Orleans, is expecting the first grandchild, so she was unable to attend her sisters' debuts in Houston. Junie and her husband, the Honorable Hugh LeBlanc, were at the Blakely Point residence when they learned of the crash.

Art Hollingsworth, a resident of Houston, Texas, was a successful businessman and philanthropist. He and his wife, affectionately known as "Weezie," were active in the community dedicating numerous volunteer hours and financial support for a host of charitable causes. In lieu of flowers, Junie Hollingsworth LeBlanc requests that donations be made to the Houston Food Bank where Mr. Hollingsworth was Chairman of the Board of Directors."

My hands were shaking as I picked up a big scrapbook. As I flipped through the pages, the photographs and captions chronicled every July 4th from the time my mother was born. The patriotic decorations I saw in the bins were in full display in some of the pictures.

There was a picture of Mom sitting on a bicycle with training wheels. She wore a white dress with American flags smocked across the front, her hair in pigtails, one tied with a red bow and the other with a blue bow. Red, white, and blue streamers were woven between the spokes of her bicycle tires and dangled from her handlebars. The caption under the picture: *Junie, 4 years old. The Inaugural Parade.*

Underneath Mom's picture was a page from the June 1969 Blakely Bay Inn newsletter:

"We are excited to announce our first July 4th parade. Weezie Hollingsworth has worked hard in planning this inaugural event, so we hope you will participate. This is an opportunity to show your creativity and patriotic spirit from your attire to the decorations for your bicycles, wagons, scooters, and strollers. We also encourage spectators to line the parade route and cheer on our participants.

The parade will start from the Hollingsworth residence at 10:00 a.m., then proceed down the boardwalk around the Inn property and finish at the gazebo where we will have ice cream and snow cones for all participants. Awards will be provided in various age categories from Most Patriotic to Most Creative. See ya on the boardwalk!"

I always found it odd that anyone could walk through our property on the boardwalk and some were even bold enough to walk down our pier to check out our boathouse. Dad explained that state Supreme Court ruled that the boardwalk was a public walkway, which meant that waterfront property owners, like us, would have to tolerate the tourists and others that traversed this part of our property.

From the pictures in Grandma Weezie's scrapbooks, I thought she must have celebrated the public access. She not only organized a parade on the boardwalk from our house, but also welcomed the onlookers, especially on July 4th. She spared no expense with the yard decorations. The white picket fence was draped in the flag garland that I saw in one of the red bins. Our fence in the pictures looked like all the others on the boardwalk; it was white. I wondered when Mom painted it purple. I wondered when the start of the parade route was moved from our house. Not only did the inaugural parade start here (obviously Weezie's idea), but also every one after that.

Each parade was memorialized in the scrapbook. One year, Uncle Frankie was dressed up like Uncle Sam. His tall "Stars and Stripes" hat looked about as big as he was. Mom wore a blue bonnet with a matching blue dress and a big red bow. She carried a wooden pole with an American flag attached to it. The caption under their pictures read: *Uncle Sam and Betsy Ross. Most Patriotic Award!*

In all the pictures, Aunt Viv and Aunt Emi wore matching outfits, except one year. That year, according to the caption, they dressed up as Benjamin Franklin and Thomas Jefferson. They must have burned up in those outfits with their gray wigs and brown coats with big brass buttons. They probably forgot any discomfort because the next page revealed: *Viv and Emi. Most Creative Award!*

Even when the Hollingsworth clan outgrew participating in the parade, there were pictures of Mom, Frankie, Viv, and Emi clad in stylish red, white, and blue outfits. They were smiling, waving flags, and cheering the participants. There was a great picture of Mom and Uncle Frankie, both laughing, his arm around her shoulder, and her head on his. The caption: 1980: *Frankie and Junie.*

I began wondering what happened to Mom's best friend, the girl who was photographed with her every year until 1981, when Mom was sixteen. The last picture of the BFFs captured them arm-in-arm with baseball caps turned backwards, both grinning from ear-to-ear, both in braided pigtails, both their lips stained red from the snow cones they were eating, and with Uncle Frankie's photo-bomb. The caption: 1981: *Junie and her bestie, CiCi (and suddenly Frankie!).* Mom looked so happy.

Tears welled up in my eyes. I wished I had known them, even for a little while. Why couldn't I have experienced even one parade with my grandparents, uncle and aunts?

It was suddenly all making sense to me—why Mom never let me participate in the parade, why we retreated to the boathouse the evening of July 3rd, why we didn't return to the big house until July 5th, and why Mom always wore black on July 4th. After the crash, Mom just couldn't bear to be in the big house for even one minute on July 4th. That is what I thought, and what I continued to believe until Farrah's visit three years later.

Chapter 4

Francie

Dad called to say that he was arriving later than usual on the eve of Independence Day. I never heard my parents argue before that phone call. Mom placed Dad on speaker phone, so she could continue the preparations with the machines she pulled out every July 3rd. She explained that the apparatuses helped pull the moisture from the air. Before that day, I believed her.

"I know what you are doing, Hugh," Mom said. "I saw Ophiuchus last night."

"Who the hell is Ophiuchus?"

"He is the northwest center of the Milky Way."

"Oh. What did this particular constellation say to you, Junie?"

I have never heard Dad use this tone with Mom. I certainly knew before now that Mom was just a little quirky; truthfully, it was more than just a little. I was even beginning to believe Bethany Brooks' characterization of my mother.

Bethany was my age and spent the summers at their family's vacation home next door. After I was too old for Becca and Luna, I asked Bethany to ride bikes one day. She said that she couldn't because her daddy would give her a good belt whipping. He thought my mother was cuckoo and instructed her to steer clear of my family.

Cuckoo or not, in the past, Dad went along with Mom's prognostications based on her cosmic energy theories. I knew he never bought into them. He would smile and wink at me when she started burning her camphor incense. He'd good-naturedly utter, "Aquarius must be in the Seventh House." But today, he sounded disgusted and condescending. His tone was just plain mean.

"He didn't have to say anything. It's the fact that I saw him. Ophiuchus was grasping Serpens."

"Junie, you aren't making any sense. Have you already been into Art's pipes?"

"No, Hugh, I haven't. Serpens is a constellation representing a snake. It means you and your penis are up to something, and guess what, I don't care. Why don't you just stay in New Orleans with her? No need to pretend for Francie anymore. She's old enough to know the truth."

She ran out of the door with Dad still on the phone.

"Junie, calm down. Junie? Junie? Junie, are you there?"

I was frozen in space. I couldn't speak, I couldn't move. My legs felt like concrete. Then, I heard Dad say over the speaker, "That didn't go so well. That nutcase hung up on me! Like I told you, she is nuttier than ever."

I heard a woman laughing.

"Well, I love YOUR nuts. And I want them now. Come here."

"I love you, Ginnie, and will gladly...." Then, the phone went dead.

I ran out to the porch and flung myself face down onto our big swing. I buried my head into the pillows and began sobbing. The porch swing, with its endless views of Mobile Bay, always calmed me down.

It calmed me down the day when Bethany Brooks called my mother "cuckoo." It calmed me down when her father, Charles Brooks, yelled at our yard guy to "start painting that damned purple fence and remove all the SHIT." It calmed me down when I learned that Charles Brooks' wife, Celeste, was Mom's former bestie, CiCi, who was right next door but whom I had never met. It calmed me down when Mom opened the complaint that Charles Brooks filed with the Blakely Point Preservation Society complaining about us. It calmed me down the day I read the complaint's contents: "LeJeune LeBlanc's gauche defacement of her yard and surroundings is eroding our refined heritage. Her activities are a menace to the boardwalk." It even calmed me down when I overheard Dorothy Reynolds, the manager of the Blakely Bay Inn's gift shop, telling some stranger that "the Hollingsworths used to be the most prominent family on the boardwalk. I just hate to think what Weezie and Art are thinking watching all of Junie's shenanigans. So sad."

The porch swing and the Bay views, my medicine for whatever ailed me, eventually were replaced with much stronger medicines to manage my anxiety and depression (I'll get to that later). That day, I felt a much deeper darkness, a deeper hole. I knew that these feelings couldn't be fixed by my porch swing because I could no longer look at the water. I was afraid of what I would do. I imagined that I was flinging myself into Mobile Bay. I was feeling the current take me away, far away.

My images were abruptly interrupted by a tap on my shoulder. I lurched so violently that I almost fell right out of the swing.

"Francie, what's the matter, darlin'?"

Farrah was standing there with a big straw basket filled with oils that Mom purchased from her shop. I threw my face back down into the pillows. Farrah began stroking my hair.

"It's OK if you don't want to talk about it, but I'm always here for you, Francie. I'll just take these things inside for your mom. Is she here?"

I nodded my head negatively and remained planted in the cushions. From the jolted rock of the swing, I knew Farrah sat down. She began rubbing my back. Then she started singing:

"When the moon is in Heaven's House, and the Jubilee aligns with Mars, then peace will heal the people and light up all the stars."

I knew the song. After Farrah, Herbert, Aurora, and Mom smoked Grandpa's pipes, they would sing the classic Fifth Dimension song, "Aquarius." Though Farrah butchered the words, her voice was sweet.

"Farrah could make a killing if she learned how to bottle her soothing spirit," Mom always said.

Mom was right; Farrah's "soothing spirit" was the reason that I didn't throw myself into Mobile Bay that day. After Farrah finished singing to me, she peeled me off the swing and said I needed to help her.

"It is time to cleanse the house. Time is of the essence," she said, convincingly.

It was the urgency in her voice that snapped me out of my melt-down. She picked up the basket and led me into the kitchen. She started removing the oils and instructed me to fill the "vaporizers." That day, I learned the real purpose of the machines that Mom retrieved from Frankie's room every July 3rd.

"This is patchouli," Farrah said. "It helps relax our emotional energy and keeps us grounded."

She placed the oils along with water into the machine and turned it on. It released vapors that didn't smell so great.

"This is neroli," Farrah said. She began the same preparation. She moved into the den and plugged in another machine. "Neroli heals your mind, body, and spirit."

"This is bergamot," Farrah said. "It releases stress and anxiety."

I liked the smell of the bergamot the best, as the aroma began filling the dining room.

"Your mom wants this one in her room," she said, so we proceeded to Mom's bedroom with the ylang ylang. "It balances energies, relieves stress, and restores equilibrium and confidence. A multi-purpose oil," Farrah said. "Junie likes ylang ylang mixed with lavender. Junie insists on myrrh for your room," as we headed into my room with a machine.

"What is myrrh for?" I asked. I was getting some insight into why our family abandoned the big house on July 3rd.

"Myrrh is versatile like ylang ylang—it cleanses and heals, it provides emotional balance, and even helps your skin," Farrah said, as she placed the machine in my room.

We placed rosemary in Dad's room. Farrah said it "warded off evil spirits." I thought that the evil spirits had something to do with Ginnie, the woman's voice I heard through the speaker.

When Mom finally showed up, she flung the kitchen door wide open and sprinted in. Farrah assured her that the cleansing was right on schedule.

"Oh, thank you, thank you, thank you, my child," Mom said to Farrah. "I can't believe that I lost track of the time on this of all days."

I never knew where Mom went. If she hadn't disappeared, I would have never learned about the annual ritual in our house the eve of every July 4th. I was getting the picture that the cleansing seemed to have something to do with the demons that Mom was convinced killed her family. But, even Farrah's oils weren't strong enough to eliminate the demons taking up residence in Mom's brain and knocking on my door. They weren't even strong enough to temper the chaos that was on the horizon.

Chapter 5

Francie

After that cleansing exercise with Farrah, I started believing that myrrh worked some sort of magic for me. It was the summer of 2005.

Dad was still AWOL, and I wondered if he was going to show up at all. Mom was gone too.

"On a boat ride with Farrah, Aurora from Daphne and Herbert," the note Mom left me said.

I was beginning to grow fond of "Les Quatre Mousquetaires" for a lot of reasons. I knew they were loyal. They loved Mom for who she was or had become. Never in a million years would they file a complaint with the Blakely Point Preservation Society.

Becca and Luna were retired as friends with whom I talked and played. But, I still wrote to them or, to clarify, wrote about them. So, I picked up my "Becca and Luna" journal and walked down the boardwalk to the Blakely Bay Inn's pool. I was so engrossed in writing about my former imaginary friends that I didn't notice the good-looking boy until he sat down beside me.

"Is this chair taken?" he asked.

"Uh, no. No, it's not," I stammered.

"I have been watching you. I've noticed that you have been writing away. What are you working on?"

I was embarrassed. I was not about to disclose to the first boy to ever initiate a conversation with me that I was writing about imaginary friends who existed in the Land of Cuckoo, according to Bethany Brooks. He would have run for the hills.

"Oh, it's nothing," I answered, as I hurriedly closed my journal.

He asked if it was my first time at the Inn. He had never seen me before. Not surprisingly, no one ever noticed me. But today was different. Bethany and her gang kept staring at us, wondering I'm sure what this hunk could find interesting about me.

I spent the rest of the morning with Henry Pritchard DeVries and learned that his family celebrated the week of every July 4th in Blakely Point for as long as he could remember. He was from Ann Arbor, Michigan. His father and mother were both professors at the University, but his mother had grown up in Florida. Her father had served in the Air Force and was stationed at the Naval Air Station in Pensacola. So that is why they "had to come every year," he said, "to continue the tradition of his mother's family."

"I've always hated it before now," Henry said, as he leaned in to kiss me after he walked me home.

After I got in bed in the boathouse that July 4th, I closed my eyes to try and relive my first kiss. I didn't know if I was more excited about the actual kiss or that a boy finally kissed me. I must have been the only rising high school junior who had never kissed a boy. I quickly forgot about Mom's demons, Dad's girlfriend, and everything else. All that seemed to matter was Henry DeVries and if he could tell that it was my first kiss!

We kept in touch, and, the next summer, the summer before my senior year, I led Henry to the porch swing at the big house. That July 3rd, I knew that Mom wouldn't venture within five feet of the house while Farrah's oils were in the cleansing process, so I was safe from any interruptions. "You and Me" by Lifehouse began playing over our speakers as Henry kissed me, putting his hand in my bathing suit top. I found myself touching him and wanting him right there on the swing, thinking that the song was prophetic.

He said to meet him the next morning in their family suite. His sisters and parents would be participating in the Independence Day Parade on the boardwalk. I looked up into the sky and silently said, "Thank you, Grandma

Weezie." Though I had never participated in the parade that she originated, without it, I wouldn't have this opportunity with Henry. It seemed very karmic.

And I did go to Henry's room the next day, July 4, 2006, the day that I lost my virginity. I was in love. I was nervous to disclose to Dad that I applied for an early decision determination to the University of Michigan. Initially, I was shocked that Dad was so supportive. But the more I thought about it, the greater the distance between us, the more he could carry on with his mistress. He communicated his support differently.

"It's a great fit! The faculty is composed of award-winning writers ranging from novelists, short story writers, and poets," he reasoned.

Dad knew that my favorite pastime was writing. He encouraged me to pursue my talent. I'm not sure he really thought I was talented, but he knew that my writing saved me over the years. I reviewed the English Department's website again.

"Along the way, you write a few pieces that, in the words of Robert Frost (the University's first Fellow in Creative Arts), 'will be hard to get rid of.'"

Turns out, numerous pieces of mine were "hard to get rid of." I was on my way to becoming one of those award-winning writers referred to on the University of Michigan's website; and at that time, I credited it to Farrah's oils.

Everything seemed to be "emotionally balanced" and "in sync with positive cosmic energy."

I finished my degree in three and half years and focused on my book, *The Adventures of Becca & Luna.* Since Henry's tuition was covered due to his parents' tenured positions, he took his time. When Henry finally graduated and passed his CPA exam, my book was published, reached record sales, and was nominated for many children's book awards. We celebrated his graduation and my book success at the Blakely Bay Inn that summer. We exchanged our wedding vows on June 22, 2012. I attributed it all to Farrah and her myrrh.

Chapter 6

Francie

After the success of the Becca and Luna sequels, my agent encouraged me to write my first novel, *Crash & Burn*. While it was fiction, it admittedly provided a glimpse into my childhood, the loss of my grandparents, my uncle, and my aunts. And, it detailed how the remaining family member coped.

The only remaining Hollingsworth family member didn't like it one bit. "Blasphemous" was the word Mom used in her critique. Aside from my mother, it was a hit—number one on *The New York Times* Best Seller list for six consecutive weeks.

My publisher paid me an advance for a sequel, *After the Crash & Burn*. The future was rocking right along, until Mercury in retrograde immediately halted the trajectory of my success.

I didn't know what was more shocking—Mom's news on my voicemail or the cool indifference in her voice.

"Your father has been shot. He is in the hospital. Thanks."

Shot?? Hospital? Then, "thanks"???? Did I hear her correctly? I replayed the message over at least five times. I knew that her telephone etiquette was odd, but seriously — "Thanks"—after the delivery of such disturbing news?

My frantic calls to her cell went unanswered. Mom detested talking on the phone; hence, she rarely answered any call. How could she not answer after her message? Henry immediately began googling "Hugh LeBlanc New Orleans."

There were a number of articles immediately displayed. We didn't need to read past the first one.

October 6, 2018

"Hugh LeBlanc, the Chief Judge for the United States District Court for the Eastern District of Louisiana, is in intensive care after suffering a gun-shot wound as he was exiting the Federal Courthouse. Judge LeBlanc is presiding over a matter involving federal racketeering charges. It is believed that Judge LeBlanc was the intended target."

Mom's cell phone continued to go into voicemail, and the land line went unanswered. I needed to start calling the local hospitals and check flights to New Orleans but couldn't seem to do much of anything except lay in bed with a pillow over my head. When Henry came into our bedroom at 3:00 p.m., the look on his face said it all.

"The Honorable Hugh LeBlanc died from a gunshot wound sustained earlier today, as he exited the Federal Courthouse. The judge's law clerk, Virginia Smith, who was by his side at the time of the shooting, suffered only minor injuries and has been discharged," the article revealed.

I learned, by now, that the "Ginnie" I heard on the speaker phone years earlier was Dad's long-time law clerk. She was, no doubt, the Virginia Smith referenced in the article. I poured a big glass of wine. Though it was seventeen degrees in Michigan, I went outside to our porch, sat on our porch swing, which replaced the one from Blakely Point, and blasted "Aquarius" by the Fifth Dimension.

Chapter 7

Francie

Thank heavens for my psychiatrist, Dr. Carmen Quinn, who was highly recommended by Henry's mother. At first, I was embarrassed that Henry discussed my anxiety and bouts of depression with my mother-in-law. Henry thought that I needed to overcome my Southern bias of therapy as taboo. His mother had been seeing Dr. Quinn for years. I relented, reasoning that if a tenured professor in the psychology department saw a psychiatrist, there must be something to it. He was right. Carmen helped me navigate through the issues relating to my lonely childhood, my parent's relationship, Mom's behavior and the death of her entire family.

I religiously followed Carmen's advice of morning meditations. They worked for a while until Uncle Frankie would enter my brain during the quiet time. Playing peaceful music to distract me from talking to him did not work. Reading aloud inspirational passages did not work. Finally, taking Valium did work.

Due to the shit storm in my forecast, I begged Carmen to give me something stronger before leaving for New Orleans. I needed all the help I could get. En route to catching our flight, Henry and I stopped at the pharmacy. Carmen called in a new prescription for me.

"Dr. Quinn has increased the strength to 15 mg, but decreased the dosage to ONCE a day," the pharmacist cautioned.

"Thank you, thank you, Carmen," I said, silently.

I had never seen "Dan, the pharmacy trainee," according to his badge, but he was way too serious in my opinion. I mean it was only Valium, not Oxycontin.

"You should only take this before you go to bed because it causes drowsiness. Side effects that you may experience are lack of coordination, confusion, blurred vision, memory loss, dizziness..." as Dan, the trainee, began rattling off the list. I interrupted him assuring him that I was aware of all possible consequences, but I had a plane to catch.

When I arrived in New Orleans, I noticed that Mom's station wagon was packed to the gills. That car was still kicking. It must have soaked up all the energy sources from the bumper stickers plastered all over the back hatch.

They ranged from various constellations to messages describing the "cuckoo" behind the wheel: "Grasp the magnificence of the cosmos," "Powered by the Chakras,"

"Eat, Sleep and Herb," "There's an Oil for That!" "Learn Your ABC's—Astrology, Bergamot, Chamomile." "Everything's Better With Ylang Ylang." The most disturbing sticker simply said "KOOK." I was pretty sure that the Brooks' family was behind that one. Mom was either unaware of it or simply approved.

I found it symbolic that Mom's reliable station wagon was headed to Blakely Point, never to return to New Orleans. It was delivering her to Herbert, Farrah and Aurora from Daphne, the only constants in her life.

As she sped off, I turned my attention to the overwhelming tasks that landed in my lap, beginning with cleaning out my childhood home and handling Dad's estate. Apparently, Dad's estate contained more than our home in NOLA's Garden District. A home in the popular Lakewood area, which was bequeathed to Virginia Hill Smith, had been purchased seven years ago for $1,240,000. Virginia Hill Smith was also the beneficiary under Dad's three million dollar life insurance policy.

I turned onto Oak Tree Drive in Lakewood. Part of me wanted to see where Dad headed every summer the minute our station wagon pulled out of the driveway for Blakely Point. From the conversation I overheard years ago, Mom clearly knew about "her." As I parked and stared at the contemporary 3,000-square-foot house, I not only wondered if Mom knew the second home but also the boy holding Ginnie's hand pulling her out the front door. The boy was a spitting image of my dad.

Before my meeting with the Executor of Dad's Estate, I agonized over what Mom would say OR DO if Virginia Smith and son showed up at the funeral service. Dad took care of that issue. He left instructions that he should be cremated, and his ashes presented to Virginia Hill Smith. Any memorials should be directed to NOMA—the New Orleans Museum of Art. I later learned that Ginnie was a NOMA board member.

Each layer of settling the estate uncovered the unsettling reality of Dad's full devotion to Ginnie.

The Executor of his Estate, the head of the trust department of Dad's long-time bank, explained beneficiaries under life insurance policies are a matter of contract between the company and the insured. The estate laws don't govern those contracts. This meant that I couldn't challenge Ginnie's standing as the sole beneficiary of Dad's life insurance policy.

Making matters worse, the second home was purchased with funds Dad inherited from his family. The executor explained that neither my mother nor I were entitled to "separate property." We could have retained someone to investigate whether it really was separate property.

"Let it go," Mom said. "Such nonsense would require negative energy."

Perhaps she was afraid of what else she may learn. Mom simply didn't care about the house or the life insurance policy, but what she did care about was his memorial request.

"NOMA is his girlfriend's request. I was his wife. I don't know or care how you go about it, but you must add that his widow wants all memorials be made to the Southern Poverty Law Center."

After we reached a compromise on both memorial requests, Mom radiated a peacefulness, a determination to put it all to rest, and to bury the past once and for all. As the sole heir of the Hollingsworth estate, she certainly didn't need the money. So, I let it go, as instructed. At least I no longer needed to worry about how to memorialize my father one day and contest his will the next.

It wasn't long before Mom buried more than the past with Dad. She was reunited with Celeste Brooks, her childhood bestie. CiCi became a fixture in the big house like Farrah and Aurora from Daphne, though CiCi just walked over from next door. Aurora and Farrah actually moved in.

"All that space seemed to be wasted," Mom said when she told me about her new roommates. "But, your bedroom is still available for your visit when you finish up in New Orleans."

When cleaning out my childhood home, I was shocked to find a thick scrapbook. The mother that I knew was not a scrapbooker. But, then again, I was learning all kinds of things about my parents. I was eager to view pictures of her and CiCi, or some other memorialization of her exuberant spirit that I recalled from Grandma Weezie's scrapbooks. As I flipped page after page, they seemed to be all about Dad. This was his scrapbook. How strange, I thought.

Several pages were dedicated to his graduation from Yale Law School in 1987, with Mom by his side in only one of the pictures. There was a commencement program identifying that Dad graduated with high honors and obtained the highest grade in Constitutional Law, Civil Procedure, and Criminal Law. He also received several advocacy awards.

Pictures from his graduation from Tulane in 1983 presented a similar story—summa cum laude, president of the Student Body, History Department's Medal for Academic Excellence. Again, numerous pictures of Dad with various friends and professors, but no Mom.

There were numerous pages with programs identifying Dad as a speaker at various events for the Louisiana and American Bar Associations. There were newspaper articles about cases where he presided. It appeared he saved every piece of paper where his name was ever mentioned. A far cry from the memorialization in Grandma Weezie's scrapbooks.

The latest addition contained a NOMA newsletter, dated July 17, 2018, reporting on the success of a recent fundraising gala. The article included several pictures of attendees at the black-tie affair. I spotted Dad in a group shot and immediately recognized one of the women in the picture, Virginia Smith. The caption revealed that Virginia Smith was the gala chairperson.

I turned the pages quickly, thinking I could read all about his documented accomplishments later. I searched for more pictures of Mom and Dad together. I didn't find any more of Mom, but I did find one of her mother. The caption read: *Weezie Hollingsworth, Chair of the 1982 Houston Presentation Ball with Debutante Isabella Hunt and Escort Hugh LeBlanc.*

I realized then that I never knew how my parents even met. I never heard them talk about their romance or wedding. Did Grandma Weezie know Dad? Was he in the picture just because Grandma Weezie was the chair of the event? Who was the woman Dad escorted? When did he and Mom start dating? Did they meet at the ball? I had lots of questions, but I wasn't going to dare ask the only person who could answer them. It would require "negative energy."

Henry and I finally made it to Blakely Point after cleaning out my childhood home that Mom had abandoned. Before checking into the Blakely Bay Inn, we stopped by the big house.

Upon our arrival, Mom and her new roommates, along with CiCi and Herbert, were having an afternoon tea party on the porch with Grandma Weezie's sterling silver tea service. One silver tray displayed scones, surrounded by strawberries, oranges, mint from Mom's herb garden, and apparently some of her other herbs. Another silver tray

The Purple Fence on the Boardwalk

displayed five of Grandpa's vintage pipes. They must have already partaken in the pipes because Herbert was playing the banjo, and the others were enthralled in their version of the Hokey Pokey:

> You put your right cheek in;
> You take your left cheek out;
> You put your whole ass in,
> And you shake it all about;
> You do the hokey pokey,
> And you turn yourself around;
> That's what it's all about.

I owed Henry a giant "thank you" for booking a room at the Inn, though we were going to be in Blakely Point for several weeks. Henry rationalized the expenditure due to the Inn's business office and all the technology required for his job. The amenities were bonuses: a workout room, indoor pool, and good coffee. Neither of us could drink Mom's bitter coffee. Despite his legitimate reasons, I thought the real reason was Henry found the Inn to be a reprieve from the hotbed of eccentric women at Mom's house.

Away from the daily activities of Les Quatre Mousquetaires, we developed a routine of our own. After breakfast, I walked down the boardwalk to the boathouse to work on my sequel, while Henry analyzed clients' revenues at the Inn. On some nights, we'd join the Musketeers for a happy hour and/or dinner. I preferred dinners alone with Henry on the Bayside Grill patio while watching the sunsets.

Mom seemed to be rocking along nicely. There was no reason to worry about returning to Michigan other than the imminent approach of Mercury in retrograde. I was worried she may snap. I told Henry that I needed to extend my stay for at least twenty-one more days.

While I was concerned for Mom, deep down, I was more worried about me.

Chapter 8

Francie

I was making great progress on the sequel. I didn't want to trade my dock views and the sixty-degree weather in Blakely Point for the icy gray views and freezing temperatures in Michigan.

Usually, I was stricken with Seasonal Affective Disorder at this time of year. While skeptic about the consequences of mercury's orbit, I knew SAD was real. It provoked my anxiety, increased my feelings of hopelessness, and froze my creativity. Worst of all, SAD challenged my sanity. Every year, I worried if this was the year that SAD would outlast the arrival of spring. I lived with constant fear that Mom's demons would take up full-time residence in my brain.

The boathouse was my refuge. I stopped relying on my Valium to get me through the day. But, that was after— after my appointment with the Executor of Dad's Estate, after meeting my half-brother (well, from the window of my car), after cleaning out the Garden District residence, and after listing it with a realtor.

After all those things were behind me, the boathouse replaced my meds. The boathouse soothed me like always. Uncle Frankie began speaking to me too. If I became stuck in my writing, he would stand over my shoulder and his peaceful and supportive energy would free me of impediments. After a break-through, I would search Tom Petty on my phone, and Uncle Frankie and I would celebrate by blasting his new favorite song, "Learning to Fly."

I also felt Uncle Frankie's presence when I took a break from writing and sat on the dock, staring at the Bay. During these times, I wondered if Uncle Frankie was just in my imagination, like Luna and Becca had been. However, his company seemed different. He wasn't just a playmate. His conversations with me were instructive. He made me see things clearly. He assured me that Mom was now happy. She found "her people" in her universe. I should stop worrying about her and focus on me, my well-being and my book. Quit focusing on the perfect, perfect, perfect life of Bethany Brooks Baldwin.

I was embarrassed that Uncle Frankie picked up on my obsession with our next-door neighbor, but I couldn't help it. Life seemed to fall perfectly into place for the Bethanys of the world. For as long as I could remember, I envied her confidence, style, and her friends. During my childhood summers, I secretly watched her from my bedroom window and ached to be more like her.

Though Bethany couldn't be blamed for the way her father tormented Mom or for his refusal to let her play with me, she didn't have to flaunt my exclusion while entertaining other girls right under my nose in her backyard. When we were older, she continued to exclude me from her clique of summer friends who would hang out at the Blakely Bay Inn pool.

She'd arrive, with her entourage, sporting her plush, lime green, oversized, beach towel and matching tote, both monogrammed in bright pink with "BB" (later to be replaced with her "BBB" monogram). When I requested a monogrammed tote one summer, Mom laughed and rolled her eyes. She said monograms were like cattle brands.

"Why on earth do you want to be branded?" she asked. "That only limits your life-force."

I wasn't a bit surprised one summer when a tall, distinguished-looking guy visited the Brooks' house for the July 4th holiday weekend. Henry met him at the Inn work-out room; he went to the University of Georgia and was a "Baldwin" from Buckhead, the upscale trendy area of Atlanta and location of his family's extensive real estate holdings. Of course, given that Bethany was the daughter of Charles Mitchell Brooks, V, the biggest snob on the boardwalk, she would have never looked twice at someone who didn't have an impressive pedigree.

Bethany Brooks hit the bloodline jackpot with Simpson Baker Baldwin. A fairy-tale wedding on their back lawn (that I watched from my bedroom window) soon followed. The BBB monogram rapidly appeared on her towels and totes, serving trays, stemware, pillows and even Adirondack chairs. I began to agree with my mother. Monograms are an off-putting and restrictive weight.

Seemingly on cue, not one but two baby swings were hung from one of the large oak trees in the Brooks' yard. Bethany and her mother would spend hours presenting the next generation, Brooks Fitzgerald and Anna Baker, to the boardwalk sovereigns. Twins were in my immediate family tree, not the perfect Brooks' family. As could be expected, I was having problems conceiving even one baby.

Worse, Bethany would spend the entire summer with her daughters at our cherished summer retreat, just like Mom and me during my childhood. That was then. Now, I was relegated to only a couple of weeks due to Henry's job with the accounting firm.

Dorothy, still the manager of the Inn gift shop, still nosy, still gossipy, still sucking up to the "A-list" of boardwalk residents, didn't even pause at our house anymore. We were deleted from the "A-list" long ago. I never told Mom what I heard Dorothy say in the gift shop years ago about how disappointed her parents would be over her "shenanigans." But I sort of got it, especially after I saw Mom swinging a broom at Dorothy one day yelling, "Shoo, shoo, shoo! Shoo!" I asked Mom why she did that to Mrs. Reynolds.

"Dor'thee is a walking and talking piece of negative energy. I don't want that toxic karmic bitch anywhere near this house."

I questioned Mom's rationale. because neither Dorothy Reynolds' toxic karma nor the other boardwalk visitors to the Brooks' home who "emitted despicable vibes," according to Mom, seemed to have any impact on Bethany. She had been blessed with twin daughters and a dashing, successful husband.

Simpson Baldwin's success spanned a much greater reach than his family's Atlanta real estate footprint. Though he still worked for a family business, he was credited with taking his father-in-law's private investment firm national in scope. It required him to travel extensively.

"You'll see more of Simpson this summer. He has a jet with his own fleet of pilots, so he'll no longer be held hostage by the commercial airlines!" Bethany relayed to Dorothy Reynolds, who was strolling the boardwalk and stopped at the Brooks' fence to visit—the white fence encompassing their perfectly landscaped yard, with "no SHIT" in it like ours.

Our yard became even more outlandish after Mr. Brooks' last complaint to the Blakely Point Preservation Society. The complaint only instigated Mom's "shenanigans." She snagged every remaining tiki torch at Herb's Earth House and lined them up and down the border between ours and the Brooks' yard. The oils she burned in those torches weren't the least bit aromatic. In addition to the tiki torches, she draped crystals throughout the branches of our big oak tree that hung over into the Brooks' yard.

Over the years, CiCi Brooks quietly enjoyed watching Mom push her husband's buttons, something CiCi was never brave enough to do. CiCi recently confided to Mom that she always loved the torches and the trespassing crystals.

"That woman is going to rot in hell," Charles Brooks yelled after Mom's additional tiki torch enhancements. CiCi wanted to garner the nerve to tell him, "If yard art is the path to Purgatory, there is a much hotter place for you!"

"It's ironic that Charles thought you were going to be 'the end of him,' instead of the fifth of scotch he drank every night," CiCi disclosed.

The fifth of scotch eventually obliterated his liver and kidneys, precipitating his move into the Fairchild Village for Senior Living. The day after his admittance, CiCi showed up with a peace offering for Mom. She and Mom have been inseparable ever since, much to the mortification of Bethany Brooks Baldwin. Bethany didn't understand why her mother wouldn't move into the village to be closer to Charles.

"What she really wants is for me to move away from you. Junie, Charles is the one that placed the "KOOK" bumper sticker on your car. He thought it was priceless. As God is my witness, I'm not going to let anyone keep me from enjoying the little bit of life I have left with my Junie, my dear, dear friend!" CiCi said. She hugged my mother. They began dancing.

I learned all these things when I joined the gang for their three o'clock afternoon tea, which was a misnomer. No tea was ever involved, unless it was spiked. I felt Uncle Frankie's nudges to participate after finishing a chapter in my book. Henry never finished working before six, and I needed a break. So, I followed Uncle Frankie's lead.

When Grandpa's "peace" pipes appeared at the tea party, I gracefully exited. As I began walking back to the boathouse, Uncle Frankie prodded me to take a walk. With Uncle Frankie as my guide, I walked down the boardwalk toward the Blakely Bay Inn.

Before I reached the Inn, I saw Henry with a woman in the gazebo. He was uncharacteristically talking in an animated fashion. He must have said something funny because the woman placed her hand on his arm and tossed her head back in laughter. Her long blonde hair was waving in the wind. I felt as if I was interrupting something special.

They were obviously more than just new acquaintances. When my thoughts were headed down a treacherous path, Henry saw me. He motioned me to come over.

"Francie, do you know who this is? It's Georgia, Georgia Murphey."

I didn't know a Georgia Murphey, but Henry sure thought I did. She seemed to think that I knew her too.

"It's been such a long time! It's so good to see you, Francie."

From my blank look, Henry picked up on the fact that I was clueless about Georgia Murphey. Was she someone from my past that was now a movie or TV star? From her perfect figure, confident aura, and Henry's demeanor, she seemed like someone that I shouldn't have forgotten.

"Georgia's family used to come to the Inn every July 4th. Now, she's a realtor in Fairchild," Henry said giddily. "Isn't that something?"

"That's great," I said, not really knowing what else to say.

"I've been filling Georgia in on Junie, her roommates, and CiCi!" Henry said laughing.

He seemed tipsy, and it was only four-thirty! He was usually entrenched with work at this time of day. Georgia seemed a little tipsy too.

"I was just telling Henry that I think it's awesome that they have patched things up. Even back then, it was clear that Celeste was jealous of your mom—well, your Mom's free spirit. Celeste has always had a fire in her belly. She put on this aloof exterior, but underneath was a wild side. A side that Charles Brooks didn't know about," she slurred.

I was curious about how this Georgia knew of Mom and Celeste's childhood friendship.

"You've got some catching up to do," Henry said to me before turning to Georgia. "While I get us drinks, tell Francie what you just told me."

Henry appeared to be stumbling, as he headed to the bar to retrieve my drink and, apparently, another round for them.

"When I ran into Henry earlier, I told him that he owed me a drink," Georgia said. "I reminded him that I was the reason you two met."

Reminded? Interesting choice of word, I thought. How could he forget? That day was as clear as yesterday to me. It was the day after I first learned about Ginnie on our speaker phone, the day after I first learned of the house cleansing ritual and THE day I thought Farrah's oils were magical. I took my journal to the pool to write about my former imaginary friends when Henry sat down beside me. "Is this chair taken?" he asked.

"That day, we were drinking lemonade with vodka," Georgia said laughing. "The things we used to do!" she flipped her long hair. "We were all pretty loopy and started playing truth or dare. Nancy Summerville asked Henry the craziest place he had sex in the Inn and with who. He took the dare. Right then, you showed up. Nancy gave him his dare—to try and talk to you. She bet him ten dollars that you wouldn't give him the time of day."

She then placed her hand on my arm, like I saw her do to Henry earlier, laughed again and continued, "Nancy obviously lost the bet."

As she was unfolding her version of that day, I learned the missing piece of the puzzle. I could vividly recall the way Bethany, Nancy, Katie, and apparently Georgia were huddled together laughing and gawking at Henry and me. Of course, I knew Bethany, my next-door-neighbor. Nancy, her brother Cannon, and Katie were also boardwalk summer regulars, but since I was never included in the clique, I never met any of the Inn guests, including this Georgia Murphey. I was confused as to why she was the reason Henry and I met and not Nancy Summerville. Didn't she just say that Nancy was the one that dared him to talk to me and bet money on the outcome?

Henry then appeared with the round of drinks.

"Can you believe that about CiCi?" Henry asked.

"Oh, I haven't gotten to that part yet; I got sidetracked," Georgia laughed.

"About CiCi... like I did every summer after my family arrived at the Inn, I would hop on a bike and head to Bethany's house. I can't remember what year it was, but when I got to the Brooks, Bethany was still at some camp and wouldn't be arriving for two more days. I remember that Mrs. Brooks looked different that day. I couldn't put my finger on it. Later, it hit me that it was the make-up. She was wearing make-up. She never wore make-up or a bathing suit for that matter, but she was in both. Later that day, I was killing time down at the marina, and I saw her on the back of this yacht. She and this man were sitting closely, drinking champagne and smoking cigarettes. Her head was on his shoulder. They disappeared below deck. I was shocked."

I was more than shocked at this story. If this was true, it probably was the reason that CiCi didn't move to the retirement community to be closer to her ogre of a husband.

"She came back the next day," Georgia continued. "I watched them a long time. I know that probably sounds weird, but I was bored. Bethany was still at camp, and I was fascinated by the discovery of this different version of Celeste Brooks. Right before she left the boat that day, she and her yacht friend started making out on the back of the boat, right out in the open. When she was leaving, he picked her up, and helped her onto the dock. She crossed her legs around his hips. He kissed her all around her neck and chest; she threw her head back laughing until she saw me. I wanted to run, but my legs wouldn't move. When she started walking toward me, I was scared. Her gaze suddenly looked exactly like Mr. Brooks' scowls. 'If you know what's good for you, you will unsee that, missy!'" she huffed at me.

I didn't know what to think of this story. Admittedly, I was just getting to know CiCi after all these years, but I watched her plenty of times out of my bedroom window while she doted on Bethany and the twins.

"Celeste was suffocating in her house. Who wouldn't be? Everybody was scared to death of Charles Brooks, and truth is, we were equally scared of Bethany. Like they say, the apple doesn't fall far from the tree, and with Charles and Bethany Brooks, it was a rotten apple."

I agreed with her on that. Charles Brooks' words, "start painting that damned purple fence and remove all the SHIT," still echoed in my head at the oddest times.

It then clicked why Uncle Frankie nudged me from the boathouse, why he encouraged my participation in the afternoon tea and why he guided me down the boardwalk. He wanted me to understand that Charles Mitchell Brooks, V was responsible for the falling out between CiCi and Mom. He wanted me to hear about the real Celeste Brooks, so that I would see her in a different light. This information was changing my impression of the perfect house next door. It was indeed time to focus on me.

Chapter 9

Francie

I felt guilty for all my bad feelings about Celeste Brooks. I also felt guilty about being miffed with Henry's invitation for Georgia to join us for dinner. He was headed back to Ann Arbor early the next morning, and I just wanted to spend our last evening alone with a quiet bayside romantic dinner watching the sunset. I knew that was a little selfish on my part since he had been such a trooper helping me clean out my family home and dealing with all the emotional turmoil of not only my father's death but also my discoveries.

"You should get to know Georgia," he said. "Since she is local, she could be someone to meet for lunch, dinner, or a glass of wine. She would certainly enjoy an invite to the Musketeer's tea parties!"

I thought about Uncle Frankie's advice—that I should focus on me. It would be nice to have a friend like the ones Mom now enjoyed. Henry and Georgia obviously went way back from their family vacations at the Inn, those past summers they couldn't quit talking about. Georgia had joined Bethany's entourage when Cannon Summerville became her summer beau. Cannon's sister, Nancy, an original member of Bethany's club, included Georgia in the group.

My disguised amusement at their stories was an attempt to conceal my true feelings. I had been an outsider then and was feeling like one now. My childhood pain was bubbling up—the loneliness from being excluded from this group and resigned to watch them from my bedroom window felt as poignant today as then.

After another mojito, my mind and body started relaxing. I was beginning to be comforted by the tales. I was learning that Mom wasn't the sole perpetrator of shenanigans on the boardwalk. Bethany Brooks and gang had been busy with their own.

Bethany was the ringleader in what I would call malicious pranks. I was glad that I had not been included in them. Bethany held a grudge too. Her payback was hell. One person she targeted was Dorothy Reynolds, the manager of the Inn gift shop.

"She suspected that we were the ones behind the disorganization of the souvenir T-shirts in the gift shop," Georgia said. "Remember how she would suddenly appear if you picked up a T-shirt? She'd be right behind you, folding it back just so, and peering at you over those fake diamond cat-like reader glasses. Remember those?? Anyway, one day when she was busy with several guests,

Bethany went in there and made a mess of the T-shirt table. She unfolded them and even mixed up all the sizes. Dorothy politely suggested to Celeste that Bethany and her 'gang' quit coming into the gift shop; it was for the Inn guests."

I found this story interesting given that Mrs. Reynolds was constantly sucking up to the Brooks. She must have really been upset to garner the nerve to even make that polite suggestion to Bethany's mother, Celeste.

"Bethany said that she had more of a right to be in that store than the stupid hired help," Georgia continued. "She made a plan to send that message. Me and Katie were supposed to distract Dorothy, so we tried on flip flops, jewelry, and hats with her watching us like a hawk. Bethany snuck up behind her and squirted red dye from a water gun on the back of her skirt. As Dorothy flitted around the shop, I heard a 'Bless her heart,' but Bethany heard the best comment: 'She either got bit by a humongous mosquito or poor thing's had an accident.' I don't think Dorothy even knew how she got the red stain on the back of her skirt that day."

My mother's so-called "shenanigans" that seemed to offend everyone were innocent and harmless and only involved our property, not others. I found it amusing how over the years, Dorothy Reynolds would hang over the Brooks' fence and ogle over Bethany's twins. If she only knew...

"Then there was the time she put eye-drops into Katie's sister's lemonade, so she'd quit following us around."

"Eye drops?" I asked. "What does that do?"

"She thought it would give her a horrific case of diarrhea, but she actually only vomited!" Georgia said, laughing.

I was relieved that I was left out of their group and their mischiefs. What a waste of energy to have allowed my exclusion to torture me over the years. Georgia was opening my eyes to all kinds of things. She could have saved me lots of nights spent crying in my pillow.

She explained that Nancy and Katie were on the opposite end of the shock spectrum from Bethany. They weren't mean, just risqué. Nancy liked to venture over to the wild side with the "townies," those who punched the clock at the Inn before returning to their homes outside its enchanted gates.

Nancy endlessly propositioned one townie, Griffin Harper, the leader of the Inn's summer camp. She enjoyed the attention of Justin, one of the bartenders, who shared inventory with her from the pool bar. Clyde, another townie, left the door to the roof unlocked for Georgia's and Nancy's smoke breaks.

Apparently, Georgia never kicked her need for a smoke break because before her next story, she whipped out a cigarette from her purse. Due to the winds blowing off the Bay, she was having issues getting a spark. I was stunned when Henry took her lighter and cupped his hand around the flame to block the draft. She leaned in placing her hand on his wrist until the end of her cigarette turned orange. The smoke that she exhaled wafted over into his face. Henry abhorred smokers, so I was more than flabbergasted at his assistance with her light and that he tolerated the second-hand smoke. He was clearly doubly loopy by now and was enjoying reminiscing with Georgia.

Henry told the story about when they "borrowed" the Inn's rental bikes and snuck out beyond the gates with a twelve-pack of beer that Justin slipped Nancy. He described how Cannon wiped out in a channel on their way back, mangling the front wheel of his transportation. "He pushed that wobbly bike all the way back, sopping wet and covered in black muck," Henry recounted.

Georgia then jumped in and narrated the time Charles Brooks caught them all in Bethany's boathouse making rum punch. They were all convinced he would have their families banned from the Inn—permanently! Bethany swore that he was drunk and wouldn't remember anything in the morning and even if he did, we would ALL get a pass due to an earlier prank that he was still belly laughing about.

After Georgia mentioned the earlier prank, she paused, and I thought it must have been an errant slip. She gave Henry a funny look, like "whoops" but then spilled her guts anyway.

"Oh, Francie, I am sorry. But, the prank was that we pulled up all the herbs from your mom's terracotta planters and threw them in the Bay. Bethany intimidated us. She was just so mean. I know that is no excuse, but I didn't know you then. I feel so bad about that now."

With that, Georgia ordered another round of drinks and instructed the server that this round was "on her tab." Henry helped Georgia light another cigarette, as the stories heated up a notch to what I found to be rather inappropriate after-dinner conversation.

"Remember the time that Griffin Harper finally relented to Nancy's flirtatious overtures? They were caught naked on the bar at Olie's, and Nancy was covered in whipped cream left over from the children's ice-cream sundae social!" Georgia said. "That story has been embellished over the years because now it is up to twenty cans of the aerosol whipped cream that was applied to Nancy."

"Then there was the time when you and Cannon were caught skinny-dipping in the Bay," Henry said.

"I was still discovering sand in my you-know-twat three days later," she said, then blowing smoke rings.

Then, they talked about Katie having sex in her grandparent's house, with whom they couldn't remember, while the rest of the family was marching down the boardwalk in the July 4th parade.

"Katie said that more than one bottle rocket blasted in her grandparent's bedroom that July 4th!" Georgia recalled.

I was relieved when this summer reunion finally ended and, perhaps, more relieved that none of them involved Henry with another girl. I was mostly relieved when Henry later told me that he would be back soon. He said the business accommodations at the Inn were excellent and that he agreed with me, the place was special. I suppose the walk down memory lane from earlier that evening made him sentimental. As I laid in his arms that night, I was hoping that he could figure out how to work from Blakely Point permanently. I wanted this place to call him back like it had Georgia Murphey.

Georgia had given us her business card. I thought that maybe I should take Uncle Frankie's advice and focus on me now, and I should take Henry's advice and invite her to lunch. That would be the perfect time to ask her to keep her ears to the ground for any potential listings on the Bay.

Chapter 10

Francie

Dr. Carmen Quinn was extremely pleased with my update the next day, during my monthly telephone appointment. I was ahead of my submissions schedule to my editor, who, along with my agent, was pleased with how the book was progressing. Since arriving in Blakely Point from New Orleans, I didn't need my meds—not once. Carmen agreed that the boathouse was my special place; I had been through a lot in the last thirty days.

And I had.

My father died, and my mother abandoned my childhood home, leaving me to clean it out, list it with a realtor, and then sell it. I discovered that my father's estate contained a piece of real estate in which my dad's son and his mother resided. The boy's mother, my dad's long-time law clerk, was the beneficiary of my dad's life insurance policy. Moreover, Mom didn't care about any of it. Meanwhile, Mom took in two new roommates and reconciled with her best childhood friend, Celeste Brooks, the matriarch of the perfect family next door, which I also learned wasn't so perfect after all.

It wasn't that I was gloating that CiCi had been so unhappy over the years, but something about all the news sure made me feel better for Mom. She must have felt like I did over the years—an outcast, a blemish on the boardwalk landscape. In reality, it was much more than a blemish, it was a pubescent teen's worst case of acne. Though it never seemed to bother Mom, I thought she had been masking her feelings.

However, even now, none of the blotches on the walls within the Brooks' household seemed to detract from Bethany's opinion of herself. She still exuded this perfectly enchanting air, even though it was evident that she was aware of her father's drinking problem. She probably sensed her mom's disdain for him too, whether or not she knew of CiCi's captain friend. She continued to treat me like a pariah.

I needed to let bygones be bygones and listen to Uncle Frankie's advice. Focus on me. Focus on the positive. "Shoo, shoo, shoo!" I said waving my hands in the air to eliminate my negative thoughts about Bethany. I was beginning to buy into Mom's philosophy that negative energy had no place in our home.

Despite Uncle Frankie's coaching and Dr. Quinn's encouragement, for some reason, I couldn't shake my gloomy state of mind today. It even seemed to escalate before the call from Henry announcing his return to Blakely Point. His return was much sooner than I anticipated. He was able to move some things around on his calendar. He'd be arriving on Thursday morning. I started thinking that the boathouse wasn't my sole cure after all. It was the boathouse and Henry. I needed them both. Without him, I was lost.

After staring at a blank page for over an hour, I started thinking that Mercury in retrograde must be affecting me. Today was the start of its twenty-one-day cycle. I justified that one Valium wouldn't be so bad. I knew I could stop taking them, but not until Henry arrived. As I was swallowing the pill, the skittish pharmacy trainee's instructions to only take before bedtime was the last thing on my mind. But I remembered when I woke up at 3:00 p.m.! I was disoriented.

The good news was that I was ahead of schedule in meeting my submission deadlines. I could tell this was one of those days where I was experiencing severe writer's block. So, I decided to join Les Quatre Mousquetaires for their afternoon tea party.

They must have started earlier than usual, I thought, as I opened the purple gate and proceeded toward the veranda. The music was already blaring, and CiCi and Mom were dancing.

"Oh, Francie, darlin'," Mom said. "So glad you are joining us." She twirled CiCi around under her arm, "we've had the most wonderful day so far, and it's only getting better!"

Did she forget what day it was? I learned quickly that she hadn't, and she and her allies were armed for it.

Aurora was already pouring me a cup of tea from the sterling silver tea service. On the sterling silver tray was also an assortment of crystals.

"Farrah outdid herself today," Aurora said. "In addition to the crystals, she made this concoction that helps with positive communication!"

"It's the start of Mercury's retrograde so I had to pull out all the stops!" Farrah said. "We have agate, onyx, rose quartz, turquoise, aquamarine, apophyllite, and hematite," as she pointed to the crystals on the tray.

"The hematite is for Junie." She picked up the dark gray crystal streaked with red. "It works with the Root Chakra to absorb toxic emotions and negative energy."

I thought that I needed to slip some of that into my purse.

"And the rose quartz is for CiCi," Farrah said laughing. "It balances the Heart Chakra."

They all laughed. Based on their reaction, I wondered if they knew about CiCi's sailor friend. But that was quickly confirmed when Mom stopped twirling CiCi, stood at attention, saluted her and said "Aye, Aye, Captain."

"Speaking of captains, Henry and I had dinner with Georgia Murphey last night," directing my comment to CiCi.

"Who's that?" Mom asked.

"She was one of those dreadful 'tour-ons' who descended upon our Bay every week of July 4th," CiCi said rolling her eyes. "She was definitely more moron than tourist."

CiCi harbored the same disdain as Mom for all the tourists who took over our boardwalk in the summer. They seemed to think that our piers and boathouses were somehow public like the boardwalk.

"Somehow she and Bethany became buddies," CiCi said. "Never cared for her, or any of the other wannabes for that matter."

"Francie, how on earth do you know her?" Mom asked.

"Well, I didn't before last night. Apparently, Georgia Murphey and Cannon Summerville were an item every summer," I said. "Henry recognized her from his family vacations here over the 4th."

"Never cared for those Summervilles either." CiCi said. "So, I'm guessing she told you about Captain Gabe?" CiCi asked while all the others giggled.

"Yes, she did."

"Bethany mentioned that Georgia moved to Fairchild, and she sells real estate," CiCi said. "I can't believe that little hussy is still spying on me. I thought we were really careful last night."

"Last night? She was talking about years ago!"

"Oh my! Guess I'm busted!" she said, while laughing and taking a big swig of her tea.

"Do tell!" Aurora said to me.

"Only with CiCi's permission."

"No secrets amongst us girls here!" she said. "And I'd like to hear her rendition of it."

I then relayed Georgia's story of heading to their house every year after her family checked in at the Inn. One summer, she noticed CiCi was wearing make-up and a bathing suit.

"While walking around the marina later that day, she saw you with a man on a yacht, drinking champagne and...well, other stuff. She saw you again the next day, and that is when you saw her and told her she'd better "unsee that, missy!"

The Les Quatre Mousquetaires were cackling.

"That little bitch followed me is what she did," CiCi said. "When I was walking down the boardwalk toward the marina, I kept thinking someone was behind me; I was hearing footsteps. You know I was scared to death of what Charles would do to me if he found out about my Gabe. I'd turn around and wouldn't see anything. I thought I was going crazy. Then I got to the stretch on the boardwalk where there aren't so many trees, near the Alexander's house, and I saw her trying to hide behind their grill on the dock. I turned around and walked right up to her and point blank asked her what she was doing. You know I never trusted those tour-ons, eternally trespassing on our docks. She fooled me, I guess, because she said that she was trying to find a spot to smoke a cigarette. I found her honesty refreshing and thought that I was being overly paranoid."

CiCi took another big swig of Farrah's concoction.

"You know, after she told me she was trying to find a smoking spot, I guess I got careless. Then, I saw her again the next day. I knew she had followed me. Gabe's boat slip is the last one on the back side of the marina. So, Georgia Murphey just didn't happen to waltz by! That girl was hiding behind a tree!"

Mom, Farrah, and Aurora were loving this story.

"I wish I would have known you then!" Farrah said. "I could have loaded you up with some fluorite."

"Yes, I definitely needed the Third Eye Chakra that day. And, I needed something the next day to keep her lips from flapping. She asked Bethany about the man she saw me with on a big yacht. Talk about toxic karma, she wrote the book on it!"

"Holy moly," Aurora said.

"That would be holy smokes, Aurora from Daphne!" Mom yelled while picking up one of Grandpa's pipes.

"You may need some hematite too since Miss Georgia has moved to town," Farrah said, picking up the crystal and swinging it around in the air. "Bless your heart, CiCi!"

I started thinking that asking Georgia to lunch was a bad idea. And even worse would be asking her to keep her eye out for a house for Henry and me. I certainly didn't want this newcomer "wannabe" infiltrating my life with negative energy, especially during Mercury's retrograde.

Chapter 11

Francie

I didn't disclose to Henry that I was becoming a believer of cosmic forces that night when we spoke. But I was truly worried about him traveling during Mercury's retrograde.

"Mom says you need to pack the crystals she gave you. You still have them, don't you?"

Henry laughed. "I forgot all about those. I may need a new supply because my schedule keeps getting all out of whack! The good news is that I'm still coming."

"Oh good! I was worried that the retrograde was keeping you in Michigan," I said laughingly. Secretly, I wished Henry knew where his crystals were.

"I'll call when I land. The Inn shuttle service is picking me up. I will be tied up on the phone on the drive from the airport and all morning. Hopefully, we can meet for lunch, unless you are in full writer's mode."

"I'm sure I will need a break by then. And I've missed you. It seems like you've been gone for weeks!"

"Doesn't it, though? I left Georgia a message that I would be back tomorrow and asked that she set up some appointments for us to check out available real estate. What do you think about that?"

"Oh Henry! You know that is what I've dreamed about. I love you so much."

"I love you too. See ya tomorrow."

After I hung up, I forgot about Mercury's retrograde, CiCi's comments about Georgia or anything else. I silently thanked Farrah and all her crystals. I was cautiously optimistic that I may not have to return to Michigan after all.

When Henry not only landed safely but early, I thought those crystals were still at work. I needed to get some one-on-one advice from Farrah about which crystal was best for concentration and put them in the boathouse. But then again, perhaps Henry was the equivalent of such a crystal. When he was in Michigan, I could barely write a page. I was hoping that with Henry's return to Blakely Point, my cosmic forces would realign, and my creativity and attention would be restored. But as I sat staring at the computer screen, I got nothing but a headache. I learned my lesson about taking my meds in the middle of the day, but I really wanted a Valium. Really bad. After Henry arrived, I would stop taking them.

Uncle Frankie advised me to go for a walk instead, that fresh air was what I needed. I could feel his hand leading me down the boardwalk once again to the Blakely Bay Inn. As I walked past the Alexander's, one of the few houses with no pier but instead a small area of sandy beach, I saw it, the Jubilee!

The rare phenomenon where flounder, crab, shrimp, catfish, and other species come ashore and appear trapped—a fisherman's version of winning the lottery. Since the marvel happens only once annually and lasts for only an hour, many try to predict when the mounds of fish loot will arrive, so they'll be prepared with their nets, gigs, and coolers for the ultimate fisherman payday.

The marine biologists have been recording these events for many decades, attempting to predict the next coming. Some of these scientists point to the requirement of a full moon, following a day of showers. Others say an easterly wind and a rising tide are prerequisites. All agree that the Jubilee happens in the summer months when the water is stagnant and oxygen levels depleted.

It's like the fish are drowning in the water and frantically seeking air. They arrive in hoards on the shore flopping, writhing, and struggling. The times I have witnessed it, they seemed frantic, like they were trying to escape the Bay. Apparently, Mobile Bay is the only place for this event, other than somewhere in Japan. Mrs. Alexander told me that fact during my inaugural Jubilee on their stretch of beach.

On the Alexander's sandy beach was where Mom also saw her first Jubilee. The Alexanders mounted a big bell near their fence so anyone who first saw it could ring the bell and alert all the neighbors. Every time I passed the bell, I thought of Dad's stories about the midnight ride of Paul Revere during the Revolution warning that: "The British are coming! The British are coming!" But on Mobile Bay, it was: "The fish are coming! The fish are coming!"

At her first Jubilee, Mom saw "old-man Miller" in his skivvies with a bucket bent over trying to scoop up dinner. She said she'd never seen an "ass crack on an old man" and hoped it was the last. She hated the Jubilee. She thought the fish looked scared; she felt sorry for them. She wanted to tell the swarms of Boardwalkers to let them be. Her first Jubilee was her last, and she forbade me from ever touching any species squirming on the Bay.

Henry had never seen a Jubilee. What I knew about its rare occurrences in the past, they were always at the crack of dawn, instead of the crack of "old-man Miller," and never at this time of the year. Though March was unseasonably warm, a Jubilee this early seemed impossible. With the calendar flipped to April, I thought this was an April Fool's joke. But no one could pull this off.

I ran as fast as I could to the Bay Inn. I knew Henry had a hectic morning, but he could not miss this. Marvin, who was a long-standing employee at the Inn, was behind the front desk.

"Good morning, Ms. DeVries."

"Oh, Marvin, it's incredible. It's either an amazing April Fool's joke, or it's the Jubilee!"

Marvin raised his left eyebrow in doubt. He looked at me like I had either been drinking or finally turned crazy like my mother.

"I've got to get Henry. Is our room available yet? Do you know where he is? Is he in the Business Office?" as I was talking a mile a minute. Henry just couldn't miss this historic moment. Work could wait.

"Yes, he checked in some time ago, but then he called and requested another room," Marvin said, and his left eyebrow raised again or was that my imagination? "Which key do you want?"

I thought this had to be a mistake. Perhaps the first room wasn't ready when he arrived. He mentioned that he was smothered in work. He probably just took the first available room, but it seemed that Uncle Frankie was talking for me. I heard myself answer and it was my voice, but I didn't know where the response was coming from.

"Oh, yes. I'll take both."

"Room 253," as he started inserting the plastic card into the electronic reader and handed me a key. "I've never seen so many faxes come in for a guest before. There is one coming in now so you may want to stop back by after the Jubilee," he said chuckling, obviously not believing me. "And there was a letter that came in for him as well. Only be a minute, I'll get it."

I thought that Marvin obviously didn't understand the historical significance of a Jubilee in April, much less April 1st. When he returned to the front desk, he said that the letter had already been delivered to Henry.

"The other room is in the Spa Building, Room 566," Marvin said, handing me the second key. "Do you want to wait on the fax?"

"No thanks, Marvin! The Jubilee may be gone by then!"

I decided to head to Room 566 first. The Spa Building was the newest addition to the Inn's amenities and the location of the upgraded work-out room that Henry frequented. Perhaps that's why he changed rooms. I ran as fast as I could. He just couldn't miss the Jubilee.

As I approached Room 566, the "Do Not Disturb" sign was hanging on the door. If Henry was enthralled in a business call, he may not appreciate the interruption. I rationalized the call could wait for the Jubilee.

I knocked gently on the door before inserting the key. When I opened the door, I knew that Marvin unintentionally violated a fundamental rule—providing a key to a stranger's room. There was a pink purse on the bed and a dress on the floor, and I heard the shower running and a woman's voice. I quickly exited this room. April Fool's I thought. Then, I ran to Room 253.

When I entered Room 253, I noticed Henry's luggage on the rack. I called his name. I called his cell. I heard his cell ringing. It was on top of a bunch of papers strewn across the coffee table. Beside his phone was an opened envelope with his name on the front, and then a letter underneath his phone.

I got your voicemail. I'll definitely help you find a house! But truthfully, when I heard your voice, I was hoping that you were calling because you were thinking the same thing I was.

I can still feel the sexual energy between us. And I sense that you feel it too.

If you want to relive our first and last time, you have my number. No one needs to know. And the TRUTH is that this time it will be MUCH better. And after, I will show you houses, and welcome you back with open arms...

Xoxo,

Forever, your Georgia

The involuntary buckling of my knees and the contraction of my gut confirmed that the purse and dress I had seen in Room 566 were Georgia's. She was in the shower, and she wasn't alone. My hands were visibly shaking as I picked up my husband's phone. I looked at his recent calls. There was the missed call from me and an earlier call that lasted over an hour from a Michigan area code.

I then went to Henry's text messages. The most recent text was a string of heart emojis from a local number. I scrolled down knowing what I was getting ready to discover. A text from Henry, "Got your note. You're right. The truth is that I can't get you off my mind. I dare you to meet me in Room 566 this morning at 10. I'm very dirty."

Part II

Chapter 12

Millie Hill

Once again, I was disgusted with myself, as I looked at my reflection in the mirror. It was a different version of the innocent, starry-eyed, but scared shitless, Millie Hill that exited the subway in Grand Central Station five years ago. Why are you so weak? You have always been strong. Why are you doing this? You have always had a fervent, moral compass. Why are you willing to throw all of it away for a man who you can't have? Why Mille? Why?

I brushed my tears away, removed the mascara stains from my cheeks, reapplied my blush, and picked up my suitcase. I hailed a cab to the Teterboro Airport. There, my married lover's private jet would whisk me away to Palm Beach.

"How are you doing, Pat?" Corky, the pilot, would uniformly ask.

"Great, Corky, hope you are!" I would respond even though I wanted to yell, "My name is not Pat! It's Millie!" I thought if the plane ever went down, no one would know I was on board. I lived alone; no one knew about my excursions with Simpson Baldwin. I unfailingly took a cab to the private airports and always paid in cash. Since I was listed as Pat Miller on the passenger list, no one would ever know that Millicent Jane Hill perished. "Pat," Simpson's idea, "androgynous Pat." He thought it was funny; I thought it was heartbreaking.

I swore that the last time I was with him would be the last time. I vowed the same thing the time before that and the time before that. There had been too many "last" times to count. The first time I made this promise was when I learned that Simpson Baldwin was married. His wife called my cell. When I answered, she asked, "Who is this?"

I responded, "Who is this?"

"I'm Bethany Baldwin, as in Simpson Baldwin's wife. Why are you spending hours on the phone with my husband?"

Despite the huge lump in my throat, I thought my voice remained composed in explaining in the most professional manner that I could muster that I was an accountant, and I worked with her husband's private equity firm. Then, I couldn't help myself. Anger engulfed me.

"I find your question highly inappropriate and unprofessional," I added. "A word of advice, if you don't trust your spouse, perhaps you should be talking to him, instead of his business colleagues."

After I hung up, I puked. I was "dating" Bethany Baldwin's spouse and had been for over a year!

Several times, I considered a therapist; the weight of guilt I carried was overwhelming, but I wasn't even able to divulge my secrets to a confidential psychologist. I was too embarrassed. I was too ashamed.

But, I couldn't resist Simpson Baker Baldwin. He was smart and handsome. He oozed confidence and charisma. And, who was I kidding? He was an amazing lover. He ignited a sexual fire in me that I thought was extinguished when I walked in on Matt with one of his classmates in a nurse's uniform. We were still in our honeymoon phase, for Christ sake!

The only thing that helped me get over Matt's betrayal was my job. Before I moved to New York, my job was a means to an end; it paid Matt's medical school tuition. Now, it was my purpose in life. It made me not only financially independent but also emotionally independent. It was my identity. In fact, it gave me great pleasure. I didn't need any man for that, or so I thought.

As the cabbie was weaving in and out of the traffic, I stared out the window at the hustle and bustle of the greatest city in America. I began reminiscing about the once pure, naïve Millie Hill, who arrived in the city that never sleeps from the sleepy town of Hinton, West Virginia, where I was born and raised.

Though accepted everywhere I applied, including Yale, Harvard, the University of Pennsylvania, and the University of Virginia, none offered me a full scholarship like the university in my home state, West Virginia University. It was where I met Matt, my future husband, and I thought it was a sign that I would never leave.

It seemed like a dream when I received my first job interview in New York City. Mountaineers simply didn't venture to the Big Apple. Mountaineers camp, fish, whitewater raft, and ski. We navigate the biking and hiking trails in the New River Gorge National Park, not the street grids of Manhattan. Like I said, I was naïve but also full of hope.

I recalled the excitement of my interview trip. I made a New York playlist to pump me up. Of course, the first song was Frank Sinatra's "New York, New York," but my list also included George Benson's "Broadway," Stevie Wonder's "Living for the City," Don Henley's "New York Minute," Billy Joel's "New York State of Mind" and my favorite, the new song by Alicia Keys, "Empire State of Mind." But when those subway doors opened, under my breath, I sang the theme song from *The Mary Tyler Moore Show*. I believed that I was going to take the town. If I weren't in the middle of Grand Central Station, I would have tossed my beanie in the air.

And, I did take it and make it. I landed a job with Vittoria & Associates, a highly-regarded financial advisor to investors or purchasers of large companies. I was part of the balance sheet management team that scrubbed the financials of our clients' targets. My biggest account was a private equity firm based in Atlanta, SBB Capital. It was flush and gobbling up underperforming private businesses. Moreover, its founder was more than easy on the eyes.

All the women in the office swooned over Simpson Baker Baldwin. Even the heterosexual men were drawn to the magnetism of this eligible Southern bachelor. After the call from "Simpson Baldwin's wife," I discovered that the "eligible" part wasn't true. Up to that point, all indications were to the contrary. Simpson never sported a wedding band. And, then, there was the rumored romance with Mary Beth Underwood. She was not only one of the few female partners in Simpson's elite Atlanta law firm, but also the lead partner on the SBB transactions.

Despite the rumored relationship, I began wondering if the flirtatious vibes I sensed were only in my imagination. Perhaps his penetrating blue eyes looked at everyone like they did at me. They made my insides burn. My moth-balled libido was the guilty party, not Simpson Baldwin, I thought. After I left Matt, I was more than bitter and perfectly content with the decommissioning of my sex drive, that is, until I met Simpson Baldwin.

"You did a fantastic job on the analytics for Project Apparel. How about dinner tonight? My treat."

"That sounds great. I'll email the team."

Simpson's investment targets were highly confidential, and any written or oral communication used a disguised reference. The current acquisition was assigned "Project

Apparel." I wondered who pegged the aliases because they were unoriginal, and they provided clues about the intended conquest, or at least industry group. Of course, I kept that to myself. I didn't want to offend the originator, especially if it was Simpson's main squeeze, Mary Beth Underwood, Esquire.

"Well, I was hoping that it would just be you. To thank you for the excellent job in leading the Project Apparel team," he said.

I could feel my face turning five shades of purple, as I looked down at the floor. I decided to tackle this uncomfortable conversation head-on.

"I think I may be blushing," I said. "Just doing my job. And, as they say, there is no "I" in team or Project Apparel, for that matter; I couldn't do it without them. But, to be honest, my group wouldn't be interested in dinner with the lawyers anyway."

"I don't blame them. The lawyers aren't invited. I just want to treat the Queen of Analytics. You have an amazing talent and are someone that I'd like to get to know better. And, the bonus is that you are very attractive. But, you must know that, Millicent."

He didn't know that I preferred "Millie." I detested being called Millicent. It sounded so stodgy. I changed my mind after Simpson Baldwin said my name. It was the way that he said it. He made it sound sexy and sophisticated; Millie suddenly sounded childish and Mountaineerish.

He took the "Queen of Analytics" to one of the finest restaurants in the city and ordered the finest bottle of wine, actually two bottles. When he suggested a night cap in his $1200-a-night, five-star hotel room, I was tipsy enough to disgorge the rumor mill.

"I'd love to but don't think Mary Beth Underwood would approve of that!"

I found it refreshing that he didn't play dumb, nor innocent. He just laughed.

"We broke up. She was too needy. She didn't like the way I looked at you. Lawyers are trained to over-analyze things, but you've got to give it to her. She was right on target with her suspicions."

With that, he leaned in to kiss me, and I didn't stop him. I didn't stop him all night long. I didn't stop him the next morning, and I haven't been able to stop him ever since. I had never experimented with any narcotic. Frankly, I didn't understand the temptation, but I was beginning to have empathy. After I learned of Bethany Baldwin, the remorse I felt after each rendezvous had to be how addicts feel after relapse. I couldn't quit. I was on a high. I was addicted.

As I tipped the driver, clutched the handle of my bag, and headed toward Simpson's private jet en route to the Breakers in Palm Beach, I vowed to kick the habit. I would end this, but not until after I returned to New York next week.

Chapter 13

Millie

We were ten minutes into a couple's massage in our oceanfront suite at the Breakers when Simpson's cell began ringing off the hook. Call after call.

"Someone forgot to silence their phone," I said. "Must be important. Maybe you should get it."

"Whoever it is will obviously call back," he said, oblivious to the persistence of the caller.

His phone must have rung ten times during our treatment, but he ignored it until our scheduled time was over.

"Sorry for the interruption," he said to our masseuses and gave them an extra tip.

"Just as I figured, it's Bethany. This should only take a minute."

Something definitely was wrong due to the number of times she called. I was worried that my last getaway was going to be cut short. And yes, I was determined that this was the very LAST getaway.

"I told you that Pat [as he winked at me, which made my stomach ache] and I are looking at the books of a prospect. Ever heard of leaving a message?"

She began talking a mile a minute, and her tone was not chipper, to say the least. He sat there patiently listening to her while rubbing my feet.

Charles Brooks, Simpson's father-in-law, had fallen. Celeste, Bethany's mother, was AWOL. Bethany was in a tizzy, but her angst wasn't from her father's fall. She was irritated that she couldn't reach her mother. She was yelling so loudly I could hear every word.

"She is either off with that crusty fisherman or with Looney Junie. I can't just drop everything and drive to Blakely Point. The girls have too much going on!"

"I'll take care of it. I'll call you when I get there."

"Get there." The bad news was confirmed. While Bethany was still ranting into the phone, I got up and went into the bathroom. I stared at myself in the mirror. It was the kick in the gut that I needed to reinforce the solemn oath I pledged when boarding Simpson's jet for the LAST time. I knew that it was going to be hard. Whenever I was with him, he doted on me and made me feel like a princess. I really believed that he loved me. Sometimes, I even forgot about his wife and twin daughters. But for that phone call from Bethany, I probably would have never learned about this other life.

Simpson didn't talk about his other life, and I certainly never asked. I preferred to pretend that it didn't exist. But, given the amount of time we spent together, there were numerous emergencies that Simpson needed to handle ASAP. Like the time when we were in the Bahamas and there were issues with the contractors—the contractors who Simpson was paying to completely overhaul the kitchen, bathrooms, and boathouse on a home he didn't even own. The estate on Mobile Bay still belonged to Bethany's parents, though Bethany would inherit it one day. Simpson didn't mind the investments. In fact, I think he would have paid for the renovations even without the future gift. "Anything to keep her there and occupied in the summers," he said.

There or not, due to the number of "crisis" calls when we were together, I began thinking that Bethany knew that "Pat" was, in reality, a female. I mean "Pat" traveled with Simpson on his numerous business trips, which often extended into the weekends. The legitimate business trips made it impossible to end things, especially when the client wouldn't accept another member on my team to handle his account. But, it was time. I had been there and done that too many times to count.

With the news of Simpson leaving, new resolve took shape. I splashed water on my face and walked back into our suite.

"Guess what, babe? We're going to Blakely Point!"

I knew that I should have headed back to New York, but I justified accompanying Simpson to one of his vacation homes. It was part of our "LAST" time together. And deep down, I knew that I wanted our last time to linger just a little longer before my self-imposed rehab.

Moreover, Simpson's home on Mobile Bay seemed a fitting place to end things. The home where his wife and daughters relocated in the summers, the one place that I had never been invited. If I saw the house, his other life would slap me in the face. That would definitely make my rehab easier, I justified. Then, I would, once and for all, be able to say good-bye.

Chapter 14

Francie

I was a mess. The Les Quatre Mousquetaires took turns attempting to reboot my Sacral Chakra, but my confidence and self-worth were burrowed so far in the depths of my despair, nothing was working. Farrah placed an APB amongst her crystal community for carnelian, which she was convinced would do the trick. It would spark a healthy robust flow of energy throughout my body, she said, which will surely HAVE to stimulate my creativity and make me forget about Henry DeVries.

Everyone was worried about me and the impact this scandal might have on my blossoming writing career. They overheard my agent's pleading messages on our answering machine, the one in the kitchen, the same one where I first learned about my father's infidelity with Ginnie Smith. I did not listen to the messages. Since learning about Henry and Georgia, I had wallowed in pity inside my room in the big house for the past three weeks. I learned of my agent's messages from Aurora, and she didn't mince words.

"Your agent is at her wit's end. She said you haven't been returning her calls and have now missed several deadlines. She says that you must let her know what is going on! She said that the publisher is getting skittish."

But it wasn't Aurora's frank warnings from my agent, Farrah's ultimate procurement of carnelian, or Mom's Kombucha tea or Jojoba oils that zapped me out of the doldrums. It was CiCi's bluntness.

"Things normally work out for the best. Look at your mom. He was a double whammy—a tour-on and from the North. So, get your whiny ass out of the bed, before you end up with bed sores, like Charles."

The way CiCi described Charles' abscesses resulting from his confinement to the bed actually made me feel sorry for the monster. Fearing a similar fate, I crawled out of bed. And after taking a long bath in Mom's oils and lathering myself in her homemade soaps, I drove straight to the pharmacy.

Dr. Quinn called in more Valium and upped my dosage to twice a day. I retreated to the boathouse and assured my caregivers that I was ready to start writing again. That was a lie. I just needed a Valium. Mom and Farrah would have lost their chakra if they knew I'd succumbed to synthetic medicines in lieu of their herbal alternatives. I thought Aurora and CiCi would understand, but I wasn't going to test the waters.

To give the chemicals a little boost, I washed the Valium down with tequila. The pain that consumed every nerve in my body fled about as quickly as Mom had from New Orleans. Now, that image seemed funny. It made me laugh.

"Good for her! Good for her! Cheers to my crazy Mama! She is one strong crazy Motha!" I yelled as I imitated the Les Quatre Mousquetaires' version of the Hokey Pokey:

> You put your right cheek in;
> You take your left cheek out;
> You put your whole ass in,
> And you shake it all about,
> You do the hokey pokey,
> and you turn yourself around;
> That's what it's all about.

My performance was interrupted when I noticed an unfamiliar woman on the Brooks' dock. She was stunning. Her almond, slightly wavy, hair rippled down her exposed back. She was wearing a blue halter top and blue-and-white striped palazzo pants that hung around her hips. She held a glass of wine in her hand. Her silhouette in the sunset could have donned the cover of a fashion magazine. Her swagger was sophisticated and worldly; it was mesmerizing.

As I sat gazing at her, a man came up from behind and grabbed her around her waist. She turned around. She put her hands on his cheeks. They began kissing. When they finally stopped, I realized the man was Simpson Baldwin. But the woman on the dock was NOT Bethany. No way.

Bethany wasn't as tall as this bombshell on the Brooks' dock, and Bethany's primary accessory was a headband. This woman boasted a sexier fashion style than Bethany, whose frumpy monogrammed sweaters not only masked her cute figure but also made her look twenty years older.

Was I hallucinating? I knew from Dan the pharmacy man that confusion was a side effect from my increased Valium dosage. But what the hell was a little confusion? I'd been confused my entire life. I closed my eyes and shook my head, trying to reboot my brain, and then looked again. The image was still there.

Simpson was carrying a wine bottle. He and the woman walked to the end of the dock. She sat down on the edge and began dangling her legs in the water. He straddled his legs behind her, as she leaned back into his chest. He started kissing her neck, until she turned around and rolled on top of him, with his legs wrapped around her. The whole scene was sensual. Against the backdrop of the setting sun, it seemed surreal. I could have watched them all night, but the sun completely disappeared into Mobile Bay.

The sun had set on a lot of things lately...my marriage, my self-esteem, my writing, my soul, and now on the perfect, perfect, perfect picture engrained in my mind of the perfect life of Bethany Brooks Baldwin. I was sad for me and surprisingly, I was sad for her.

The next morning, I kept rehashing the romantic picture I witnessed the night before. It couldn't have been real, I thought. I finally rolled out of my bed in the big house, poured a big mug of coffee, opened the purple gate, and crossed the boardwalk to my once writing haven. I saw Bethany, and she seemed to be on a mission. She was walking up and down her dock—or crawling was more like it. If I didn't know better, I'd think she was counting every nail in the pier. I thought to myself, "… and she thinks our family is odd."

Then she must have seen something. She was clutching it between her thumbs and index fingers, holding it up to the sun and examining it carefully. To me, it looked like air, but not to her. She laid down in the spot and began beating the planks of her pier. She seemed to be having a break-down. This time, I was more than sad for her, I actually felt sorry for Bethany Brooks Baldwin.

After her tantrum, she stood up straight, brushed off her pants, and began walking back to her house. She resumed her walk of confidence, that walk of arrogance, with her nose pointed to the sky. I watched her until the gate on her perfectly painted white fence slammed shut, the fence beside our hideously painted purple one.

Part III

Chapter 15

Louie Trahan

I'm a Coast Guard Captain for Sector New York in Staten Island, the largest USCG operational field command on the East Coast. Within the maritime community, this region is known as "The Buck Stops Here."

I am lucky to be in Sector New York. It offers the greatest opportunity to climb the Coast Guard ladder. But, career advancement or not, I miss my roots. Yes, Louis Gustave Trahan is Cajun to the core.

I miss everything about my former post in Baton Rouge, Louisiana. I miss the 200 miles of waterways of the Mississippi River, Atchafalaya River, Red River and the portions of the Gulf encompassing my former area of responsibility. I miss the crawfish and boudin sausage. I miss the jazz music. I miss the Spanish oak trees. I miss the bayous and swamps. I miss the sticky sweltering days when even at 6:00 a.m., my sunglasses instantly fogged up from the thick humidity. I even miss watching *Hee Haw*, the old country variety show, with Dad.

The needy side of me misses Southern women, and everything that comes with them: their accents, their style, their smell, and even their coyness. All the things that are lacking in the aggressive girls on Staten Island.

When first arriving in New York, I tried to disguise my Cajun accent, thinking that the "redneck blood" that ran through my veins would limit my movement up the ranks. As it turned out, my Cajun toughness distinguished me in my sector. The northern members in my division were more in awe of the fact that I swam with alligators and killed snakes than my impressive rescue record.

I also entertained the members of Sector New York with my wealth of useless knowledge from all the movies and classic television sitcoms that I had watched with Dad. I liked the nicknames pegged by my northern buddies: "Bayou Lou" and "Louie Louie," the shortened version of Louis from Louisiana.

"Bayou Lou's" imitations of famous movie and TV lines seemed to help ease the stress of our job and provide a little levity. I was beginning to honor the upbringing that grounded me and germinated my bad ass image. It was finally serving me quite well.

As for the serious side of my job, I held more awards and decorations than anyone, except for our sector commander. In that regard, I was following in Dad's footsteps but a long way from rivaling his remarkable feats.

But like Dad, the lives lost were the only thing that mattered.

I finally understood Dad's obsession with the movie, *The Guardian*. Growing up, I knew very little about his career in the Coast Guard. Mom told me questions were forbidden. Now, I knew Dad was living vicariously through Ben Randall, Kevin Costner's character. Dad was reliving his twenty-five years of service in the United State Coast Guard as a rescue swimmer. He, like Ben Randall, only kept track of the number of people he lost, not saved.

I wished I understood it then. But, at the time, the only thing I appreciated was that *The Guardian*, which played repeatedly, was a welcomed replacement for Dad's fixation on *Survivor*, *Law & Order*, CSI and their spin-offs.

One thing I did understand then was that our house was dramatically different before I unexpectedly came along. All the pictures of Dad and my three older brothers illustrated the contrast.

My three older brothers were two years apart and then ten years elapsed before me. Instead of rough housing and all the other things that one experiences during childhood with brothers, my childhood was akin to that of an only child. Worse than the lack of bonds of brotherhood was the complete absence of a father.

By the time I arrived on the scene, my father's downward spiral had started. Instead of having playmates with whom to go fishing, hunting, or to play football or baseball, I spent most of my time in my room reading about such pastimes.

There was not one picture of Dad coaching me at a little league game or Pop Warner football, or with any prized fish from Doyle's Bayou. I was never offered the opportunity to shoot one deer or duck, like each of my brothers. Their best ones were mounted and displayed in our den. Hell, I never ranked high enough for a possum or raccoon shooting adventure.

If I spent any time with Dad, we watched movies or TV shows. Dad's recliner in the den was my contribution to the family. He had rarely left it since the day I was born. I discovered why when I was seventeen years old.

That night will be forever seared in my brain. I scored the winning touchdown against my high school's archrival, a team we hadn't beaten in eight years. It was a diving catch as the time expired. I felt like a hero as my teammates carried me off the field to the deafening cheers in the packed stadium. Better yet, I felt like I was going to get lucky with Monica PreJean. It was the way she was shaking her poms-poms and yelling, "Louie, Louie, he's our man!" It was the way she was smiling at me. It was the look in her crystal blue eyes.

When I got home after the post-game celebration at Monica's, I ran in to tell my parents about my winning touchdown catch. Dad, as usual, was sitting in the recliner and watching *The Guardian*. Apparently, my excited entrance interrupted a climatic Coast Guard rescue scene. Dad wasn't the least bit interested in my heroic catch. He was furious. It was like he was possessed.

"God damn it! Can't you see I'm busy! You son of a bitch, you made me miss the best part."

He had been mesmerized by the movie since its release and probably watched it fifty times. So, he hadn't "missed" anything. Maybe, it was the effects of my hyped-up testosterone from the near hookup with Monica, or simply years of rejection. Whatever the reason, my suppressed feelings came boiling to the surface.

Any other father would have been in the stands, thrilled and proud of the epic moment, instead of parked in a recliner watching the same movie over and over. I snapped.

"God damn you. What kind of father would prefer to watch a fake scene in a movie over hearing about his son's football game? Real life! Your own flesh and blood! I scored the winning touchdown tonight against the Bulldogs. But forget it. Sorry I interrupted the movie that your sorry ass has been glued to for the past four weeks."

He jumped up from his recliner. It was the fastest I witnessed him move in the last seventeen years. He cold-cocked me in the jaw.

"Don't you ever talk to me like that! I am your father."

"Father? You are the worst excuse for a father that has ever existed," I mumbled, already feeling the effects from his punch.

This time, I was prepared. When his fist came toward me again, I ducked. The force of his missed swing unbalanced him and gave me a chance to lock myself in my room.

"No one talks to me like that! Come out and fight like a man!" he yelled pounding on the door.

"Pierre, Pierre, calm down," Mom said. "I've rewound the movie to the part you missed."

After I locked myself in my room, Theo called. My thirty-one-year-old oldest brother was more of a father to me than my real one.

Theo wanted to treat "the MVP" to breakfast to celebrate the victory over the Bulldogs. Theo didn't mention anything about breakfast during his congratulatory bear hug at the football game. Perhaps I didn't hear that invitation due to the mayhem, but I thought the more likely scenario was that Mom had reported the incident to him.

Theo took me to our favorite spot, the Waffle House®. We always ordered the same thing: a pecan waffle with chocolate chips, with a side of country ham. At some point, we learned to split our "scattered, smothered, covered, country" hash browns order.

If you were regulars like Theo and me, you knew the Waffle House® vernacular for the hash browns: "scattered" meant spreading the shredded potatoes on the grill so they could get extra-crispy; "smothered" if topped with diced onions; "covered" was the addition of American cheese; "country" was topping them off with sausage gravy. The hash browns were our very favorite, but that day, I couldn't have any of my favorites. My jaw was killing me. I needed soft food. I ordered scrambled eggs and country grits. I explained the reason why.

But, Theo knew and was prepared to talk about it. So, at seventeen years old while sitting in a booth at the Waffle House®, Theo relayed the cause of Dad's mental collapse.

Three months after I was born, Dad responded to a plane crash in the Mississippi River. The conditions were especially bad that day. The waters were particularly rough and dangerous and blanketed by a dense fog. He swam to an older man and woman, who were struggling. Dad was securing them onto floats, when the man ordered him to save his children. He couldn't see anyone else but heard a young man's voice screaming for help. He followed the pleas through the fog. The young man was holding onto his teenage sisters but losing his grip. Dad instructed the girls to hang on tightly, as he pulled their brother toward the boat.

"Dad said the young man became so heavy. He had never before felt a grip like this man. Dad said that his hands felt like they were in a choke hold. He couldn't fight the man's strong, sinking pull. The last thing he remembered was the surface of the water over his own head and then darkness."

Theo told me that Dad's crew resuscitated him. He had survivor's guilt because he failed to save the family. He didn't adequately secure the parents before following the father's direction to save his children. But, the failure to secure the parents wasn't merely what haunted him. It was also his loss of focus.

"Well, you know about the Trahan hands; you could grip a basketball when you were six!" Theo recounted. "The size of Dad's hands and his focus were legendary, his trademark."

Theo told me about one of the numerous stories that circulated through the Coast Guard. During down times, Dad would play darts. He wouldn't stop until he hit five consecutive bull's-eyes, which one day took five hours. After his success, he said, 'That took too damn long,' and he started again.

"During the rescue, the size and power of the man's hands threw Dad's concentration," Theo continued. "His once unyielding intensity was rocked, and it rocked him to his core. Dad never lost that many people during any rescue. He never lost an entire family or his focus until July 4, 1989."

Theo's explanation made me realize that Dad's withdrawal from me, his lack of interest in my activities, and his irritability and anger didn't have anything to do with me. It had everything to do with that family of five and his abject failure. By then, however, my psyche was severely damaged.

Like Dad's obsession with his new movie, I found myself obsessed with the family. I craved more information but didn't think I would ever crave a breakfast from the shoebox-shaped diner again.

From the news accounts I located, the King Air-200 was owned by Arthur Francis Hollingsworth, III. Mr. and Mrs. Hollingsworth's twin daughters, Vivian Louise and Charlotte Emerson, were presented at the Houston Debutante Ball. Frankie, short for Arthur Francis Hollingsworth, IV, piloted the plane that departed Houston en route to Blakely Point, Alabama to join the remaining family member. The Hollingsworth family celebrated every Independence Day at their summer home on Mobile Bay, a family tradition for many generations.

After all these years, that family came crashing to the forefront, just like that Beechcraft King Air-200, when I perused *The New York Times* Best Seller's list. The current number one, *Crash & Burn*, was written by Francie DeVries. It was spine-chilling, and I don't mean the book, but its author. I learned that her mother, Junie LeBlanc, was the sole survivor of the Hollingsworth family that perished in the Mississippi River that July 4th. Junie wasn't on board the plane because she was pregnant.

After finishing Francie DeVries' book, the daughter of Junie, the only granddaughter of Art and Weezie Hollingsworth, the only niece to Frankie, Vivian and Charlotte, there was an emptiness in my gut that even hot dogs, hamburgers, deviled eggs, and cobblers couldn't fill. An immense sadness settled over me and couldn't be erased, even by booming fireworks.

That incident continued to haunt me every July 4th, like it did my father. He felt responsible. I felt guilty.

If Dad hadn't been resuscitated, my childhood wouldn't have been so lonely, isolated, or sad. I wouldn't have silently cried myself to sleep thinking that my unplanned conception was responsible for Dad's withdrawal. His spirit and zest for life drowned in the Mississippi River that day alongside the Hollingsworth family. He might be breathing but that was all.

Chapter 16

Louie

Every July 4th, I tried to think about the sacrifices of our founding fathers and the lives lost in our fight for freedom. I attempted to honor the day, honor the heroes, and celebrate our liberation.

But, every year that family drew me back to the waters of the Mississippi. Dad would forever mourn the loss of that family. He would forever be scarred by his remorse.

I attempted every distraction from the upcoming July 4th celebrations, even scheduling my semi-annual visit to the dentist before it closed for the holiday. I hated the dentist, but the time on the subway from Brooklyn to Manhattan, then my time in the chair with my mouth wide open, took my mind off of the upcoming festivities. The most effective distraction was the horrible toothpaste they used, though they promised every six months that a more palatable version was available.

The purported new and improved cinnamon flavor left me feeling queasy. I hadn't eaten since 5:00 a.m., hated cinnamon and gagged at the cinnamon paste that slipped down my throat during the excessive rinsing by the inexperienced hygienist. I wondered if this feeling was the equivalent of what morning sickness felt like for expectant mothers. I thought I was going to vomit.

I dashed into the nearest market for a box of crackers. You'd think I was speaking Latin when I asked the clerk for the cracker aisle.

"Did you say, crack an owl?" the confused clerk asked.

Out of nowhere, this very attractive woman appeared, rescuing the clerk.

"Crackers are on the second aisle. South Carolina?" she asked.

"Try again."

"Alabama?"

"Nope, Louisiana. I'm Louie Trahan," extending my hand.

"Millie Hill," she said. I instantly thought her hand was as soft as butter. I didn't want to let go.

"So, Millie, I'm guessing you're a Tennessean."

"Close, but no cracker for the cracker. I'm betting you'll never guess."

"I'll take that bet. If I'm right, you'll have to let me treat you to a beer."

She curled her hair around her ear, smiled and gave me a thumbs up. From our sparse conversation, I could tell she was more than a pretty face; she was smart and quick. She wasn't going to say another word to provide any more clues about her accent. Don't screw this up, I told myself. No room for a casualty here. I definitely wanted to have a drink with this Southern belle.

The USCG's taxing training for an Aviation Survival Technician prepared me for pressure situations. I was drilled in keeping my emotions in check, so why was my stomach tumbling, like the first time I rode a roller coaster?

My training served me well. I pushed my nerves aside and my counterintelligence experience kicked in. A clue...her environmentally friendly canvas grocery tote donned the logo of the "The Spa at the Greenbrier." I would have never guessed West Virginia was her origin.

I didn't want to jump the gun. A beer with this hottie was on the line. She did have a classy aura about her so perhaps she had only been a guest at the posh resort.

The closest thing to a resort for me was the Pipestem Resort State Park, ironically in West Virginia. There, I camped, hiked, and fly-fished, not been pampered with a mud bath, a deep tissue massage, or hydrotherapy from the region's natural mineral springs.

I didn't want to spook her by totally checking her out, but I quickly did a full body scan. I needed something else, some other clue. The shoes, the shoes confirmed my initial thought. The shoes were hiking boots, and not just the hip stylish kind. Instead, they were substantial, over the ankle boots for a serious hiker.

"Weeeeelllll," she finally said interrupting my analysis, as she pushed her hair behind her ear again. The way she strung out one syllable into four, I knew she was trying to throw me off.

"West Virginia," I said confidently.

"Seriously? What the hell?" she said clearly irritated.

By her reaction, I thought that I totally offended her. It occurred to me that if you're not from West Virginia, you would wonder why someone thought you were! So, I quickly decided to come clean.

"Well, only because of your Greenbrier tote, and your hiking boots. Other than that, I was leaning toward Georgia. You remind me of the girls I've met in Athens...all beautiful, by the way."

"Nice attempt at a save! But no need to backpedal. Hinton, West Virginia to be exact. Go get your crackers. I want that beer."

We talked for three hours at the bar, with our grocery bags in tow. Afterwards, I walked her home.

"Thanks for the beers and for carrying my groceries! I'd ask you up for another beer, but I have an early date in the morning with a lot of numbers on a balance sheet. I'm already dreading it. I had so much fun with you, Louis Gustave Trahan."

I didn't think her excuse was a brush-off. I loved the way she said my name while pushing her hair behind her ears. Was I imagining things or was she blushing? Too many beers, I thought. I wanted more than anything to spend more time with her. After three hours of talking, I learned a lot about Millie Hill. I knew where she worked and what she did. Like me, she loved Southern novels, Southern movies and Southern food. It seemed like the only thing we didn't agree on was what we liked best with grits: she liked hers with trout, while I liked mine with shrimp.

I revealed that I didn't live in the neighborhood, but my dentist did. I would have to take the subway back to Brooklyn.

"I had fun too. I will never dread going to the dentist again," as I leaned in to kiss her on the cheek. She returned the favor and kissed me on the cheek, lingering a bit before slowly retreating. She looked up at me with her big brown eyes.

"Can I call you?" I asked.

"Yes, that would be great," she replied as she retrieved her cell from her purse. "What's your number?"

After she entered it in her phone, my cell rang.

"Now you have my number, so no excuses."

I answered it.

"Hey, I'm busy right now. I'm with this smoking hot woman that I really want to kiss."

"Go for it!" she said into her phone.

And I did. It was long and inviting.

"Damn, damn, damn those balance sheets!!" she said, when we finally stopped seriously making out on her condominium steps.

"It's okay, I understand. Gotta long day ahead of me myself. But I would like to propose another bet."

"I am willing to entertain the bet."

"If you don't have July 4th plans, I'd like to cook dinner for you—shrimp and grits."

"That sounds great, but what are we betting?"

"If you don't like shrimp and grits better than trout and grits, I'll have to fix you breakfast. If you agree with me, you have to fix me breakfast. And just fyi, I'll want mine in bed."

"And just fyi, so will I."

We made out again like two teenagers. She not only stayed over on July 4th, but also the entire weekend. I stayed with her the following weekend. After our first night together, Millie revealed that she loved my accent and my nicknames of "Louie Louie" and "Bayou Lou." My nicknames were far better than the nickname given her after her arrival in New York, "Millie Hillbilly."

Who would have ever imagined that I would fall in love with a mountaineer in New York City? If not for my Cajun accent, I would have never met her. Until I met the hillbilly from West Virginia, I dreaded the sight of a Waffle House®, and I dreaded July 4th. Millie breathed new life into me.

As I placed a triple order of scattered, smothered, covered, country hash browns after my shift, my insides were exploding with a giddy euphoria. They were bursting with all the colors that light up sky on the fourth of July.

Chapter 17

Francie

Since going back on my meds, I was definitely less depressed about the demise of my marriage, and I was more relaxed—too relaxed!! I couldn't concentrate on my writing. It was bad enough that my days were getting confused. Even worse, my reality was getting blurred. I started questioning if I really saw Simpson Baldwin with another woman and Bethany Baldwin having a temper tantrum on their dock.

A talk with my agent bought a little more time for my next deadline in my anticipated sequel to *Crash & Burn*. I wanted to go in a different direction and promised it would be worth the wait. Of course, I didn't tell my agent that I hadn't written one word since my last submission.

I wasn't going to worry yet about my lack of progress. Mom and her roommates were celebrating the ending of Mercury's retrograde. Despite the fact that there could be lingering effects during the two weeks following the retrograde, they decided to enter this shadowy period on the offensive—hitting the Retroshade right "in the nose."

Plans were complete for entertainment, party favors, decorations and food. Herbert strummed his banjo, and Aurora from Daphne supplied wide-brimmed hats and colorful, plastic sunglasses for each guest. Mom strung green, purple, and white blinking lights throughout all the Spanish oaks and draped them along our purple fence. The blinking lights and the various oils that Mom added to the tiki torches were to hold at bay any unwelcoming forces.

No cheese, crackers, or finger sandwiches were even considered for the guests. Farrah prepared a variety of root vegetables, including carrots, radishes, turnips, sweet potatoes, and a colorful array of beets.

"Roots pack a dynamo of energy and minerals needed to tackle the Retroshade," Farrah said.

Since the Retrograde had affected communication, Mom always made pralines for the party. She pronounced them "plaaah-leens," not "pray-lenes," and quickly corrected any mispronunciation.

Mom was renowned for her "plaaah-leens." I assumed she just touted their communication aid as a gimmick to show off her culinary skills. After she replaced her famous recipe with Aurora's, I doubted my theory. I decided to delve into the connection between pralines and communication.

Mom's explanation made me feel guilty that I thought she, of all people, would have an ulterior motive.

"Since the 1860s, pralines were the means for African-American women to make a living in New Orleans," she said. "These women were pioneers in 'product branding'— they connected this delightful confection of butter, sugar, milk, and pecans to New Orleans' culture. Product branding is the ultimate communication skill."

By serving pralines, Mom found a way to honor Aurora's family too. Mom replaced her concoction with Aurora's ancestral recipe to honor Aurora's heritage and the strong women in her family. Aurora's great-grandmother made and sold pralines in her confectionery shop, one of the first African-American, woman-owned businesses in the French Quarter.

I would never view pralines the same after this. They added another dynamic to the independent spirit on the porch. I was suddenly aware that some of the Boardwalkers present at the party were the same ones who previously shunned and even frowned upon Mom's eccentric ways. They were having a glorious time. Perhaps, given their advanced age, they were tired of pretending to be something on the outside that they weren't on the inside, or maybe they were just plain tired. Whatever it was, they stripped their prior facades and were laughing, singing, dancing, drinking, and munching on pralines!

It was a boardwalk reunion of sorts. The Alexanders, owners of the Jubilee bell, were there. Old-man Miller, now a widower, was also present. I never could look at Olin Miller without remembering Mom's story about his "ass crack," when seeing her first Jubilee. As he was shaking his booty at this reunion to Herbert's rendition of "Sweet Home Alabama," I saw the infamous ass crack and cracked up.

The spirit in our yard was happy; no, it was extraordinary. The Retroshade was initiating an awakening, a spiritual revival, and an elimination of any and all pretenses. That is, until the end of Mr. Miller's dance with CiCi.

"I am having such a wonderful time," Mr. Miller said. "Who would have ever thought that I would be dancing with CiCi Brooks! But I must admit, after seeing your daughter carrying on with her husband on your dock, I know things aren't always as they seem!"

After Mr. Miller's outburst, he must have picked up on the shocked looks among the Les Quatre Mousquetaires, especially after CiCi removed her sunglasses and looked at him with her eyebrows arched over her wide eyes.

"How about you and me take a walk?" CiCi asked Mr. Miller, as she refilled his drink, took him by the hand, and swept him away from the crowd.

After all the guests left, CiCi recounted her conversation.

"So, Winston and I were out that night trying to catch some red fish," Olin Miller said. "Winston was driving the boat on our return, so I was just taking in the sights of the Bay. You know, it's beautiful at night with all the lights reflecting on the water from the boathouses. And those lights seemed like they were shining right down on Simpson and Bethany—like a big spotlight."

"Well, what were they doing? Sounds awfully romantic."

"It was. I mean I didn't mean to stare but it could a been a movie scene—the water, the lights, two naked bodies on a dock. They were oblivious to anything and everything around them."

"That doesn't sound like Bethany at all! You know those tour-ons trespass on our docks all the time. I can't tell you the things I've stumbled upon over the years."

"No, it was definitely them because Winston was trying to be funny, and he honked the horn. Simpson shot up like he'd been struck by lightning. Winston hit the horn again several times, you know, guy stuff. Definitely them. I ran into Bethany the next day and apologized for interrupting their frolic and honking the horn."

"What did she say?" CiCi asked.

"She didn't say anything, but she didn't have to. Her glare said enough. She was blistering mad. I apologized again but she just went stomping off."

"And ladies, I'm telling you now," CiCi said. "If he saw Simpson Baldwin, it wasn't Bethany with him. I only hope for Simpson's sake that Olin was wrong because hell hath no fury like Bethany Baldwin on a good day."

I knew then that everything I had seen was real. That I wasn't confused or hallucinating. That Simpson Baldwin was with another woman, and Bethany crawled around on that dock likely looking for evidence. And based on her reaction, I think she must have found something. Knowing that I wasn't going crazy should have made me feel better, but it didn't. It made me think of Henry and Georgia. It made me think of Dad and Ginnie. It made me chase down too many Valiums with too much tequila.

Chapter 18

Francie

The next few days weren't any better. I started sleeping in the boathouse. That is, if what I did at night could be called sleeping. My sleep pattern was so erratic; I didn't want to disturb Mom or her roommates, but what I really didn't want was their worry and the load of sacraments they'd spring on me if they learned of my schedule.

I would pass out at 8 p.m. but only sleep for several hours before waking up. When I gave up trying to get back to sleep, I would slip out to the dock. While the rest of the world was fast asleep, I found peace from the Bay—the water lapping against the dock's pilings, the moon's reflection on its surface, the clicks of the cicadas, and the hoots from a nearby owl.

"What wise words do you have for me you ol' hoot owl?" I asked. "It's easy to judge from your lofty spot. Come out in the day when the world is spinning out of control, and then see how smart you are!"

Sometimes, I wasn't all alone with the hoot owl; Uncle Frankie would join me on occasion. He would try to comfort me about Henry.

"It's part of life's passage to suffer from a broken heart," he'd say. Perhaps he was interpreting the hoot owl when he told me that "when the suffering stops, you come out of it on the other side stronger and a hell of a lot brighter."

I didn't know about the stronger part, but I was beginning to understand the brighter part of the equation. Henry was the only boy or man that I had ever been with. Shoot! He was the only boy who ever noticed that I existed. We never discussed our commonalities, our goals, or our weaknesses. Simply put, I fell in love with the first man who paid attention to me because he paid attention to me! How silly! How stupid of me to fall for someone as shallow as he was—someone who would be attracted to Georgia Murphey. From my limited time with her, I sensed her insecurities, her manipulation, or as CiCi put it best, her "wannabe" status. More power to them both!

Uncle Frankie helped me see things clearly, and he brightened my spirit. So why was it that I couldn't regain my concentration? Why was I continuing to mope around? I was beginning to act and feel like a sloth. The more sleep I got, the less energy I had. I rarely ventured out of the boathouse; but when I did, I knew Mom noticed I wasn't quite right. I couldn't recall a time in my life when she doted, but she was doting now. She even invited me on a bike ride, and I had never seen the woman on a bike! But, it was the invitation to a Blakely Point Preservation Society meeting that threw me for a loop.

I never heard Mom even utter the formal name for the Blakely Point Preservation Society. Instead, she referred to it as the "Boardwalk Po-Po." I learned at an early age to steer clear of its members, especially its president, Charles Brooks. Over time, she warned me about others.

"Now, watch out for Collier Duval; she's a pot-stirrer and member of the Boardwalk Po-Po. That's Priscilla Hodges. She will try and worm information out of you; she's a part of the Po-Po. If they try to talk to you, tell them to 'talk to the hand 'cause the face don't give a damn.'"

I knew now that this group were the ones constantly behind some petition about our yard and my mother's tea parties or other "shenanigans." So, I was speechless when Mom asked me to attend their meeting. She laughed when she saw the look on my face.

"Not the meeting with the snotty Boardwalk Po-Pos, it's the meeting after THE meeting," she said, while making quotation marks in the air.

So, more out of curiosity than anything else, I agreed to attend "the meeting" after *the meeting* at Edward Bastian's house. I learned that Edward was a member of both societies. He was the mole, so to speak, who would not only divulge the Po-Po's latest tactics but also other inside society information. I think Mom was given a preview, thus the reason for my invite.

Edward lived down the boardwalk in the opposite direction of the Inn. I couldn't remember the last time I ventured down to this end of the boardwalk. I forgot that my favorite house growing up was on this side. The house changed ownership more than a dozen times. It was known as the "Yellow Awning House." In addition to the signature massive yellow awnings, the expansive wrap-around porch still looked the same and still won the prize for the most rocking chairs on the boardwalk.

Edward Bastian's house was next door to my favorite house, well my old favorite house. Our house is now my favorite. As long as I could remember, I was embarrassed to be associated with our house. Now, I embraced the purple fence and our yard that the Blakely Point Preservation Society characterized as a "carnival" and a "spectacle."

I grew to love our unwavering house, warts and all. It was us. I was now ashamed that I wanted to belong to other families on the boardwalk when growing up. Though I had pined for a "normal family," if I learned anything from Uncle Frankie, it was that "normal" was an oxymoron. "Don't ever, ever believe that anything is normal because when you do, it will bite you in the ass," he advised.

I was learning that he was right. I had even grown to appreciate Mom's "enhancements" to our yard. "Bring it on, Momma," I would yell from the dock while the rest of the world was asleep.

128

Chapter 19

Francie

Mom opened the gate on his white picket fence, and we walked down the slate steppingstones in the meticulously groomed lawn to his small, charming bungalow. That evening, I learned that Edward Bastian's other neighbor was the Summerville family (Nancy and her brother Cannon). Funny, I never noticed the Bastian's house when riding my bike past Nancy's, longing for the day I might be invited to join her gaggle of girlfriends. I must have been too preoccupied with the goings-on at the Summerville's house to notice anything else. But, as ass-crack Miller so eloquently announced to CiCi, "things aren't always as they seem."

The Bastian bungalow, which Edward inherited, was evidence that the amount of square footage wasn't the measure of charm or class. This home could have donned the cover of *Southern Living*, *Architectural Digest*, or any publication dedicated to exquisite style. The furniture in Edward's den was upholstered with fabric from the finest Parisienne boutiques. The clothes he was wearing spotlighted his love of understated fineness—fitted cotton pants, a linen shirt and Gucci loafers.

He welcomed both Mom and me with a peck on each cheek, and I noticed his cologne. It was not overpowering, but it was just enough to emit an inviting aura, a freshness, and a confident vibe. Edward was a man who understood himself. He was totally comfortable in his skin, and his skin was unblemished, smooth, and clean-shaven. Even his perfectly shaped bald head was glowing.

Edward picked up a silver tray with flutes of champagne garnished with a strawberry.

"Dom for the lovely Dames?" he asked laughingly, as he offered his expensive bubbly. "Shall we?" He held up his glass for a toast. "Here's to preservation!"

After our toasts, Mom quickly cut to the chase and wanted an update about her recent provocations discussed at the meeting.

"Junie, Junie, Junie, my dear Junie," Edward said with a grin. "You will indeed be happy, or not, to hear that your tomfooleries were not the topic of discussion. Ironically, it seems that their attention has been turned toward your neighbor."

"Oh, Edward, you can't possibly be referring to CiCi! That would send Charles Brooks over the edge!"

"Well, karma's a bitch. However, the scuttlebutt involves Bethany, not CiCi."

"Charles Brooks ruined that child," Mom said, as she patted me on the knee.

Apparently, Mom picked up on more than I had given her credit. Growing up, I blamed her for my outcast status. I felt a wave of remorse for thinking that way. She did know. Was her lack of intervention a sign of helplessness or was it intentional? Was it that she wanted me to find my own way? If the latter, what she didn't know was that I still didn't know my way.

"Seems that Bethany has offended a host of Boardwalkers lately," Edward said. "She has exhibited erratic behavior and even dropped the 'f-bomb' to Priscilla Hodges. According to Priscilla, she simply inquired into what Simpson was up to lately. Collier Duval added that Bethany has become a 'regular' at the spa, spending a 'lot of money' on rejuvenation services and products. Collier believes that there is trouble in paradise and that Bethany is 'sweet' on someone at the Inn."

"Well, you know I don't care anything about such nonsense," Mom said. "I'm just relieved I don't have to deal with another petition! Francie must be my good luck charm. She'll have to accompany me to our next meeting!"

I started wondering if my mother was trying to be a matchmaker (which would be so out of character for her). Edward was obviously single and around my age, he wore cologne and was quite dapper. But all the what-ifs swirling around in my head were answered quickly as he refilled my champagne glass.

"Junie tells me that you have been working on a sequel to *Crash & Burn*. Xavier and I can't wait for its release. He will be beside himself to know that THE Francie DeVries visited our home. We'd love to host a party for you when your sequel is published."

"Where is that handsome Xavier?" Mom asked. "I was hoping Francie could meet your better half."

Xavier was obviously Edward's partner. Mom clearly was aware of their relationship. I was thankful that I acquired this knowledge before questioning her about her motives. That would have totally signaled to Mom my shaky frame of mind. My original instincts were confirmed. She simply wanted to get me out of the boathouse, bond friendships with some of 'her people'—those she trusted unconditionally.

"When Xavier returns from his business trip, we'd love for you to be our guests for dinner."

"Oui, Oui, Monsieur," Mom said. "That's a date! Francie and I accept."

"I know you are a fabulous Cajun cook, but nothing compares to Xavier's French specialties," Edward said.

"Just say when," Mom said.

But when the "when" was decided, Mom suddenly had a conflict. She insisted that I attend.

"It would be good for you to get out, socialize with some interesting people your age," she said.

I knew that she was right. Since the demise of my marriage, other than Mom's friends, my only company was Uncle Frankie, and I certainly couldn't decline a dinner invitation due to a previous engagement with a ghost.

In addition to my mother's doting, Aurora and Farrah had also become quite attentive. On the day of the dinner, Aurora brought me a dress from her shop; it was a little too Bohemian for my taste but certainly seemed more appropriate for a French dinner than the boring options in my closet.

"You look beautiful!" Aurora said. "The dress fits you perfectly; it accentuates your exquisite figure."

I was starting to feel like I had three mothers. I appreciated their support and encouragement, but I was an adult now, not a child (although I did ask Luna and Becca to say a little prayer for me as I began walking down the boardwalk to Edward Bastian's dinner party).

Either their prayer was answered, or I didn't need a prayer. Edward welcomed me at the door, with a kiss on both cheeks, while leaving the scent of his signature cologne in the air.

"You must meet Xavier, my 'better half,' according to Junie! Xavier, come meet Francie DeVries!"

I thought I probably blushed as a tall, lean, and very sexy Frenchman walked in. Same kisses, same cologne. I couldn't pinpoint the aroma, a combination of so many scents but it mostly smelled like welcome. A welcome to a gathering of unpretentiousness and transparency. Xavier was as charming as Edward. I instantly felt at ease.

Our first glass of some fancy pinot gris was served with a charcuterie platter with brie cheese, apricots, pickles, prosciutto, pâté, and candied walnuts. Then came the gougères, a pastry filled with Gruyère cheese.

Edward giddily revealed how he and Xavier first met. He accompanied his mother to Paris to visit his younger sister. After graduating from high school, she left for college on the west coast and was studying abroad for the semester.

"She fled Jasper as fast as she could and never turned back."

"Jasper?" I asked.

"Yes, my hometown."

"I've never heard of Jasper."

"It's forty miles northwest from Birmingham and an hour north from the center of universe."

I certainly knew Birmingham, and if there was another 'center of the universe' in Alabama, my first guess would have been Mobile. So, I was confused. Edward picked up on my muddled state instantly.

"Tuscaloosa; you know, Nick Saban, Roll Tide."

I was still confused.

"Football, Francie! Football! Like in Louisiana where it's Baton Rouge and the LSU Tigers."

"Ah yes, how could I forget? I didn't go to LSU, but Michigan, where football is also king. I guess I was too busy working on my children's book or hanging out with Henry. I'm embarrassed to say that I never attended a single football game. In retrospect, I should have gotten out more," realizing that my college experience was quite shallow.

"I get what you're saying. There were lots of times I regretted that I wasn't more like my baby sister. I never appreciated her desire to broaden her perspective and experience different cultures. Then, I thought her 'thirst for intellectual enlightenment' was just weird."

Unlike his sister, Edward took the road most traveled in Jasper, which led him to the University of Alabama. He never even applied anywhere else. Everything that he heard about the abundance of beautiful girls was confirmed on the very first day of his freshman year. Since the percentage of girls enrolled at Alabama was much higher than men, Edward had an unlimited supply of dates. It was during that time that Edward discovered his true self.

"I never viewed my sister as eccentric anymore but wise beyond her years. I began to admire her. I admired her broad-mindedness, her progressive views. But for her, I would have never met Xavier."

"Didn't you enjoy your college years?" I asked. At this moment, I was so envious of Edward's sister and her sense of self at such a young age.

"Oh yes, I did, unquestionably. My experience at Alabama aided the discovery of my sexuality. I mean if none of the hottest girls I had ever seen did it for me, there was no denying it. I did meet some exquisitely fabulous girls along the way."

"All those 'exquisitely fabulous' girls still call him," Xavier said. "Often! He could make a killing from a call-in show dispensing his wisdom on finding the perfect partner in life."

"Xavier is not only drop-dead gorgeous but also has a wicked sense of humor," Edward said laughing. "I do believe that each turn in our life path—whether good, bad, or ugly—is essential in our growth as we journey through this life. Dwelling over the 'what-ifs' or 'do-overs' of the past consumes energy that should be conserved and tapped for what lies ahead. We can't think about all the things we should have done along the way because we can't retrace our steps. Only move forward."

How had I never come across Edward Bastian growing up on the Bay? My early years would have been drastically different with a wise friend like him. Then again, as he so poignantly said, every path is essential. If I met Edward earlier, there, most likely, would have been no Becca or Luna, which meant no best-selling children's books. Without my best-selling children's books, there would have been no first novel or a sequel. And Henry? While following Henry to Michigan wasn't ideal, Becca and Luna would have never come to life without my creative writing supporters there.

"So, when did Xavier come into the picture?" I asked, shaking myself from my thoughts.

"He was what was lying ahead! At that time in my life, the last thing I wanted to do was to go to France with my mother to visit my over-achiever sister. I was struggling to find a job and had no idea what I wanted to do. I only agreed because I planned to spend my days in the local Paris pubs, not fancy white-tableclothed cafés. I gave in on the first night. Xavier was our waiter. He had me at duck foie gras. I didn't return to Alabama with Mom. In fact, I stayed in France for five years!"

"Oh, how romantic!" I said.

"Yes, and in addition to those local pubs in Paris he was dying to experience, I introduced him to better ones in the south of France," Xavier said.

"Yes, he did. As well as La Poutargue, the caviar of Provence, razor clams in the French Riviera, and the macaronade, stuffed squid and mussels in Sète."

By now, Xavier replaced the charcuterie platter and the gougères with a goat cheese salad and substituted a rosé for the pinot gris.

"I've never heard of Sète."

"Oh darling, Sète is the 'Little Venice' of the Languedoc and on the coast of the Mediterranean. Xavier took me on a boat tour. We wove through the canal network for panoramic views of the city."

"And don't forget the Joutes," Xavier added.

"Oh, yes. Francie, you and Junie must let us take you there. Junie would adore the Joutes. They are Sète's version of jousts; but, instead of knights on horseback, there are two boats with high platforms supporting a jouster holding a lance and a shield. It's quite the spectacle!"

During this story, Xavier served a Bordeaux with our lamb chops and pommes dauphinois. I didn't think I could eat another bite, the pommes dauphinois was so rich and, apparently, Xavier's specialty so I certainly didn't want to offend. Edward explained that Xavier perfected the thinly sliced layers of potato using a mandolin, and he preferred whole milk in lieu of a heavy cream. The cream stifles the Gruyère! It's superbly rich, oui?"

"Yes, divine," I said. "Better than a dessert!"

"Oh, honey, wait for it...the dessert is dazzling! Poire belle Hélène!"

When he explained that this was a poached pear concoction, I had to pass. Even with all the food, I was more than inebriated. I was afraid that a poached pear may cause me to regurgitate my entire meal!

"It does sound fascinating. Would it be too much trouble to wrap it up? I want to share it with Mom. I know she will be beside herself that she missed all of this."

"Of course, except for the vanilla bean sorbet! We will have you again. We do love us some Junie!"

"How did you and Mom meet?"

"The Blakely Point Preservation Society! My grandmother was the bane of their existence long before your mother."

Edward then explained that his grandmother, Gertrude, was a close friend of my grandmother, Weezie. Like the Hollingsworths, his mother's family spent every summer on the Bay. As with my family, tragedy took his grandparents.

En route to their home one summer, a drunk driver crossed the center line and hit them head-on. They were killed instantly.

"Mother wouldn't set foot in the house after the accident. I encouraged her to sell it. But she couldn't—too much family history. It fell into disrepair over the years and became the subject of many preservation society petitions," Edward explained.

"I do remember your house now! It was covered with ivy! When I'd ride my bike down the boardwalk, I'd speed by your house. I thought it was creepy."

"Indeed, it was! The ivy was creeping into the house! I wanted to demolish it; Mother wanted to preserve it. The more that I visited, the more that I fell in love with the house, the Bay, all of it. I got into several disputes with the 'So-ci-et—y,'" Edward said mocking and exaggerating a Southern accent, "over my renovation plans. Eventually, I beat them down, and our little American bungalow was created."

"It's stunning. I'm so glad you saved the house, preserved your mother's memories, and stood firm with your vision. Your 'American bungalow' is a wonderful addition to the boardwalk."

Soon after its restoration, the Blakely Point Preservation Society "rewarded" Edward with an invitation to join its exclusive group. Given the tactics used against his mother and him, he was more intrigued than interested. But after attending the first meeting, he learned that Junie LeBlanc, the daughter of Weezie Hollingsworth, his grandmother's friend, was the current "momentous blemish on the boardwalk." Edward decided to meet this 'crazed mad woman.'

After Edward met my mother, he was captivated by her spunk, her raw genuineness and everything else that drew you in. He loved Junie LeBlanc. So, Edward not only gave Mom a heads-up about all the petitions but also the ammunition to fight them. Not only her private advocate, he drafted all her responses. Edward had saved the purple fence, the glass orbs, the crystals draped through our oak trees, the yard art, and even the herb garden. No wonder Mom referred to him as "one of her people."

I thanked my hosts profusely for my most memorable evening before leaving. It was memorable and a much needed escape. I felt as if I was swept away to the south of France—worlds away from the tightening grip of my depression. Nonetheless, as I traversed the slate steppingstones, I quickly returned to my depressing reality. I heard voices, familiar voices, in the direction of the Summerville porch. One was Georgia Murphey.

Chapter 20

Francie

Instead of lifting the latch on Edward's gate and heading down the boardwalk to the boathouse, I backed up and headed toward the boundary between the Bastian and Summerville properties.

"I'm sure you're wrong, Georgia," the voice of Nancy Summerville said. "You know I wanted you to be in our family! But, that was selfish of me. It was obvious to all of us that you and Henry had a thing. It was destiny. I saw it. Bethany and Katie did too. And I guess if his weirdo ex was ever around the two of you back then, she'd have seen it too. We need more wine...be right back."

It wasn't the "ex" part that made me sad, but Nancy calling me a weirdo. She was right. And currently, the "weirdo" was sitting in Edward Bastian's yard likely soiling her new outfit from Aurora with grass stains. I couldn't move. Uncle Frankie told me not to worry about stains. Stains can be washed away. I felt the weight of his hand on my shoulder, silently instructing me to stay put. Then, I almost jumped out of my skin—a ring, a phone ring. If they discovered me eavesdropping, my certifiability would be all but confirmed. Then, I realized it wasn't my phone ringing.

"It's so weird that you are calling. I was just talking about you!" I heard Georgia say. "I'm at Nancy's, and you know what she just said? She said you and I were destined to be together, so why are you doing this to me?"

There was a long silence.

"I don't believe you! Why would you meet her in Mobile the day you were supposedly stuck in Michigan?"

Then a long silence again and the slam of a screen door.

"Nancy's here. I'm putting you on speaker; tell her. I want a witness."

"Why hello Nancy. It's Henry."

When I heard Henry's voice, I was shocked at my reaction. Nothing. Not one twinge of jealousy. Not anger. Nothing. Absolutely nothing. In fact, he sounded different, like someone I didn't know. A stranger. A stain in my past. I now understood Uncle Frankie's message: "Don't worry about the stains. Stains can be washed away."

"I'm sure you both have heard the rumors whirling around about Bethany's prick husband," Henry said. "Anyway, she reached out to grab lunch, she needed a friend. That's all. Just trying to help."

"That makes a lot of sense Henry," Nancy said. "The simplest thing would have been to give Georgia a heads-up; we do live in a cocoon."

"That's the point. I guess because I live in Michigan, and we have known each other forever, she feels like she can trust me. To tell you the truth, it made me feel good to have someone's trust. Take me off speaker, please, and give Georgia the phone."

Georgia took her phone. As she headed inside, I heard her say, "I want to trust you. That's all I want."

Uncle Frankie was telling me it was time to leave. But, I refused. I was glued to the grass watching Nancy, waiting for Georgia to reappear. When Georgia walked back onto the porch, she was visibly stumbling, perhaps from the wine. She could barely keep her balance as Nancy helped her light her cigarette.

"You, OK?" Nancy asked.

"I just can't shake the feeling that something is going on with Henry and Bethany. Call me crazy but you'd think I'd be worried about Francie and worst yet, Looney Junie. I've been on pins and needles waiting for the backlash from those two nuts but have not heard even a peep from that bat-shit crazy family."

"Bat shit crazy," "looney," "weirdo." I flinched thinking about all the names given to Mom and me over the years.

"I think we all have a little crazy in us," Nancy said. "I've come to admire Junie LeBlanc. She has always been true to herself, something that I sure haven't been."

"Yeah, me either. You know that a part of me loved Cannon, but I must admit what I loved more was the life I wanted with him and you—summers here, raising our children together. I idolized your family and all the other boardwalk families. I only got a little glimpse into your life during those two weeks in July. I was so jealous of you, Katie, and even Francie! Your big boardwalk houses, your boathouses, and your family traditions."

"Well, you should know by now that everything is not all sparkles and picnics."

"I know that now, but I used to stare at all the framed photos in your house, picturing myself in them. My favorite is the one where you have no front teeth and wearing overalls with a red-striped shirt. You're standing beside Cannon with your decorated bikes for the parade."

"I love that picture too! Those were the happy days for sure."

"I longed for happy days like that. I'd imagine my children's pictures on the shelves documenting their first-hooked fish, their first success on water skis, their first Jubilee, and of course, all the parades. But, that was all a fantasy. I was chasing all the wrong things. That became crystal clear when Cannon dumped me the spring of senior year no less!

I had planned every detail for our wedding from my dress to the flowers and music!"

Georgia lit another cigarette. CiCi appropriately pegged her a "wannabe." But, I found myself feeling sorry for her.

"Yeah, that was a really dickhead move on his part. I was caught in the middle. I did get a huge laugh at your payback. I should have reached out to you then. I'm sorry about that. Why didn't you ever try to reconnect with Henry after that?"

"Oh, I did, and we did. Things picked up where we left off. I am ashamed to admit that during the summers, Henry and I hooked up A LOT. But in my defense, the hookups were only when Cannon wasn't around, like the week when y'all were both still in summer camp, or when he was on one of those fishing trips with his boarding school friends. I had sex with Henry long before Cannon. But, I was an idiot. Every time Cannon returned, I'd ditch Henry and run straight to Cannon."

Everything was becoming clear to me now. Henry never noticed me. I was simply the target of a dare but worse, I was used to get back at Georgia for her preferring Cannon over him—for Georgia's wishes for a "Boardwalker."

"So, what happened with Henry? You said you reconnected."

"Well, he was dating Francie who was also at Michigan. Can you believe that she followed him there? Talk about a doormat. Even if I had been with Henry then, no way I would have gone to college somewhere that cold. Anyway, we met for a weekend in New York. We had crazy sex all weekend. We even laughed about how he and Francie first got together. You remember that, right?"

"No, I don't. I was too preoccupied with trying to get into Griffin Harper's pants!" Nancy said.

"Aw yes, Griffin Harper and the whipped cream! That story is legendary. What I really want to know is how many cans of whipped cream y'all went through?"

"He is the only one that knows. I was just the recipient! Anyway, finish the story about how Henry and Francie met. I never could figure out how those two got together, such an unlikely match."

"Seriously! No one could. I was the only person who really knew...of course, other than Henry."

I started to leave then. I didn't want to hear the truth or dare story all over again. After hearing Georgia's first version of those events the night we had dinner, I wondered why Henry took the dare instead of truth. But after I discovered them in the shower and read her note over and over before finally tossing it into the Bay, I knew that she was the reason.

"Anyway, it was the July 4th when you, me, Bethany, Katie, and Henry were drinking lemonade spiked with vodka by Justin, remember Justin?" Georgia asked.

"Oh my gosh, Georgia, you do have some memory. Yes, Justin, the bartender, who was our source for all of our alcohol."

"Because he had a major crush on you! Anyway, we were all at the Inn pool and pretty drunk. We started playing truth or dare. You asked Henry the craziest place he had sex in the Inn and with who. He looked at me because we both knew the answer. With me in the shower! Clearly, he couldn't tell the truth with you there. So, he took the dare. And right then, Francie showed up. The timing was weird because I don't recall ever seeing her out anywhere, much less the pool. You dared Henry to go talk to her. You told him that Francie's family was like royalty, no way she'd give an Inn guest the time of day. You even bet him ten bucks."

"It's all coming back to me. I guess Henry remembered it."

"Yes, we talked about everything that weekend in New York. He said that your last comment got to him...like he wasn't good enough for the boardwalk society. You know that is the reason Henry and I had such a connection. We were both just short-term guests in the fairy-tale world of Blakely Point. I told him that if he hadn't taken the dare, he would have never met Francie, and that we could have been together. 'It didn't matter if I took the dare or not, you would have never dumped Cannon' was his reply, before he led me into the shower where we replayed the scene that prompted his taking the dare. But the sex was much wilder than it was that summer. Like really wild. I knew then that Henry was my true love."

Part of me wished I listened to Uncle Frankie and left before hearing all of this. Henry used to frequently travel to New York. I remembered the trip Georgia was talking about. I offered to go with him. He gave me every excuse in the book. How stupid I was to have believed all his work conflicts! He'd said that he would be by himself all weekend. When he called to "check-in," he claimed he snuck away because he "missed me so much." Add incredibly naïve and stupid to my list of names.

"This doesn't make any sense, or maybe I've just had too much wine. What happened? How did he end up married to Francie?"

"He was going to break up with her. Every night when we talked, I would ask if he did it, and he kept making excuses...but then the last time we spoke, he said that her book was getting ready to be published. She received a big advance. It was not a good time. I needed to be patient like he had been with me all these years. Then, I learned that they were engaged!"

Any lingering doubts of Henry and me reconciling were completely erased. When Henry was returning from his New York trip with Georgia, I learned of my book deal. I remember it like it was yesterday. I cooked his favorite meal and put champagne on ice. I was excited to share the news of the publication and the advance. He proposed to me that night. He was shopping for wedding rings in New York. The ring was being sized, so he didn't have it. After

149

my news, it seemed like the perfect time to propose. "A double celebration," he said. What a crock!

"Oh, Georgia. I never knew," Nancy said. "I totally understand why you wouldn't call me, but I just wish I could have been there for you."

"I know. Me too. I almost called you so many times. Anyway, when I found out, I went crazy and drove straight to Ann Arbor because he kept ignoring my calls. He was furious! He said to let it go. Francie provided him something that I never could. He was the most important man in her life. He couldn't ever settle on being second. I couldn't hate him because he was right. He was second all those years. But, I think the real reason was that Francie could provide him the ticket into the Blakely Point boardwalk society. I desperately wanted that with Cannon. Henry wanted it too. I guess both of us were tired of being just ordinary inn guests."

"Now that you're older and wiser, you should enjoy your relationship, embrace it! I mean it was fate y'all reconnected after he and Francie split."

I wondered if Nancy would think it was "fate" if she knew the facts behind the reconnection? No way Georgia was going to reveal to Nancy that she WAS the reason behind our split, I thought.

"That's what I thought," Georgia said, "but I am telling you there is just something not right now."

Nancy refilled their wine glasses.

"Everything will work out. I do think what Henry said is true. There are certainly rumors floating around about Simpson Baldwin and another woman. I believe them because the man hit on me last year."

"Seriously?? Do tell."

"It was last New Year's Eve, the party at the Inn. Cooper went to the bar to get me a drink. That arrogant ass waltzed over to me and whispered in my ear. 'I've been watching you all night. Seems things are pretty chilly between you and Coop. Just so you know, I'm ready to be whipped,' he said, laughing. 'Get it, Reddi-whip?' He stuck his tongue in my ear lightly and then hard. Then, he just walked away. Bethany was staring a fucking hole through me. I know that stare. I have given that same stare to Cooper too many times to count over the years. But I was TOTALLY innocent. She has been ice cold to me ever since."

"Girlfriend, he did the same thing to me! Right after I moved back, he called me and wanted to look at a house. He wanted his own house, not one that Bethany would eventually inherit. I showed him the 'Yellow Awning House!' You could have been neighbors! Anyway, he asked me if I ever had fantasies when I showed houses? I said, like what??? 'Like having sex with a client in the owner's bed.' He pushed me down on the bed in the master!"

"He is a sick man. What did you do?"

"I wanted the sale, so I couldn't slap him, which is exactly what I wanted to do; it would have been a humongous commission! I told him that he was a very attractive man, but he was married to Bethany, and she was a childhood friend. When I said that, he forced himself on me and started kissing me. I told him there was another showing, and we needed to leave."

"Quick thinking!"

"I thought so until he said that wasn't true, he checked the schedule! He got up and said, 'Honey, you just lost yourself a big, fat commission.' Bethany found out I showed him a house without her and was royally pissed. Bethany Baldwin doesn't forgive or forget. She always gets even. I think that's what she's doing with MY Henry—using him to get even!"

"I don't know about that, Georgia. Simpson is truly a piece of shit, but a great-looking, powerful, and rich piece of shit. I don't think Bethany would give that up to get even."

"So, you're saying Bethany just ignores her husband's messing around and doesn't do anything about it? I'd get even for sure!"

"I don't know. I'm not one to judge. Given all my issues with Cooper, I have learned I'm not as tough as I thought I was—it's best just to go along."

"That's not the Nancy I know. I guess that's where we're different. I've waited too long for Henry. Nothing or no one is going to interfere with our destiny. I even warned Bethany to stay away."

"Seriously? I'd given anything to be a fly on the wall during that conversation. What did she say?"

"She said I was still pathetic. She and Henry were friends and that she was married."

"I told her marriage didn't stop her mother or her husband from fucking around. She slapped me and went stomping off."

I finally relented to Uncle Frankie's tug on my elbow. He led me back to the boathouse. As I chased Valium with vodka, I felt sorry for Mom's orchestrated set-up of what was admittedly a splendid evening, yet one ending like all others. I was going to bed alone.

I vowed to erase the past. I turned on the Fifth Dimension's song, and as it played, I told myself that tomorrow was a new day. It was the day that I was going to take over my destiny. It was the age of Aquarius.

Part IV

Chapter 21

Millie

It's normal to suffer a relapse during a period of rehabilitation, I rationalized, as I boarded the train to meet Simpson Baldwin. This time to the Hamptons. I kept my resolve for five months, actually five months, three weeks, four days, and twelve hours to be exact. It seemed like five years. I was depressed beyond depressed. Work could not even come to my rescue because I serviced the SBB Capital account. I knew exactly what Simpson was doing—giving me the space that I demanded and making me miss him terribly. So, when he called after five months, three weeks, four days, and twelve hours, I accepted his invitation.

I could feel the electricity weaving through every nerve in my being from his anticipated touch. Yes, everyone has relapses. It is to be expected. It is part of the process. I needed this. I needed his big, strong hands all over me. I wasn't stupid. I knew the ecstasy would be fleeting, and temporary. But, I was ready.

I was ready because I knew, without any doubt, that this time was the last time. I had accepted a new job with a new company, and SBB Capital wasn't a client. In fact, my new job was not only in a different city but also in a different country. I resigned yesterday and would find the right time to disclose the news to Simpson. The news that Millie Hill was headed to London.

I would start my new position in two months, so I viewed Simpson's invitation to the Hamptons as eerily psychic. A sign. A door opening for an appropriate closure. I needed one last hurrah. I had the upper hand now. I would soon be across the pond.

The power that was pumping through my veins may have impaired my judgment, I thought, after half of my coffee ended up on my blouse from an unanticipated jerk of the train. My blouse was my only blouse. I thought it had been sheer genius to show up with no luggage. Instead, my stunt backfired on me.

Simpson always teased me that I packed as meticulously and analytically as I reviewed a balance sheet. Every outfit was organized by every day with some extras for the unexpected. It was my nature and training to be over-prepared. "Impeccable precision is such a turn-on," Simpson would say. When he said that, the words echoed in my head over and over. It was the first time I experienced an eerily psychic moment.

The first person that uttered those same words to me was Bayou Lou, several weeks after I returned from a fabulous trip with Simpson at the Greenbrier Resort. Simpson selected the fabulous resort because he wanted to experience my home state. Even though I was on Cloud Nine, or more like Cloud One Hundred, after being with him, our "dates" were sporadic, at best. When we were together, I was reassured that he was the one, but then weeks would pass before Simpson would even call me. It was during those down times that I questioned if I was just in his rotation of women. He could have anyone. It was too early in our relationship for me to broach with him if we were an item, if we were committed.

When I met Louie, it seemed like it was a sign, a sign that I needed to be spontaneous and go with the flow. I was young and already divorced. "Don't put your eggs all in one basket," my mother's constant advice would begin ringing in my ears. So, that day at the market, I decided to listen to my mother.

I had been seeing Louie for over three months when Simpson ordered a week-long trip to the Breakers in Palm Beach. He needed my analysis on a new target.

Before Louie entered my life, I knew with certainty the number of days and hours that transpired since Simpson's previous communication. Though the length of time between the calls was unpredictable, his greetings and closings were anything but. His patented opening: "Hey there. Sorry I haven't talked to you in a while. Been all over the place. I had a brief moment and wanted to check on you." This was followed by business chit-chat and then predictably ending with, "I've got to slow down and carve out some time to spend with you. I miss you!"

I laughed to myself as I mouthed his standard greeting, but my reaction to an invitation for a rendezvous was vastly different. I felt nauseated when he said, "We will be working hard all week but 'as they say, all work and no play makes Simpson a dull boy.'" He planned "a lot of play for us."

Of course, Louie understood my professional conflicts, my required travel. Before Louie, I used to dread the return to the accumulated mail, the wilted plants, and an empty refrigerator. After we exchanged keys to our apartments, I'd return home to watered plants, fresh flowers on the table, wine chilled, a Cajun meal simmering on the stove, and my mail stacked in neat piles. It wasn't like he just sat around doing nothing while I was working my ass off. His job made mine look like a walk in the park. I saved corporate shells from making poor investment decisions. He saved human lives while putting his on the line every day. He admired me, but I admired him so much more.

But, I was in a no-win situation. Simpson's company was one of our largest clients. His private jet would pick me up at Teterboro Airport.

I was determined to keep the trip strictly professional and tell Simpson that I was in a relationship. In fact, I was going to disclose that I was falling in love. My plan floated into the sky along with the private plane when I saw him. We weren't even "wheels up" before he popped champagne, and his large hands were all over me. I didn't have the skill set to resist this man. My rehearsed speech hung over me like a thick fog the entire week while we were in the shower, while we were in the bed, and while he was covering every inch of my body in oil.

On our last day, I gained clarity. I knew what was waiting for me at home: Louie's black eyes, the darkest eyes that I had ever seen, would be twinkling radiantly, his muscular arms would wrap tightly around me the moment he saw me, and his Cajun toughness would make me feel secure. Plus, my plants would be watered, mail sorted, fresh flowers on the table, and a fabulous meal prepared. The thought of Louie gave me the necessary strength. I just blurted it out.

"I'm seeing someone. I know we've never discussed being exclusive, and I assume you see others too. I really like this guy, and it could progress into something serious. I felt like you should know."

Recalling that conversation, I think it was the first time I observed Simpson Baldwin a little rattled. Actually, he was pissed.

"I guess I'm just old-fashioned, but it didn't occur to me that seeing others was a topic for discussion. I don't share well, Millicent. Never have. Perhaps it's a weakness. I haven't thought of you as the needy type. We're both very busy people. But, if you can't tell how much I adore you, then I'm not the man for you."

It was the comment about me being needy that got to me. That is the last thing I wanted to be, but admittedly, I was enjoying the attention from Louie. After catching Matt with the "nurse," I buried my emotions, along with my desire for any man. I felt that Matt robbed me of more than the "till death us do part" ending. He robbed me of my self-esteem and my confidence. Those qualities led me to New York—to make my own way. Now, it seemed that my need to be desired and wanted was paramount. Louie had more than delivered.

"I didn't know you felt this way," I said. "We are both very busy. Our professional lives are important to both of us. I don't know. I guess I haven't been able to get my head around being so connected when we're together to going weeks without seeing each other or even having a phone conversation. It would be nice to hear your voice, if only for a minute, before weeks pass."

"Well, I do think about you every single day, more than I'd like to admit. So, in my weird way, I am with you. I'm glad we had this talk because I do know that I'm an odd duck. We all have different needs. But I am one hundred percent here for you. I'll make you a promise, if you make me a promise."

"Shoot," I said, as he began rubbing my feet.

"I will do a better job. I'd love to promise that I'll call every single day, but since it's a promise, I want to keep my word. I will commit to call several times a week. But, you must promise that you will stop seeing him. Like I said, I'm no good at sharing a woman who I love with anyone else. And, I do love you."

Was that he loved me all I needed to hear? Louie had quickly said that he loved me. Maybe it was too quickly. Then all the notes. Every night we spent together, he'd leave a note on the bathroom mirror and another one clipped to a magnet on the refrigerator—"Good morning, I love you!!" I loved the notes, every single one. After Simpson's comment, I started thinking that Louie was enabling a needy side of me. This was not a good formula for a lasting relationship, I thought. I needed a man who challenged me. A man who was as emotionally independent as I was. I knew what I had to do. I had to end things with Louie, not Simpson.

Initially, I made work excuses...new projects, would be gone several weeks, missed him too (which I did). Finally, I ended it. I came to New York for work, not romance. I was falling in love with him, and it was distracting me from my goals, from my job. He deserved someone who could give him more than I could, someone who could love him with their whole being. Obviously, he was a tough guy. He appeared to take it well. But after delivering the news, I puked. One year later, I puked again when I learned that Simpson Baldwin was married!

By then, that man had me, hook line and sinker. Simpson kept his promise about calling me more often. But, apparently, his wife snooped on his phone and noticed the number of calls, especially the lengthy ones late at night.

Louie had likely moved on. Even if he hadn't, it was wrong to try to rekindle things. It would be so unfair to sweet, kind Louie. So, married or not, our relationship continued though I got queasy every time I heard the word "affair." The forbidden word wore me down. Instead of hating Simpson, I hated myself. I ached over the worse decision of my life-sticking with him instead of Louie. Louie loved me for who I was from the start. He loved "Millie."

I changed my professional name to Millicent after the "Millie Hillbilly" taunting. When I told Simpson that my name was Millie, he responded that Millie wasn't sophisticated enough for me and that Millicent fit me to a tee. He never once called me Millie. Those facts alone should have been enough to see he wasn't right for me. I guess as they say, "hindsight is 20-20."

I was finally ready to end it with Simpson. I didn't bring any luggage on this trip. My first splurge after landing my job was the purchase of my cherished Ghurka leather rolling bag. It cost almost as much as my proceeds from the sale of my car. I justified the indulgence because, in New York, luggage was my car equivalent. My job would involve a lot of travel and with successful professionals. I certainly couldn't show up with my worn-out canvas duffle from college.

The idea of leaving my Ghurka bag hit me while I was packing for my trip to the Hamptons and watching my favorite movie, *Steel Magnolias*. Clairee and Ouiser were fighting on the park bench, and Clairee commented that she loved Ouiser more than her luggage.

Simpson knew how much I loved my luggage, and he loved the way I packed it. As he and Louie said, "impeccable precision." I did love Simpson Baldwin more than my luggage, but it was time to get even.

I wanted to see another rattled look on his face. So, when he ask for my bag, I was ready to relish in his perplexed confusion. It made me laugh. It made me feel dominant. I knew he would immediately be off kilter when I responded, "I don't have any luggage. This is my only outfit."

Given that it had been five months, three weeks, four days, and twelve hours since our bodies were last entwined, I wanted him to wonder if I changed my mind, if I was meeting him only so he could see me, touch my hair, my lips, my skin, and want me so badly before I walked away. I wanted him to squirm. I wanted him to feel out of control even for just a skinny second.

After all, I wasn't planning on leaving the room. I was going to have some serious closure sex. It was going to be Earth shattering and all about me. It wasn't like the Hamptons didn't have marvelous shops if I needed to venture out of the room. I tried to contain my smirk when Simpson asked for my luggage.

"I don't have any. In fact, this is my only outfit."

As I said the words, I carefully examined his face. I wanted a permanent snapshot in my brain of the glimpse of uncertainty, of doubt, the look that I hadn't seen on his face since my announcement about seeing someone else. That was three years ago! On this last trip, I wanted to witness just a smidge of helplessness or weakness from the poised Simpson Baker Baldwin.

If it happened, I missed it. Without skipping a beat, Simpson said, "I agree a shopping spree is in order. I am going to spoil you rotten. I've missed you...A LOT!" He squeezed me tightly and began nibbling on my neck. "God, I want you right here, right now!"

At that particular moment, I didn't care that my strategy was a bust. I didn't care that the driver was enjoying his show from the rearview mirror. I didn't care that my damp, coffee-stained blouse was crumbled up in a heap on the floorboard. As we were turning into our $1200-a-night chic hotel, I almost blurted that I didn't bring a bag because I loved him more than my luggage. I resisted. I had an upper hand to preserve. Instead, I delivered my news.

"I resigned from the firm yesterday. I'm headed to London! As they say, an offer I couldn't refuse. I'm really excited. We're going to celebrate all weekend; I hope you're rested."

I kissed him long and hard, keeping him from uttering a word until the car stopped. I quickly put on my blouse before the driver opened my door. I headed straight to the bar and ordered a bottle of the most expensive champagne.

If the time with Simpson taught me anything, it was it took a lot to one-up or daze Simpson Baldwin. He was one smooth operator. He met me at the bar.

"I like the way you think. Let's take this to our room," and for good measure, he ordered another bottle.

After what seemed like an hour in our king-sized bed where we christened every inch, he sat up and brushed my hair behind my ears and put his hand on my cheek.

"You know that I love you. Deeply. And, I love your body. But, I love your brain and independence more. They are what attracted me to you from the beginning. And speaking of independence, I have a little surprise for you too. We're going to Blakely Point for the 4th!"

"Blakely Point?" I asked, very confused.

Over the years, it was hard to miss that July 4th was the most cherished holiday for the Brooks and Baldwin families. They were together every year at the large spread on Mobile Bay.

"On Sunday. I've fantasized for years about spending July 4th there with you. I know our relationship hasn't been ideal. I hope you understand that it has not been ideal for me either. When you have children of your own, you'll hopefully understand. I adore my girls. If I left Bethany, I'd be persecuted. It would be more scandalous than any public whipping in a town square. She is a bitter, vengeful woman; she has threatened me that I would never see my girls again. Trust me. I've floated the idea of separation numerous times. We're both so damn unhappy."

"I'm sorry. I really am. I do understand. For the record, I've never asked you to leave your wife. But it's time, Simpson. It's time for me to move on. Let's just enjoy this last time."

That's what we did. Turns out we didn't have the time or the need for shopping. It rained like cats and dogs, which was fine by me. Simpson doted on me more than ever before. We tried every spa service offered, and when we weren't in our spa robes, we were in bed. Our time together passed way too quickly.

Though I was dying to ask him all weekend how he could possibly pull off a holiday tryst at Blakely Point, I sure as hell wasn't going to broach the subject. He would see right through me. It would send a signal that I wasn't ready to say good-bye. I counseled myself that I had the upper hand. This was not the time for any weakness. If the subject came up again, I knew I would cave. I wanted more closure sex, I wanted more of Simpson Baldwin.

I stayed strong and didn't ask. The price I paid was that I didn't sleep a wink on our last night together, or so I thought. I obviously dozed off because when I woke up on Sunday morning, Simpson was gone. I thought turnabout is fair play. I showed up with no luggage, sprung my news on him, and had not agreed to go to Blakely Point. Now, he was the one who was gone, luggage and all. In the end, he won.

The knot in my throat extended all the way to my stomach. Despite my supposed upper hand, I chalked up another one to consistency. In our relationship, the lowest of crashes always followed the highest of highs. I should be numb to it by now; it was the same feeling I experienced after each time together. In the past, I was able to push through the dark abyss because another trip with Simpson was on the horizon. Now there would be no more trips. And, I had barely survived the five months, three weeks, four days, and twelve hours before I relapsed. How was I going to survive forever?

I hugged my knees to my chest and fought the tears. I began having second thoughts about my new job. Was it really the best opportunity for me professionally or simply an opportunity to just run away? One thing I was good at, for sure. I ran away from West Virginia. I ran away from my marriage. I ran away from Louie Trahan. I understood the first two. I was running to something better. But running from Louie to Simpson reversed the positive trajectory. I was spiraling backward. Nothing good can result from running TO something to run away FROM something, I thought. The door clicking jolted me back to reality.

"Can you come later?" I asked the cleaning crew.

"Yes, now and later," was the response, not from the cleaning crew but from Simpson. He was holding two mimosas. "I was hoping you were still in bed. I went to pick up your outfit that I had cleaned. While I was out, I thought some champagne was in order."

He took off his shirt and stood in front of me beside the bed. I unbuckled his belt and unzipped his pants.

"Good morning to you too," I said to his wide-awake flexed muscle. I was determined it would be the best ever. Something neither it nor Simpson would ever forget. It was turning into an Oscar winning performance until we heard, "Housekeeping," as the door opened.

Simpson grabbed a pillow to cover up himself.

"Still here. Come again."

After the door shut, he walked over and placed the "Do Not Disturb" sign on the knob. Then, he pulled the covers back and got on top of me.

"Come again?" I asked.

And this time, both of us did. He then handed me a mimosa.

"I'd like to propose a toast. Here's to the most talented, smartest, beautiful, and damn sexiest woman I've ever met."

"Thanks. That was sweet," I responded, as I started to click his glass.

"I'm not done. And, here's to celebrating Independence Day on the Bay. I'm not going to take no for an answer. Corky is on the way now."

I justified my acquiescence. After all, I didn't accept; I just didn't refuse. I viewed those responses very differently. I didn't have to inquire as to the reason the house was available. In his typical fashion, he had carefully planned every detail.

His daughters abhorred spending the obligatory holiday at their grandparent's house. They wanted to stay in Buckhead. Their neighbor was throwing a big party and "all their friends would be there." He perfectly laid the groundwork for his absence.

A new "target" would be closed for the holiday. The acquisition was highly confidential, so it was an opportune time for his team to descend upon the premises unnoticed for his evaluation. He booked a spa day for his girls and Bethany as consolation for his absence.

"Surprisingly, Bethany didn't have one of her tirades. Her mother isn't even going to be at the Bay house. She's going to be on a 'cruise,' which is code for with her captain friend, which completely unnerves Bethany. It's all perfect."

"Perfect, except isn't the boardwalk crawling with people this time of year?"

"Yes, but I'm not planning on being outside, other than our bedroom balcony. Another one of my fantasies. Hopefully, it will be better than what I've imagined over the years."

"But I have no clothes."

"Exactly. But there's enough clothes in that house, I'm sure we can find something, if necessary."

I really didn't care about the clothes. I thought it made our last time together even more erotic. I began imagining myself in one of his $500 custom shirts. I wanted to leave my scent behind. Upper-hand, I thought. Plus, I did love him more than my luggage.

Chapter 22

Bethany

Were my insides really tingling? It had been a long time since I felt any tinge of craving for a man. But, there was no denying it. I was feeling something different. And, it felt good.

"Bethany Baldwin?" my designated spa esthetician asked.

Simpson booked spa treatments for the girls and me as a token of his feigned disappointment for missing the Pooles' shindig. He left the engraved invitation on the kitchen counter.

Join us on July 4th as we celebrate
With a red, white, & blue BBQ
By the Pooles' pool!
5:00 until...
Fireworks included.
Hosted by: Claire & James
Sallie & Lexie

Seeing that invitation, my insides tingled but from anger, not excitement. The same rage that erupted every time I suspected a new member of Simpson's harem. There were many over the years, and, but for Olin Miller, I likely would have continued to live in my world which teetered between suspicion and justification.

When my suspicions reached a breaking point, I'd cross-examine him (his words). His standard response was that I needed to find another hobby and stop watching the "trash talk shows" that occupied my day. It was the intonation in his voice that was more unsettling than his cold denials. They sounded like pity.

After Olin's disclosure, I knew that all my previous hunches were on target. I began recounting them all. The first one, or I should say the first one that I was aware of, was Mary Beth Underwood. Of course, Simpson spent a lot of time with her. She was his lawyer. I naively viewed their trips as strictly business, until the invitation to her law firm's lavish holiday party. Simpson "felt obligated" to go.

Simpson Baldwin wasn't beholden to anyone but himself. The fact that he felt obligated to attend was baloney. Yet, I made an excuse for him. I came up with a reason. This one was that the firm did a great deal of work for him. He would enjoy all the attention and the sucking up from the piranhas, including Mary Beth Underwood.

When Simpson went to retrieve our drinks from the bar, Mary Beth suddenly appeared and introduced herself. It was her arrogance coupled with her condescension that put me on edge. Oddly, Simpson arrived with three drinks, and it was the way they looked at each other. It was more than just professional respect. It was the familiarity. It was the way her eyes kept darting over to me during their conversation, the way she was assessing me. It was her fake laugh.

"I'm so glad you made it!" she said shrilly to Simpson. "And you too, Bethany," she said flatly.

Then, there was the week-long trip to the Breakers, one of my favorite destinations. Of course, Simpson didn't invite me to tag along. When I announced that I would be joining him, his reaction said it all. "Out of the question," he said. "Totally inappropriate and unprofessional." He could not be viewed as using company funds for his wife's benefit.

After that trip, I stooped to checking his phone. The numerous late-night calls to a New York number were eating at me. After too much wine one night, I called the number. At that moment, I didn't care, until the woman's chastisement of my mistrust. When Simpson never mentioned it, I assumed the woman never divulged my call.

I started thinking I was overly paranoid. I became remorseful. I regretted my weakness. I regretted the look I gave Nancy Summerville at the New Year's Eve party at the Inn and my abandonment of her as a friend. I regretted my accusations to Simpson about Claire Poole. I regretted badgering the airport staff for the passenger list on the company jet.

Simpson didn't know that I obtained the plane's logs after every trip. It had been almost six months since "Pat Miller" was listed as a passenger. I kept this intel to myself because, after all, Pat Miller could be a man. From my research into Simpson's employees, there was no Pat Miller at SBB Capital. I even asked Dad if a "Pat Miller" had been employed by Brooks Investments.

This Pat Miller was a consistent "advisor" since the time the company purchased the private jet. I found him, her or it as odd as I did the plane. Dad ran the company like he did everything in life, with a tight fist. Other than Dad's agreement to a name change from Brooks Investments to SBB Capital, I wasn't aware that Dad relinquished his majority ownership. No way he would agree to such an outrageous expenditure, unless Simpson maneuvered a flip in their respective ownership percentages as well. I knew how to find out.

I asked Dad about "Pat Miller" the same day I inquired into the new "SBB" asset. I anticipated an outburst, not a burst of a smug grin. Dad seemed as enamored with Simpson as his flock of women.

"We are a national company now, thanks to Simpson. His time is too valuable to be wasted sitting in airports, making connections, suffering delays or any of the other bullshit.

It was time to rescue him from being held hostage to the commercial airlines!"

That meeting was worse than a dead-end. In addition to gloating about the company's new jet, Dad didn't know a Pat Miller. Leave it to me to come up with an explanation, especially after Dad's glowing praise of his son-in-law. Simpson utilized a swath of lawyers, accountants and other consultants. Though, I found it odd that this "Pat Miller" had completely gone dark, he or she may have simply changed jobs.

One thing was certain about Pat Miller. The timing of Pat's omission from the passenger list coincided with Simpson's uncharacteristic moodiness. The moodiness was completely out of the ordinary until it was cured during the trip with the Pooles.

After Claire and Simpson disappeared for two-hours on Friday and Saturday, I was convinced they were involved. It was his upbeat spirit upon reappearance, the way I caught them looking at each other, coupled with the timing of "Pat's" omission from the passenger list. I was convinced that Claire was the new "Pat."

I used to ignore Claire's effusiveness around Simpson. She was our neighbor, and the mother of my daughters' best friends. I was used to women ogling over Simpson. In my early years, I relished it. The most successful, best looking, and most charming man in the room was MY husband. But with each passing year, along with our complete abstinence, it began taking its toll.

Upon our return home, the girls headed directly to the Pooles' pool so there was no better time to reveal my suspicions. The denial that proceeded was different. He snapped. The unruffled and indubitably collected Simpson Baldwin lost his shit.

He was hitting golf balls; he had no idea what Claire was doing. It was merely coincidental that they were both gone for two hours on two consecutive days.

"You are a raving lunatic," he yelled. "I'm more than tired of your berating and your accusations. Just get the hell out of the house."

It scared me to see Simpson lose his cool. He was the master of control. I worried that I was going crazy. I worried that I was wrong in my distrust, but I sure wasn't going to be the one leaving.

"You will be the one leaving, and when you do, I will ruin you. Do you hear me? RUIN you! And you can kiss your precious girls on your way out the door because you will never see them again! EVER AGAIN!"

"I'll never leave," he responded coldly. "So, put up or shut up."

When he said that, I knew it was a confession, Simpson Baldwin style. Who was I kidding? Simpson's "carrying on" was previously confirmed by Olin Miller's comments. With one sentence, Olin Miller exposed a truth that I second-guessed for years. I always created different alternatives and justifications. Now that I absolutely knew the truth, what was I going to do?

I loved my 10,000-square-foot home. I loved my neighborhood. I loved my lifestyle. Simpson was powerful. I was nothing without him. I kept my mouth shut about Olin's comment. When I saw Pat Miller on his plane's passenger list the following week, I kept my mouth shut.

I also kept my mouth shut about my real July 4th plans. I wasn't about to attend the Pooles' party with Simpson. I wasn't going to stand by and watch Claire flirt with my husband right under my nose. I was going to get even. It was going to be an efficient pay back to not only Simpson but also to Georgia Murphey. I never forgave that suck-up wannabe for blabbing about Mom and her yacht friend, and then showing Simpson a house behind my back.

I accepted an invitation from Henry DeVries for lunch in Mobile. The last lunch was completely innocent, but I was feeling this one held more promise. Whatever happened afterwards, I was going to be prepared. While the girls were getting *manis* and *pedis*, I would be indulging in a facial and bikini wax.

Serendipity reinforced my scheme. Turns out, Simpson would be holed up in some conference room out of town scouring company financials. The girls were excited to spend the night at the Pooles' and could care less if their parents attended the party. Mom would be with Captain Gabe.

Poor Claire Poole, I thought. I caught myself chuckling aloud thinking about the hours she would spend getting all dolled up for Simpson. I would have tolerated a brief appearance at the Pooles' party solely to delightfully absorb the disappointment on Claire's face when I showed up alone. But, for once, I wasn't going to be alone. While the world would be watching fireworks light up the sky, I was hopefully going to be enjoying the fireworks sparked by one Henry DeVries. Like mother, like daughter, as they say.

Chapter 23

Simpson

While Millicent and I were in the air, Claire was blowing up my phone. A huge turn off, but with Millicent leaving for London, I needed to keep her in the wings. Claire was a nice surprise.

Over the years, I picked up on her flirtations, but they reached a new level in recent months. I certainly wasn't expecting an out-right proposition, especially during our joint family's mountain weekend. Propositions were common, but I was selective. I was in complete control of my mistresses, and any trysts were totally on my terms.

I laughed as I thought about the winner of all propositions—Georgia Murphey. Nancy Summerville was a close second. I couldn't decide what turned me on more, their boldness, creativity, or that they were both Bethany's so-called friends.

Georgia recently moved to Fairchild and obtained her real estate license. The "Yellow Awning House" was on the market once again. I was intrigued when she said, "You have never struck me as someone who would want a hand-me-down house. You, Simpson Baldwin, deserve to be the king of your own castle. I'd love to show it to you. And, from what I hear, the master bedroom is to die for."

She did that, and more. I surmised that Georgia wanted me to see something other than the house when she showed up in a tight, low-cut dress. My speculation was confirmed when we entered the master bedroom. She disclosed that she often fantasized about having sex in a stranger's bed, as she plopped down on the king-sized mattress. I removed her dress, and her fantasy became reality.

Then, there was Nancy Summerville. I knew she wanted me over the years, but she presented more of a challenge. I did love a challenge. She had yet to ever proposition me, but one of my strengths was capitalizing on opportunities. I saw the disdain on face at the Inn's New Year's Eve party standing by herself watching her husband gyrate on the dance floor with some guest of a member.

I decided to bait her. I asked her if the Reddi-Whip story was true, and if it was, how many cans? She responded, "Meet me in the bathroom off in Olie's Bar, and I'll tell ya." I did and she arrived with some. After that, I'd never view whipped cream the same.

When Nancy and I returned to the party, Bethany turned into Sybil. Her head was spinning around. "Where have you been? Why do you smell like whipped cream?" And she cast a hellacious glance at Nancy, who was infamous for that story.

Every woman I wanted, I got, and even some that I didn't. No one dumped me. But Millicent had and continued to avoid me for almost six months. Claire was a timely substitute, though, our trysts presented its own challenges. She was my neighbor and the mother of my daughters' best friends. I had been more than intrigued when she suggested the perfect spot for a "rendezvous." She delivered more than I imagined, winning the kinky prize that weekend. Now, she won the prize for the timely delivery of information.

"I've tried you several times. I know you told me not to leave a message, but you're not answering. Since Bethany is going to Blakely Point, we can get together! I have on the outfit you bought me. Call me so we can make plans. I miss you so much!!!"

It wasn't the "I miss you so much" that got to me but the part about Bethany coming to Blakely Point. After we landed, I kissed Millicent and then apologized that I needed to return a business call.

"After this one, no more. I'm all yours."

"No problem," she said. "I understand. I'm going to hit the restroom."

When Millicent was out of sight, I called Claire.

"I'm sorry that I am just getting your calls. I have been on my plane due to an unexpected business issue. I hate it, but I am going to miss the party. I thought Bethany and the girls were coming."

"Yes, the girls are here and spending the night. There was an emergency with Bethany's father, so she's headed to Blakely Point. I was looking forward to us getting together with her gone. I am so bummed! I can't stop thinking about last weekend."

"Oh babe, I can't either. Send me a picture of you in the outfit. I'll imagine me taking it off you and...."

"On its way!" she said.

"Talk soon."

I immediately called my father-in-law's facility and learned that he was doing great. He was playing Scrabble in the recreation room. I was more than curious about the so-called emergency. Frankly, I didn't care if Bethany caught me with Millicent. I knew Bethany wasn't going anywhere. It was Millicent that I was worried about. If Bethany was at the house when we showed up, I knew Millicent would bolt. I wasn't going to miss our last time together.

I quickly called Bethany. Unsurprisingly, she didn't answer.

"Finished up early. Didn't take long to discover the prospect wasn't going to work. Turns out for the best because I have a better opportunity. I am going to take my new prospects to play golf at Blakely Point. Have fun at the party."

If I didn't hear from her before our arrival, I would execute Plan B. I'd book my favorite private cottage at the Duc de Bourbon, a secluded historic property turned boutique hotel in Mobile. It wasn't the Bay house, but it had delivered with others in the past. Experts always have a back-up plan for the unforeseeable. I wasn't going to miss one second with Millicent.

Chapter 24

Bethany

Seriously??? I could not believe Simpson's message. The one time in my life that I made plans to do something just for me, it was imploding. After lunch with Henry, I planned to invite him to the house for a July 4th cookout and to watch the fireworks. I even fantasized about my version of "carrying on" and hoped Olin Miller got his eyes full with me on the dock this time.

I hoped that I wasn't misreading Henry's increased text messages. They seemed to have escalated from friendly banter to hints of something more. I certainly wasn't skilled in this sort of thing and second-guessing myself all these years had become part of my composition. I didn't even know who I was any more.

My heart sank abruptly and painfully after the incoming text: "Change of plans. Lunch at a restaurant was a bad idea." My eyes filled with tears and the screen became blurry. "Get a grip," I told myself. "You ARE a raving lunatic," as Simpson had called me. What did I expect?

I felt so silly about my excited preparation for an imagined romantic encounter. When my tears and my racing heart subsided, I took a deep breath and began reading the rest of the snub.

"Change of plans. Lunch at a restaurant was a bad idea. Most closed for 4th. I'm packing a picnic."

I read it again and again. My heart began racing, but this time it was not due to disappointment, but elation. I was happy from head to toe. I couldn't remember the last time I felt this way. Simpson wasn't going to ruin this for me.

I desired an evening with Henry following the picnic. I was feeling quite smug about my idea to call the Duc de Bourbon, a boutique hotel in Mobile. I first learned about it from a credit card statement. Simpson explained it was a room for a consultant with whom he had met. His secretary used the wrong credit card to book the room. He told me to cross-examine her.

Of course, I didn't believe him, and he knew I wouldn't call his secretary. After that discovery, I added the boutique hotel to my surveillance when Simpson would disappear during our extended summer stays on the Bay. Now, it was Mrs. Simpson Baldwin who was going to experience the lovely, secluded hotel.

When I called, I actually laughed upon learning my narcissistic husband already booked the Emmanuel Cottage. "Do you need a room as well?" the helpful clerk asked. "No thank you. The cottage will be perfect."

I thought about poor Claire Poole who probably outdid herself in the party preparations in an attempt to impress my husband. Instead, he was going to be entertaining someone else. And, this time I was going to enjoy keeping my mouth shut. While Simpson was at the Duc de Bourbon, I would hopefully be with Henry watching the fireworks from the boathouse and creating our own fireworks in the bed. Though many years had passed since we had considered "jumping" each other's "bones" there, this time, we both were more than receptive.

I smiled thinking about my rendezvous. I even smiled thinking about Simpson's rendezvous. His, however, was getting ready to be inflicted with some little snags. I called him. Not that I needed any cover, Simpson sure didn't care, but since I lied about an emergency with Dad to decline hussy Claire's invitation, I would follow through.

"Got your message. Relieved you are going to Blakely Point. Dad needs some scotch. He is in a dither, and Mom is not answering his calls. The girls are spending the night at Claire's, so I was headed to visit with Dad and pay Ricky $300 cash for the yard work. Poor thing needs it for the holiday. Since you will be there, you can take care of Dad and Ricky. And, change the air filters."

I immediately called Ricky, our yard guy, and told him that Simpson would be dropping off $300. I knew that I already paid him, but he should consider it a holiday bonus, and keep it between us. I also told him to discuss with Simpson his landscaping proposal, and in great detail.

I spent the rest of the evening trying on different outfits perfect for a picnic. I didn't have time in the morning for an anxiety attack over what to wear before the hitting the road. I didn't think I would sleep a bit that night thinking about Henry.

For the first time in a long time, when I looked at my face in the mirror before going to bed, the lines of anger and resentment had dissipated. I was shocked to see a happy woman looking back at me.

Chapter 25

Simpson

For once, I wasn't agitated at Bethany's orders. I would do whatever to keep her in Atlanta. I laughed that these tasks would take her all day to complete; I could knock them out quickly.

The only slight complication was that Ricky lived about thirty miles from Charles' facility and in the opposite direction. But, Ricky wasn't far from the Duc de Bourbon. I decided to check into the hotel first in case I needed that option to escape the nosy Boardwalkers.

Before knocking out Bethany's "to-do" list, I would tend to my own—the things that I was going to do with Millicent in the bed. After I completed my list, I would open some expensive wine and leave her relaxing on the dock. That should distract her from my "errands." There were worse places to have to wait.

Chapter 26

Henry

Wouldn't you know it! Georgia figured out that I was in Mobile. When I landed, there were ten missed calls from her. Her stalking tactics and resourcefulness could not be underestimated. I immediately reverted to airplane mode, cancelled my rental car, and hailed a cab.

A note was waiting for me when I checked in. Admittedly, Georgia was hot as a match, but she was also needy and possessive, with a screw or two loose. I couldn't say there were any regrets. She was the ticket out of my marriage and the ticket to a sweet financial settlement.

I wasn't proud of how things ended with Francie. But, I had been more than a supporter over the years. I had been her life raft. It had been more than tiring; it had been exhausting. Francie was always on the precipice of a breakdown. Trying to pour comfort and confidence into her was like pouring into a bottomless vessel. Georgia's sudden reappearance in my life came at a perfect time. I needed my own break down. I needed to live a little. I needed raucous and uninhibited sex. I certainly wasn't going to leave Francie for Georgia Murphey, but as they say, things happen for a reason. Turns out, Francie yanked off her band-aid when she left me. It freed me as well. I could have Georgia any time I wanted, and my availability opened an unexpected door with Bethany.

I had heard all about Winston and Olin's sighting of Simpson and Bethany upon return from a fishing trip one evening. If I was a betting man, with my prior knowledge of that slime ball, I'd wager everything I obtained in my settlement that Simpson was entertaining someone else on the Brooks' dock that night. Even from my limited exposure to the boardwalk society, I knew he was a playboy.

Francie and I certainly weren't part of the Bay social scene. We never attended the various dances and parties held at the Inn for the boardwalk residents. The only amenity that I took advantage of was use of the Inn's workout facility and spa. I was trying to beat the rush from those who resolved to work-out more and arrived in droves on January 1st every year after their hangovers wore off.

During my New Year's Day work out, I finished an hour on the treadmill before hitting the steam room. Simpson wandered in and dropped his towel.

"I need to purge the demons," he announced.

"That fun, huh?" I asked.

"Well, you're looking at the newest member into the Reddi-Whip club! Let's just say my initiation more than lived up to the hype; it surpassed all expectations."

Of course, I knew the reference. The story of Nancy Summerville was legendary and, apparently, she continued to offer herself à la mode for dessert. If I learned anything over the years, it was that there was nothing sacred among the Boardwalkers.

Certainly, Bethany couldn't be in the dark about her husband's flings. If he aired his dirty laundry to me, he obviously wasn't too discreet. Perhaps they led their own lives. Now that I was released from my shackles, I decided to dip my toe in the water. I thumbed through one of the Boardwalk directories and located Bethany's email.

"How about lunch next time I'm in town? Would be nice to catch up," as I hit send on my generic message.

She not only accepted immediately but also provided her cell number. We exchanged what I would call vanilla texts about logistics. The lunch went much better than anticipated. Our conversation was so easy, so refreshing.

We had long finished our lunch, the dessert we shared, and our coffee. While the waiter clearly wanted to turn the table, I didn't want to leave until I found out more about her marriage. She provided the opening when she mentioned that she heard about my split with Francie and asked how I was doing.

"This may sound insensitive but to be perfectly honest, I never could figure out how you two got together," she said. "But as they say, 'opposites attract.'"

"Until they don't," I said.

"I know it was hard splitting with Francie for lots of reasons. Don't take this the wrong way. You certainly know her better than I do, but I always sensed that she was a little off, you know?"

"Yes, I know all too well. I got tired of trying so hard to make her happy. That burden was wearing me down."

My statement seemed to trigger something. She teared up.

"I know all too well about burdens. I wish I had an ounce of your strength. Henry, my marriage is a fraud. One big, tremendously fat fraud. I have spent the majority of my energy over the years trying to catch Simpson with other women. And for what? What would I do if I discovered the truth? Well, I learned what I would do. Absolutely nothing."

"I'm sorry. If you need someone to talk to, I'm here. I would have appreciated a friend's ear when things were going south with Francie. I obviously don't talk to anyone in Blakely Point, hell, I'm scared to cross the county line."

"Thanks, Henry. I appreciate it. Don't be surprised if I take you up on that sooner rather than later."

I paid the tab and walked her to her car.

"I have made some good business connections here that I don't want to lose. So, I have lots of reasons to visit Mobile. I'd like to do this again."

"I'd really like that," she said.

I hugged her—an appropriate hug for a friend that was hurting. But, it was the way she hugged me back that made me think there was a chance of something more between us than the "catch-up" lunch. Her grip was so tight, it was like she didn't want me to let her go.

"Like I said, call or text me any time," I whispered in her ear.

Within seconds, Georgia was blowing up my phone. I still couldn't figure out how she discovered my early arrival or my lunch plans with Bethany. But, she did, and she went completely nuts.

Georgia served a need. I enjoyed being with her, but the pleasure was limited to the bedroom. She was getting way ahead of herself with where we were going. She pleaded for me to stay at her place when I was in town. I had explained that Fairchild was just too close to Blakely Point. I cared for Francie and certainly didn't want to contribute more anguish to her delicate psyche. The real reason was that I was enjoying my single life.

With Francie under foot while we were in college, not to mention my parents, who were professors at my university, I had never experienced any freedom. And, for once in my life, I felt liberated, and I wasn't about to be chained down. Between the sheets, Georgia was incredible, but she was beginning to suffocate me. She was constantly nagging me about my whereabouts. She was acting like a wife!

After our lunch, Bethany and my text messages escalated. Unlike Georgia, she wasn't nearly as transparent about her desires, but I was picking up more than friendly signals. I was excited about my second date with Bethany until a note was delivered to me by the hotel front desk clerk when I checked in.

"Call me after you check in. I've been trying to call but your phone goes straight to voicemail. You didn't tell me you were getting here today. But, I'm so excited and more than ready for a shower!! I love you so much!!!"

Given that Georgia knew I was in town, I suspected that she was somewhere nearby. Waiting and watching. The last thing I needed was Georgia crashing our picnic and Bethany getting caught in the middle of Georgia's craziness. But, I wasn't going to waste an opportunity for another date with Bethany. I had an idea.

Chapter 27

Bethany

When I was an hour away from Mobile, my head began spinning. I questioned whether I could go through with even a simple picnic with Henry, much less the evening that I had dreamed about all night. Our text messages leading up to this day made me feel like a teenager again. I smiled thinking about them. I couldn't remember the last time that I spent two hours selecting an outfit. However, the closer I got to Mobile, the more my emotions were swinging like a pendulum—from exhilaration to doubt, fear to guilt.

If I bypassed Mobile for Blakely Point, I knew what was in store—a party for one. I would be consumed with Simpson's enjoyment of one of his women in the Duc de Bourbon. I would be the very last thing on his mind.

I began wondering when Dad was the last thing on Mom's mind. What had been the last straw? How did she meet "Captain Gabe?" When had their affair began? Clearly, since Dad's move to the assisted living facility, she was less discreet about her absences. Her "girls weekend trips" were replaced with week-long "cruises." I stopped my third degree inquisitions, it only escalated matters. Like a rebellious child, my comments only incited her.

"Don't think you can show up in my house and tell me what to do. If you can't keep your mouth shut, then stay away! Capiche?" Mom said.

So, I started keeping my mouth shut with Mom just like I did with my husband. The result was that I seemed to be the only one in my family who was miserable. So, why was I questioning a lunch with an old friend?

My wavering was interrupted by an incoming text. It was Henry: "Having second thoughts about picnic. Call when you can."

My first reaction was *yeah, me too*. I didn't know if I could handle another unforeseen complication or change. If I was learning anything about myself, it was that I was obstinate, as Mom pegged me. "You will learn that everything is not black and white. You've picked that up from Charles," Mom would yell during our arguments.

After all these years, it was evident that Dad's inflexible and headstrong traits, in addition to his callousness, had rubbed off on me. I wasn't proud of all the nasty things that I spearheaded over the years. They were all coming home to roost, I thought. Payback was not a way to go through life. The payback, I thought, was now turning on me.

Driving in silence, I worried that Henry was second-guessing our picnic. I took the next exit and pulled into a parking lot. I realized how much I wanted to see him. I hadn't been so excited in years. From making my spa appointment to selecting the perfect picnic outfit, I was excited about what could unfold. I tried to brush away the thoughts of me alone in Blakely Point toasting my dismal life with a bottle of wine. I took a deep breath before calling Henry.

"I'm sitting out on a large, covered balcony, on the eighteenth floor with an unbelievable view of the city and a nice breeze from the river. Then it hit me, this is the perfect picnic spot. What do you think?"

I was so relieved he wasn't cancelling that I didn't care if we picnicked in the hotel parking deck.

"I think that sounds lovely! I'm about forty-five minutes out. Do you need anything? I'm happy to stop."

"I've got it all covered. I'm glad this worked out. Call me when you're in the lobby. I'll have to come get you. You need a key to access my floor."

I turned on the radio hoping that music would distract me from any further reconsideration. Of course, the one time I wanted to listen to the good ole radio, I couldn't. I couldn't figure out the new audio technology in my car, and one of the girl's playlist began blasting some song. The screen revealed it was someone named Katy Perry. The song playing was "Fireworks." Since it was July 4th, I was intrigued.

As I listened to the lyrics, I was overcome with a sense of empowerment. Time to start being true to myself and quit hiding behind a façade. It was time for me to start living. And perhaps it was even time for me to bury the hatchet with Junie LeBlanc and accompany my mother to one of Junie's tea parties.

Chapter 28

Henry

When the elevator doors opened, I saw Georgia sitting on a sofa at the hotel bar area. Thankfully, she appeared to be consumed with something on her phone. Bethany's eyes were on me. I was pretty sure that she didn't notice Georgia, but not a way to begin a date. I turned my phone on silent. After the elevator doors shut, I hugged Bethany and kissed her cheek.

"You look great! I bet you're exhausted."

"Actually, not at all. I'm used to making that trip. It's interstate all the way."

"Well how about thirsty? I am a bad host. I started without you. I've been enjoying a bloody!"

"That sounds good," she said.

Nothing like alcohol to loosen you up, and she needed it, I thought. She seemed stiff and uncomfortable. I hoped she wasn't offended by my revised plan. After seeing Georgia in the lobby, I knew there was no other choice.

"Enjoy this view while I make your drink," as I led her to the spacious balcony with unobstructed views of the Mobile River. She was more relaxed when I returned with her drink.

"Cheers!" I said. "Happy 4th!"

"Thanks. It's beautiful, isn't it?"

"Well there is nothing like Blakely Point, but this is a close second. I'm happy that you were willing to tear yourself away from your paradise to join me."

"Me too. To be honest, it would have been strange rambling around that big house all alone. Over the years, the commotion and all the activities jammed into the holiday exhausted me. I never took time to just enjoy it— celebrate the moment. Now that the girls are older, they want to be with their school friends. They hate spending the 4th here. They don't have a gang like we did."

"Until I met all of you, I dreaded leaving my friends in Michigan. After that, I hated to go back. I was envious that you all got to spend all summer on the boardwalk."

We started reminiscing about all our adventures, the card games by the pool, playing horseshoes on the beach and all the drinking games that we invented along the way.

By now, Bethany was having her second drink, and I was feeling no pain with my third. I reminded her of the time her father caught us in their boathouse making rum punch.

"Yes! I do remember that. You and Georgia were convinced that Dad would have your families banned from the Inn for life."

I wanted to kiss her. I wanted to kiss her now like I wanted to that day. Georgia and Cannon had taken their rum punch to the dock. Bethany and I were busy making another batch when I saw them through the window. Georgia was on top of Cannon. His hands were up her shirt. I wasn't oblivious to Georgia and Cannon's relationship, like he was to ours. Hell, Georgia and I were together earlier that morning in one of the pool cabanas. I knew where she stood, but it didn't make it any easier to watch. She wanted a boardwalk pedigree, not a hotel guest.

I recalled that the boardwalk pedigrees of all pedigrees was beside me making more rum punch. Her family, particularly her father, controlled everything on Blakely Point. Everyone was scared to death of him. He was not only rich, he was powerful. Someone like her would never give me a second thought.

That day, I thought the rum punch had gone to my head, explaining the vibes I was sensing from Bethany. She seemed more risqué that afternoon. She dipped a spoon in the mixture and slurped it.

"This batch packs some heat," as she leaned into me and held the spoon up to my lips. "Wanna taste?"

I thought she may be giving me the green light to taste more than the punch. I questioned if I was misconstruing the moment from being all worked up watching Cannon and Georgia on the dock. All I wanted was to take her to the bedroom that I noticed on the way to the kitchenette. Before I could decide whether to make a move, Charles Brooks came stomping in, yelling profanities. Major buzz kill!

I needed food! The recollection of that moment was exciting me. I didn't want Bethany to see the bulge growing in my pants, not yet anyway.

"I bet you're starved. Can I get you anything? I have a smorgasbord of food."

Things were going well. Take your time; don't rush this, I counseled myself.

"You have any cheese and crackers?"

Shit! When I shopped for our picnic supplies, I obviously wasn't thinking about a picnic that was a Blakely Bay Inn style picnic: cheese, gourmet crackers, an assortment of fresh fruit, salads, assembled in a straw basket, complete with a checkered tablecloth and chilled wine. The Blakely Bay Inn would serve a romantic and classy picnic, befitting the woman that was on my hotel balcony in downtown Mobile, instead of her beloved Blakely Point. I was suddenly embarrassed that my "picnic" supplies resembled a fraternity tailgate at a football game: potato chips, fried chicken, chicken wings and potato salad! What was I thinking???

"Sorry! My bad. How about some potato chips?"

She laughed. Thank goodness, I thought.

"I'm OK right now. I'm just enjoying this view, and the company. But, help yourself."

I did want to help myself...to her. I definitely needed something to eat to temper my raging testosterone. I didn't want to turn her off with greasy fried chicken breath or fingers.

"I'm good. I would like to propose a toast. Here's to memories on Blakely Point. Here's to making new ones! Here's to Independence Day!"

"Cheers to that!" she said.

My drinks and thoughts of her naked in my bed must have totally gone to my head. Was I misconstruing the way her eyes looked at me, the way she tilted her head when she clicked her glass to mine? This time, I wasn't going to question the vibe I was sensing but go for it.

"I have a confession to make," I blurted. "Fair warning, you will probably be shocked."

"I don't think anything could shock me after all these years. What is it?"

"OK. But don't slap me! When we were making rum punch in the boathouse, I was getting ready to kiss you right before your dad walked in!"

"Really?" she asked, with a poker face. "I have a confession too. I couldn't figure out why you didn't then and why you never tried."

That was all I needed. I stood up, grabbed her hand, and pulled her out of her chair.

"I didn't think you would be receptive. How about I make up for it now?"

"I thought you'd never ask."

I started on her neck and then moved quickly to her lips. She was more than receptive. She was really into it. I led her into the room, removed her shirt, and kissed her chest. It was over an hour before we enjoyed our picnic on the balcony with nothing on but the hotel bathrobes. She even loved the chicken wings!

It only got better. We drank champagne while soaking in the jacuzzi tub, then retired again to the bed.

"I love that you invited me here. It really is lovely. Don't take this the wrong way," she said, as she rolled on top of me and wrapped her legs around me, "but I'd love for you to be my date on Blakely Point for the Inn's fireworks. I'm sure you remember how wonderful they are!"

"Right now, I can't think. You're distracting me," I replied, as I kissed her breasts.

"Does that mean 'yes?'"

"Yes, I'd love to."

She kissed me, then whispered in my ear.

"Do you remember that there's a bed in the boathouse?"

"I most certainly do. Before your father caught us making the punch, I was considering jumping your bones there."

"Funny, I considered the same thing! I didn't know if you'd be 'receptive.'"

She said the last word while making quotation marks in the air.

"Are you making fun of me?"

"Sort of, but I'd really like for you to stay there with me tonight."

"Invitation accepted. Hopefully, we can continue this," I replied. I rolled on top of her.

She needed two hours. She needed to run some errands. It was now past six. Certainly, Georgia wasn't still waiting in the lobby.

After Bethany left, I looked at my phone, anticipating a bombardment of messages from Georgia. I was right. Except, it was more than a bombardment. It was a barrage. I was prepared.

I had observed Cannon's manipulation of Georgia over the years. I took a page out of Cannon's playbook. I decided to go on the offensive. I needed to keep her far away from Blakely Point. I wanted to spend all night with Bethany. I took control.

"What's your problem? I've told you a thousand times, I have clients in Mobile. Business is my reason for being here. I was at a picnic. My company wouldn't accept my absenteeism due to a hot woman in Fairchild. Though if they saw you, they would definitely understand!"

"I don't understand why you don't tell me these things!"

"It was last minute, and I knew I would be tied up all day. I couldn't be tempted with distractions. I've set aside tomorrow for an uninterrupted day with you. From your tone, it sounds like you are not interested."

"Don't be silly! Of course, I am interested! I love you so much! I have an unbelievable day planned for us. See ya tomorrow."

Crisis avoided, I thought. I decided a long hot shower was in order. I needed to be refreshed and ready for Bethany and the fireworks... all of them.

Chapter 29

Bethany

As I was waiting for my car at the Valet stand, I saw her. There was no denying it was Georgia. I mean her car was covered in one of those incredibly tacky wraps. "For that perfect home near the Bay, Georgia Murphey is the way. Call today!"

And there was no question that she saw me too. She was stopped at the light, looked in my direction, and did a double take. I started to wave at the deranged madwoman, but she immediately picked up her phone. I suspected she was calling Henry. That bitch wasn't going to ruin my evening. So, though I wanted to give him a heads-up, I was becoming quite adept at keeping my mouth shut. He'd learn soon enough, and I was more than curious as to how he was going to deal with this time bomb.

As I traveled through the Wallace Tunnel, I began thinking that Henry probably knew that Georgia was stalking him. That was likely the reason for the change in the picnic venue. Come to think of it, that was likely how she learned of our first lunch.

I smiled thinking that her attempted intervention backfired—and badly too. I was still glowing from the activity all afternoon in his bed, in the jacuzzi tub, and back in his bed. This would be a test for sure. If Henry made up some excuse about another change in plans and cancelled on me, I would know the real reason. That would be the end of him. I was never again going to settle for being less than the most important person in a relationship. I sure as hell wasn't going to play second fiddle to Georgia Murphey. No way.

En route to Blakely Point, I became disgusted with my own stalking of my husband over the years. I was no better than Georgia, I thought. No more. No more stalking that is. I was going to use my energy to get even.

When I exited the tunnel, I decided to give my neighbor a call. She was in the middle of entertaining her July 4th guests, so I was banking on her not answering. I was right.

"Claire, it's Bethany. I'm sure you're busy with your party. Anyway, turns out Simpson headed to Blakely Point. I was already on the road, so since the girls are with you tonight, I am taking a little detour to check on the mountain house. Thanks again! Hate we're missing the party. Happy 4th!"

I knew Claire would be in a tizzy that Simpson blew off the party, i.e. HER. I threw out the mountains hoping that she'd start calling him thinking he would be all alone. I was smirking as I changed lanes for my exit onto Scenic Highway 98. Then, the site of Georgia's obnoxious wrapped car in my rear-view mirror wiped the smirk right off my face. I wondered if that psycho was following me! I decided to have some fun with her too.

I stopped for gas. I stopped at the market for wine. Then, I stopped at a roadside firework stand and bought some sparklers. Henry and I could have fun with those later on the dock with our wine. I spotted Georgia's car at every stop. I wasn't the reigning *Where's Waldo?* champ in my household for nothing. Georgia wasn't even half a challenge. She was not only completely psycho but also an idiot. I wanted to yell at her, "You can't hide in that obnoxious car!"

She kept a safe distance from me all the way to Blakely Point, but she may as well have been in an Ice cream truck blasting "Pop Goes the Weasel!" I forgot to ask Henry what he would be driving. Knowing her, she probably knew the make and model of his rental car and had likely affixed a tracking device. She would be doing multiple drive-by's until he arrived. I knew this because I was just like her, I thought pitifully. But no more. I kissed that part of me good-bye when I was kissing Henry DeVries all afternoon.

Georgia was the wild card. She could spell disaster for the romantic night I planned on the dock, under the stars, watching the fireworks, twirling the sparklers, and then a night in the boathouse.

I really liked Henry, and he offered lots of potential. Even so, I started rethinking the evening I planned and began cursing Georgia Murphey. I began cursing the accessibility of the boardwalk and our dock. We stomached more than our share of those "dreaded tour-ons," as Mom called the Inn's guests. The worst uninvited guest of all would be Georgia Murphey.

Henry said he would let me know when he was on his way, but I hadn't heard from him. I was going to stay the course, though I was getting worried about another "change of plans" message. I walked through the house, out the backdoor, opened the fence, walked across the boardwalk, and headed down the dock to the boathouse with the wine and sparklers. As I was putting the wine in an ice bucket to chill, I heard a voice coming from the dock.

A trespassing tour-on immediately came to mind when I saw a woman sitting on our floating dock. She was sitting on one of my monogrammed beach towels and was wearing one of my straw hats! She was drinking a glass of wine and kicking her legs in the water. I slid open the boathouse window and gasped as I heard my husband's voice.

"Sorry it's taking so long," Simpson said, through this woman's speaker phone.

"No problem. I have been enjoying this view. It is so beautiful at this time of day."

"Well, I'm on my way. You can have your way with me the rest of the night."

"Good! Because there is something I want."

"Besides me?"

"No, but with you. I found an anchor. How about we anchor out in the Bay to watch the fireworks?"

"Great idea. See you shortly. And, one more thing, I love you."

Whoever this was had taken one of MY grandfather's antique anchors, MY family heirloom, and it was beside her on MY dock while she was talking to MY husband sitting on My towel and wearing MY hat! All of them were mine! MY husband, MY family's property, MY dock, MY beach towel, down to MY fucking hat! I snapped. It was, as they say, the straw that broke the camel's back.

Chapter 30

Henry

I was revived after my shower and was more than excited to continue this day with Bethany. No better place than Blakely Point, though I would have to be careful. I mean my ex-wife lived next door. I quickly learned that the LeBlanc's proximity to my date was the least of my worries—seven missed calls, seven voicemails, and text after text from Georgia. I thought I had placated her with my work excuse. Obviously, I had not. I didn't even need to listen to the voicemails, the texts conveyed the message.

"Work, my ass! I just saw Bethany at the hotel. What the hell are you doing? You better have an explanation!!!!!"

"I'm waiting Henry!!!! This better be good!!!!!!"

"You piece of shit!!!! I know you are ignoring me because you are a lying piece of horse shit. HORSE SHIT!!!!!!"

"What are you doing? Trying to figure out how to wiggle your way out of this one????"

"If you don't call me ASAP, we are OVER, you hear me? O-V-E-R, OVER!!!!!"

With each nonresponse, Georgia's ire escalated. After the afternoon with Bethany, I no longer needed Georgia in the wings. I was more than ready to end it. I had a multi-generational Boardwalker with more class in her perfectly manicured pinkie finger than Georgia Murphey could ever hope to attain. So, I didn't care one bit about Georgia's rants. But, I did care about Bethany.

I cared about Bethany's reaction if I proposed yet another change of plans and her disappointment of missing her cherished holiday on the Bay. Based on Georgia's messages, I knew she may be hanging out in the lobby waiting for me to leave or stalking Bethany. Who was I kidding? There was no "may" about it, the only question was "when" she would appear.

I poured a stiff drink and headed to the balcony to think. I could already hear the crackling of a variety of amateur fireworks in the distance. I recalled all the July 4th's when Cannon and I entertained Bethany's gang, including Georgia. After the fireworks when everyone retired to their large boardwalk homes, Georgia and I would sneak into the Inn's pool and have sex on the lounge chairs. But that was then. She used me then like I was using her now. I didn't need her anymore.

After all these years, I had an invite to Bethany's. Though I wanted more than anything to spend the night in her boathouse, my room was safer. Georgia couldn't even access my floor. And, my balcony did provide the best view in Mobile for the city's fireworks later.

I decided to come clean with Bethany. Let her know that Georgia had been at the hotel, for who knows how long, and that she saw her leaving. That the boathouse was probably not a good idea. I knew she'd be disappointed, but I was more concerned that she may end things before we even had a chance to get started.

Bethany didn't need any more drama in her life. She had tolerated more than her share of lies. Hopefully, she'd appreciate hearing the truth from a man, and she'd appreciate that this man wanted her badly, and only her. I started replaying our afternoon back in my head—no way she could dump me on the heels of that.

The chime from my phone startled me, then, a text. I rolled my eyes as I anticipated more berating from Georgia. But, the message was from Bethany. At that moment in time, I began believing that there was something to the cosmic forces that Francie and her mother trusted.

"Change in plans. I'm headed to you, if that is OK. Will explain. Call me."

I called her immediately. I knew instantly something was wrong. Her voice was edgy.

"Georgia saw me at the hotel. She followed me home. I don't think the boathouse is a good idea."

"I'm so sorry. But, we will enjoy the evening here—room service, watching the fireworks on the balcony. What do you think?"

"I bought wine and sparklers but left them in the boathouse!" she said exasperated.

"Don't worry about anything! What's your ETA?"

"According to my phone, I'm thirty minutes away. I'm at the bridge, and it's already backed up."

She sounded all out of sorts. Her voice reflected an uneasiness that caused me to think there was more to the story. I was sure Georgia had done more than followed her.

With our afternoon still fresh in my mind, I was optimistic that after a long kiss, a strong cocktail, and the killer view from my balcony, Georgia Murphey would be a distant memory. I was planning on showing Bethany an Independence Day that she'd never forget!

Part V

Chapter 31

Francie

I thought I was doing well, but to hear Dr. Quinn's confirmation was reassuring. Carmen said that I sounded better than I had in months. My agent, my editor, and my publisher's agitations were pacified.

I was back on track with the publication schedule for my sequel. They liked the new direction and agreed that it was shaping up to be worth the wait. I withheld that my new direction wasn't sparked by my imagination or creative thinking, but by my real-life neighbor, Bethany Brooks Baldwin. I was envious of her perfect husband, her perfect daughters, and her perfect life. However, I had begun to see nicks in the façade of the house next door, so I wrote about them. They had given me lots of material recently, but not enough.

I was in severe writer's block. My sequel came to a screeching halt. There was no path forward. There was no ending. I was stuck in quicksand. It just so happened to coincide with the end of June. By the time July 3rd arrived,

I felt like I was sinking in the quicksand. I was all alone, staring at a blinking screen. All I could think about was the past.

From the minute I took my first breath, every July 3rd and 4th, my family couldn't celebrate the moments of our country's history because we were drowning under the recollection of our own family's tragedy. This year, that torment was only being experienced by me. Mom had finally turned the page.

The Les Quatre Mousquetaires had joined CiCi for a two-week cruise on Captain Gabe's yacht. When the invitation was extended, I insisted Mom go. In retrospect, she didn't ask for my approval. But, I knew that if she sensed that I was on the verge of a break down, she would have stayed. Even I didn't feel this one coming.

Both of us had been rocking right along in the month of June. I was in a groove with a good balance between writing all day and human interaction at night. Edward and Xavier smothered me with friendship and spoiled me with fabulous dinners. I attributed my rapid progress in the sequel to their boundless support and encouragement.

We had standing dinner dates for Tuesdays and Fridays. During our cocktail hour, I would read. Our "story hour," as Edward called it, did more than stroke my ego. My friends inspired me to stay on track, and I felt more accountable to them than I did my agent.

They were already planning a party to celebrate the completion of my sequel upon their return from a vacation in France. I was on a mission. Totally attainable, I thought, since Edward and Xavier, Mom, and the Musketeers were all away.

A name change was definitely in order for Mom, Herbert, Aurora, and Farrah. Now, they were more than close compadres. They were "significant others."

During the last year, I began questioning if Mom appreciated more than just the inventory of Herb's Earth House. She seemed to glow in his presence. He made her smile. He made her laugh. When I asked her about it, she didn't deny her crush on him, she simply responded, "Herbert would never be interested in a 'cuckoo' like me," acknowledging the name that Charles Brooks pinned on her years ago. 'Til then, I thought I was the only one who tormented over that name.

As it turned out, Herbert was "cuckoo" over the "cuckoo." Watching their relationship finally take seed, like all the plants in our yard from Herb's Earth House, made my heart sing. Now, Aurora and Farrah were another story. I definitely didn't see that one coming. I was truly happy for all the couples: CiCi and Captain Gabe, Mom and Herbert, Aurora and Farrah. The craziest thing of all was that no one mentioned the upcoming ritual of the cleansing of the house. Then again, the oils were no longer needed.

Seeing them off, along with Edward and Xavier, I experienced more than a wave of loneliness. It was a tsunami, and tsunamis and writer's block were not a good combination.

I hadn't taken any Valium in over a month. Everyone has relapses. It is to be expected. Part of the process, I reminded myself, as I took several chased with tequila. I went out on the dock hoping that Uncle Frankie would join me. He hadn't talked to me lately. Perhaps he felt abandoned because I didn't need him as much. But, I needed him now. Hell, I would have even talked to that darn hoot owl. I started to go back inside. I stayed when I felt my uncle's hand on my shoulder.

I noticed Bethany Baldwin sitting on her dock on her monogrammed beach towel with her floppy straw monogrammed hat. I suddenly recalled Mom's disdain for all things monogrammed.

"Why on earth do you want to be branded? That would limit your life-force," Mom's unwavering position on the subject.

Maybe Uncle Frankie was attempting to rescue me from my writer's block. I could certainly incorporate Mom's quote into my sequel. After all, nothing else was original about it. It was about Bethany Baldwin's perfect life that wasn't so perfect after all. All of her BBB monograms didn't change the fact that they were indelibly linked to a wild animal who was never going to be branded.

And Bethany's "cuckoo" next door neighbors? The ones whom she alienated, ostracized, and persecuted—they were living life and doing just fine, thank you very much! But, that's where I was stuck. So what? What's the point? What happens next?

Maybe what comes next is that it was time to take the high road—walk over and strike up a conversation with Bethany. She was obviously alone, just like me. I wondered where her girls were or, better yet, her husband. I must have been more than a little loopy. I even thought I heard Uncle Frankie instructing me to stay right where I was.

The Valium and tequila were taking hold. A number of ideas began popping in my brain. That is, until I heard Bethany's voice, but strangely, it didn't sound like her voice at all.

"Still on the dock. It's so peaceful. I know why you love it here. Take your time, I totally understand. But we may need more wine!"

The sun was setting. My medication was kicking in. Everything was blurry. But I thought I heard, "You bitch! You can't have him!"

"Who are you?" I heard. There was more commotion and then a splash. I closed my eyes. I woke up hours later to the fireworks. There was no one on the dock. What a strange dream, I thought. But, it was exactly the kind of dream that I needed. Thank you, Uncle Frankie. You are a life saver, once again.

I finished my novel not only before the return of Edward and Xavier but also before Mom and all the others aboard the Love Boat. Edward's and Xavier's party for *After the Crash & Burn* was hugely successful. The novel held a record number of pre-release sales. My tide was finally turning.

Never in a million years would I have imagined that the events of my lonely Independence Day would have been the spark I needed. The curse of July 4th was over, at least for the remaining members of the Hollingsworth family.

Part VI

Chapter 32

Louie

There is something to be said about a stressful and demanding job. Most of the time, you don't have the time to think of anything else. When there is no one in your life to share the rare, free moments, you no longer covet them, you hate them.

When the memories of times with Millie came crashing back, I tried hard to block them out. I had tried really hard to get over Millie Hill. OK, admittedly, when I visited my dentist, I'd stop by the market where we first met, and I'd grab a beer from her favorite neighborhood pub hoping to bump into her. The worst part, that I would never ever admit to anyone, were the strolls by her complex on my way to the subway station, which were in opposite directions!

I understood her explanation, at least initially. But who just tosses true love away for a career? Why couldn't you have both? When thoughts about her intruded into my brain, I tried to comfort myself that a true soulmate wouldn't choose work over me. Like Millie said, I deserved someone who could love me unconditionally. That someone didn't seem to exist; or, perhaps, I hadn't given anyone that opportunity. I compared every date, even the ones that I slept with, to Millie. But, there was no comparison.

The strong, tough Louie Trahan would never, ever stoop to this level. But, the weak one needed to see her again, even if only to lay eyes on her just one more time. I needed to either confirm that the girl I continued to ache for was real or only a fairy tale. If the latter, it would be the closure I needed to move on. Though, I worried that if the former, how would I fight for her?

I did find some solace in my plan because it was the result of happenstance or better yet fate, not the actions of some scorned lover. The plan was precipitated by an invitation to a twelve-year high school reunion. I ignored the first, third, fifth, seventh and tenth reunions. Then, I had shaken my head upon receipt of the invitations. There was life after high school, I had thought, adventures beyond the East Baton Rouge Parish line.

It was more than my homesickness for Louisiana or my lovesickness for Millie that piqued my interest in this event. It was the handwritten note from Monica PreJean, the Reunion Committee chair, that ultimately drew me to the reunion.

Every boy had madly yearned for Monica PreJean, the hottest girl in our class. All of us immature horny boys called her: Mon-if-I-could-get-in-pre-jeans. I came close during the party at her house after the victory over our archrival. I removed her sweater and bra and was in the process of removing her jeans. Her hand was touching my rock-hard self. The sensation shooting through every nerve in my body was better than the feeling that I experienced only an hour earlier in scoring the winning touchdown.

I cursed Dean Perry so many times after that evening that he unknowingly was incorporated into my profanity expressions. "Damn it, Dean" was a more powerful emotion than just simply "damn it." Funny how even the origin of "Damn it, Dean" had slipped my mind. I knew it was a sign that time was like a magic eraser. I couldn't even remember who drunken Dean was with when he yanked the curtain back in the changing nook of Monica's pool house. I do remember it killed the heated moment.

Both of our respective dates were overserved by the spiked punch. The "Oh shit!" slur that erupted from the also overly served Dean when he laid eyes on Monica's beautifully exposed breasts ruined everything. Monica quickly retrieved and replaced her clothes and left me sitting on that bench trying to extinguish my activated testosterone hormones. As I sat there, "Damn it, Dean" was all I could say. I said it the rest of that year under my breath whenever I encountered Monica, more often than not, with Tristan Poirrier.

I read her note over and over. I was confident the invite to the reunion was more than that, it was a proposal to reconnect.

"New York is a long way from Baton Rouge! (Yes, I've kept up with your success over the years!) It sure would be great to see you again. I'm betting the years have been kind to you."

Monica PreJean

I wondered what happened to Tristan and Monica. I wondered if Monica was still single or kept her maiden name. I wondered if she was still the hottest girl in the class. I had experienced a lot over the past twelve years. High school seemed like forever ago, and my recall was hazy. Even Monica PreJean's face was blurry (and the part of her that I thought was seared in my brain was likely skewed from all the other breasts I had seen over the years, whether in the flesh or otherwise).

I began looking for my senior yearbook. If I was going to attend the reunion, I needed to refresh my memory on names and faces, especially the face of Monica PreJean. I searched for over an hour and then it hit me. Millie found my yearbook and wanted to look at all my pictures, including my dorky senior head shot. She even thought that the head shot was cute, but she really liked the action shot where the photographer caught me leaping into the air for my heroic touchdown pass. Surprisingly, the one that really turned her on, or so she said, was my senior superlative. The one that no guy relished; we all secretly desired "Best Looking" or "Most Athletic," but I was voted "Most Dependable." Such a patsy accolade, I thought then, but it sure seemed to come through for me that night.

Without that recollection, I would have never checked the nightstand on the other side of the bed, the side that had been Millie's. But it was there, right where she left it. Along with the yearbook, there was an extra fob for the electronic entry to her complex and a copy of her CD with the playlist she made for her bus ride from West Virginia to New York.

As I flipped the fob in my hand, I poured a stiff bourbon, inserted the CD, and listened to: Frank Sinatra's "New York New York," George Benson's "Broadway," Stevie Wonder's "Living for the City," Billy Joel's "New York State of Mind," and Alicia Keys' "Empire State of Mind." But, it was Don Henley's "New York Minute" that made me weep.

Things could turn upside-down rather quickly. The part of the song that really got to me was fighting for a true love because they're hard to find (that was my interpretation of it anyway). So, my strategy was formed.

"Found your extra fob, will be in your neighborhood soon, so I'll slip it in your mail slot. If you're around, maybe we can grab a beer and catch up. Hope all is well."

I even wrote my message down so I wouldn't blurt out that I missed her like crazy, thought about her every night, and wanted her back. I needed a script for sure. I even recorded my delivery. It needed to convey a strength, indifference, and dependability. I practiced so many times, I started feeling foolish and came close to ripping it up and throwing it in the trash, along with the fob and the CD. But, Don Henley's lyrics resounded in my head.

I took a big swig of bourbon, wiped my sweaty palms on my warm-up pants, took a deep breath, and gripped the paper with my lines. The paper's shaking confirmed that my hands were trembling. I placed my script on the table and took another swig of bourbon for good measure before dialing Millie's cell.

Her phone rolled directly into voicemail. God, it was good to hear her voice; her message gave me time to compose myself. I thought I recovered nicely; my voice didn't crack, and I performed my delivery exactly on cue, I thought.

A week passed with no response. I knew no response was a response. It was a harsh, very clear one. So, I don't know why I walked by her place. If I ran into her, I again rehearsed what I'd say, but this communication would simply cut to the chase.

"I left you a message letting you know I'd be in the area. Thought you may need your extra fob. Was dropping it off."

I didn't run into her; I did, however, run into Rosie. What is the politically correct name for a 'mailman' that is a woman? Mailwoman, mailperson? Anyway, I ran into Rosie, the USPS worker.

"Boy, it's been a long time since I've seen you!" Rosie said. "My route was moved but now I'm back! I thought Millie either moved or you've gotten lax about getting her mail. Her mailbox is overflowing; I can't stuff another thing inside. Wait here, I have a container in the truck for everything."

I didn't say a word. I assumed that Millie was on a lengthy business trip. When Rosie arrived with the container, I began wondering if she moved and failed to leave a forwarding address. That didn't make sense. Millie was overly organized and meticulous in everything she did.

"Thanks Rosie. Glad you're back!"

It wasn't illegal to deliver someone's mail. I wasn't going to open it. What if the fob no longer worked? What was I going to do with all the mail? Please work, I silently prayed as I placed the fob up to the pad. I breathed a sigh of relief when the door clicked. The fob also worked on the pad in the elevator. The 6th floor button lit up; the elevator began ascending. I started to just leave the container outside Millie's door. But, like in the past, I began to sort the junk mail from the important mail. There was so much of it that I checked out the postmarks. The mail had been accumulating for four months!

I wasn't expecting Millie to answer but rang the doorbell. I couldn't restrain my unsettling feelings. I decided to call her office number. Obviously, she wasn't in town, but I knew her voicemails were transcribed into her emails, and she checked those constantly. I was surprised when someone answered, but the voice was not Millie's, but a "Stan."

"I'm sorry, I am trying to reach Millie, well, Millicent Hill. Is she available?"

"No. She doesn't work here anymore. I have her old number. Can I help you? I filled her position."

"No. Not a professional need; just an old friend. Do you have her new contact information, by chance?"

"No, I sure don't."

Now, I was really feeling uneasy. It was the feeling I got during every Search and Rescue, the same adrenalin. I told myself I was overreacting but better safe than sorry. I called my best buddy at the NYPD, Antonio Rodriguez. *Damn it, Dean!* I got his voicemail.

After his introductory apology for being unavailable, I heard his standard ending, "if this is an emergency, call 911." I almost did just that, but that was not a good move, I thought. I did leave a message for him to call me as soon as possible.

I wasn't a detective. My training wasn't in figuring shit out, it was rescuing people after shit went down. My instincts told me something wasn't right. I wanted to go in, but that was more outrageous than calling 911. The wise thing to do, I decided, was to call Antonio again. Same voicemail.

"Hey listen, Bud. I am tempted to call 911, but it's a situation involving an old girlfriend. I am at her place, will explain that later, but she hasn't picked up her mail in months. I have this feeling something's not right. Call me back please."

My mind was racing through scenarios. While waiting on Antonio's call, I decided to go to the market. Maybe I would recognize someone. It had been a long time, but perhaps there was still a familiar face, and I could ask about Millie.

There was not one recognizable person. I knew something was terribly wrong when my voice asked for a pack of Camels and a lighter. I blamed it on Dean Perry, on Tristan Poirrier, and on Monica PreJean. The last cigarette I smoked was the night after Monica PreJean's party. It seemed fitting for some reason. I went through half the pack while I paced the block waiting for Antonio to call me back. I was feeling nauseated by the time he arrived.

When we entered Millie's condo and I saw her dead plants and the expiration dates on the food in her refrigerator, my dread escalated. The packed Ghurka leather rolling bag and her laptop confirmed my suspicion. She never went on a trip without them, even for a weekend and no way, for several months. I knew at that moment that something was more than not right. Something was terribly wrong.

Chapter 33

Simpson

Millicent seemed to have disappeared into thin air. Her cell went immediately into voicemail. She wasn't on the dock or in the boathouse. I did a full sweep of the big house. I was more than perplexed.

When I called to apologize for the delay, she was perfectly content. Charles had set me back an additional thirty minutes. That old codger "was finishing up a game of Bingo, and he'd be with me shortly," one of the caretakers said. Of course, an assisted living facility's definition of "shortly" differed drastically from mine.

After the delay with Charles, I thought about blowing off Ricky. It wasn't my problem that he lived from job to job. But, if he didn't get his cash, he'd call Bethany, which meant she would start blowing up my phone. This was not the night to be getting harassed by her checking up on the completion of my errands. Then, Ricky decided to talk my ear off about what he was doing with the landscape.

Millicent had been enjoying herself on the dock with wine when I told her that I was on the way back. And I was...but only from Ricky's. The traffic on Scenic Highway 98 for the Inn's fireworks was horrific. I made up time by picking up the filets I promised from Olie's Bar. Olie even offered to meet me in the turn-about, so I could stay in my car. That idea alone saved me at least thirty minutes.

During our last conversation, I didn't pick up on any anxiety, but on second thought, she did request that we take the boat out in the Bay to watch the fireworks. Perhaps, she got nervous about being spotted with all the activity in preparation for the show. There was always a mad rush for the strategic placement of chairs for the best view of the display. Maybe, she took a stroll on the boardwalk. The sun was setting. She could be waiting for a little more darkness before reappearing on our dock.

She certainly couldn't get lost. I opened the Silver Oak Cabernet to breathe. I was hoping to woo her big time with the fine wine and filets. I even planned to offer her a position at SBB Capital and double her pay. Hopefully, after our romantic evening, she would change her mind about the move to London.

After an hour passed, and several more unanswered calls, I began thinking she got spooked somehow. Certainly, any anxiety wasn't caused by the LeBlancs, the only neighbor with a view of our dock but who disappeared every July 4th.

For some reason, I started thinking about Claire's irate text message to me.

"I sent you pics of me in the outfit but crickets!"

I stopped reading it then. It was clear that she was pissed that I had not texted a response telling her how sexy she looked. What was it about women where they think they own you after a good lay? She was married for Christ's sake. I picked up my phone and read the rest of her rant.

"Since Bethany went to the mountains, I thought you would be alone," it continued. "Or are you?????"

Bethany in the mountains? Since when? She didn't mention that tidbit when she reeled off her to-do list. When thinking about Bethany in the mountain house, also property she would inherit, it hit me. Millicent found one of the antique anchors collected by Bethany's grandfather. Surely, she didn't decide to take the boat out herself. The Bay may look calm, but it wasn't a lake.

I ran across the yard and back to the boathouse. It didn't occur to me to check on the boat before. But, it was there. Perhaps she fell asleep, too much wine while waiting on me. I checked the bedroom in the boathouse. No Millicent. Then, I noticed something I hadn't before—white wine chilling in the ice bucket and a pack of sparklers. Millicent abhorred white wine.

Clearly, Bethany had been at the boathouse. She likely confronted Millicent. Millicent left and was probably angry, very angry. I sat out on the dock watching the fireworks from the Blakely Bay Inn fill the sky waiting for fireworks from Bethany. I was prepared for them, as best I could be, having no clue about the exchange between them.

My explanation to Bethany about a strange woman on our dock was simple—tourists from the Inn would commonly walk the dock to ogle our boathouse. That was a fact, and the other fact was I hadn't been there. It wasn't like she caught me in bed with Millicent. A close call, I thought, because a couple of hours earlier, she would have. If there were inquisitions about the rumpled bed, I simply took a nap. Though I never took naps, she couldn't prove otherwise. There's a first for everything.

I concocted an explanation for every possible angle. However, I didn't hear from her. Not once. When I woke up the next morning, there was still no Millicent nor interrogation from Bethany.

Chapter 34

Louie

Despite my insistence that something wasn't right, Antonio said there wasn't enough to open an investigation based only on the "instinct" of an old boyfriend.

"Bud, it's been a long time since you were seeing her. Her habits may have changed over the years. And, there's no missing person report in the database on a Millicent Jane Hill in New York, West Virginia...anywhere. I won't list all of the possible explanations, but one is quite plausible. She has a new job and is possibly in another city, or even state."

The information I knew about Millie's family was limited. Her father died of black lung after years of working for a coal mining company in West Virginia. Her mother lived with her brother, Billy Hill, who was also a coal miner. I didn't believe her when she told me his name. If that bit of information circulated around her office, even changing her professional name to Millicent wouldn't have stopped the teasing.

I couldn't recall the town, but they talked every week. I did know that.

Antonio explained that he didn't have enough evidence to request cell phone records, and even so, he sure couldn't contact the family. Millie was not the first person who failed to timely retrieve the mail! He couldn't say that the basis for suspicion was that he accompanied an old lover to her condo and saw dead plants, expired food in the fridge, a packed suitcase, and a laptop.

"You need to stick to your day job, Louie. But, I do appreciate that you didn't reach your rank in the Coast Guard without some intuitive abilities. So, for you, I'll call her former employer and see what I can find out."

I knew he was right, looking at the facts from the outside, someone who didn't know Millie. If you knew Millie like I did, or at least thought I did, her laptop and packed Ghurka bag would be the only evidence needed to launch a full investigation. But, I wasn't a detective in the New York Police Department. I had no choice but to sit tight and wait.

After three days, I was antsy and restless even though I logged forty-two hours at work during this time period. Instead of crashing when I got home, I medicated myself with bourbon and Camels. I kicked the habit before, and I could do it again. Now was not the time.

I knew Antonio was busy, like me, but how long does a phone call take? Millie wasn't a priority to him, like she was to me. The more I thought about it, Antonio probably believed my judgment was impaired or tainted by my terminal lovesickness.

After too many bourbons on the fourth night, I grew concerned that Antonio thought I pulled him into a sketchy situation, using the accumulated mail as a reason to snoop on Millie. I didn't want my professional reputation polluted by any of this. So, I didn't press him. I painfully awaited an update.

When he finally called, my emotions flipped from initial relief to agony. The relief was that my judgment hadn't been impaired; that any possible misgivings Antonio may have harbored about my intentions were restored. But, that relief quickly vanished.

Millie had accepted a new job in London. He started to close his unofficial investigation, but her condo didn't support signs of a long-distance move. He followed up with her new employer. She never reported for her job two months ago. Follow up calls to her weren't returned. Her voicemail was full.

Antonio pulled her cell phone records. The last calls were with a Simpson Baldwin on July 4th.

"Millicent was part of a team that represents my company," Simpson revealed, when Antonio called him.

"We worked together over the years. She called to let me know that she had taken a new job. I can't recall the name of the company, but it is in London. I haven't heard from her since. Is everything OK?"

"Call it twenty-two years of doing this, but that man knows more than he communicated," Antonio said. "There were two calls on July 4th, and they weren't placed from Millie to him, but from him to her. Both lasted about a minute. He was the last person who spoke to her. There were several more attempted calls that evening from Simpson Baldwin to her, and the next day as well. Let's just say there have been numerous calls between them over the last year. Could all be legit. As he said, she worked for his company; she definitely won the prize for calls from him. No one else is even a close second."

"It wouldn't be out of the question for her to work on a holiday," I interjected. "She worked a lot! It doesn't make sense that she would take two calls, not others, then go dark."

"I contacted the family. You were right. She called weekly until the month of July. Her brother said she was taking a couple of months off between jobs, so he knew she was busy, packing, and finding a place in London. After two weeks passed, he tried to reach her a couple of times. Her phone went directly into voicemail. He just assumed she was busy."

"I know I haven't seen her in several years, but I did know her. None of this matches up to the Millie I knew. I don't know what to do."

"Nothing is what you will do. Don't go rogue on me and get involved. I've requested an official investigation. So, head's up. You will be contacted. I disclosed everything, even the entry into her condo. They may find your prints."

"Well, you have the information that I have. I'll do anything. Just tell me what and when."

"Officer Barrett will be contacting you and taking your statement. Given our friendship, I can't be involved with that."

"I understand. I am taking some vacation time in a couple of weeks. I'm attending a high school reunion in Louisiana. So, the sooner the better."

"I'll pass that along to Officer Barrett. I shouldn't have told you what I've learned, so let's keep all this between you and me. Now that the investigation is official, I'm sorry that I can't talk to you anymore. I wish I could be there for you, man because none of this sounds good. Be patient."

"No, it doesn't. And thanks for every..."

I couldn't finish my sentence. Antonio wrapped his arms around me. His embrace confirmed my worse thoughts—Millie was dead. I believed that this Simpson Baldwin was somehow connected to it all.

Chapter 35

Simpson

Before the call from the NYPD asking questions about Millicent, I assumed she was in London trying to start a new life, one without me. She made it quite clear that our last weekend together was just that—The Last. I hoped to change her mind that night with steaks, expensive wine, fireworks, and an offer at SBB Capital. Then her disappearance coupled with evidence that Bethany had been there, I was certain Bethany was behind her departure.

Another clue was Bethany's complete silence about how I spent my 4th, including zero questions about Charles and the scotch, Ricky and the payment, who I played golf with, when I got home, what maintenance I completed, where I got dinner, when I got home from dinner, did I watch the fireworks, with whom, where, and what time I went to bed. The Bethany I knew, the ultimate combination of Inspector Clousseau, a prison warden, and the Wicked Witch of the West, had literally transformed overnight into a combination of Glinda the Good Witch of the South and Hoda Kotb! I was not attributing the conversion to fresh mountain air.

So, I contacted my people. These people were on retainer to locate dirt on my targets, and by that, I mean the CEO's, the CFO's, well any C-suite executive whom I could influence with uncovered dirt. There was usually dirt, and more often than not, it was more than just dirty, it was rotten. This intel had saved me millions over the years.

Not only did my people help me in my professional life but also in my personal life. I treated my affairs the same way as my business targets. I learned everything about them down to their credit card purchases. I knew their weaknesses; I knew their habits, and I knew how to counter any threats of exposure once things went south. And, they typically did go south.

All women became jealous and needy at some point. They wanted what they could never have, me. My people also came through on those rare occasions when I succumbed to an easy pick-up on a business trip. I wasn't dumb enough to hire a prostitute. I was never desperate enough to search "one-night stands in the area" on dating sites. All I had to do was sit at the bar at a five-star hotel, order a martini, and within minutes, a smoking hot woman would appear. I referred to it as the "James Bond" moment.

I never disclosed my real name, didn't care if I got theirs. It was all irrelevant. But one thing was as certain as the sun setting, the tide receding, and the excellent sex, they always gave me their number. And though they didn't know my name, I took no chances. My people were conducting background checks on them the next day, my version of being very careful.

Long before I laid eyes on Millicent, I turned my people loose to find out all about her. She was a target from the minute I heard her voice and read her analysis of the balance sheet of an acquisition target. When I saw her picture on the Vittoria & Associates' website, my primary go-to financial consultant, I was smitten. She never disappointed, that is until the disclosure of a boyfriend. I didn't see that one coming. After that, I called for a 24/7 surveillance. Unless they completely botched their job, she kept her promise to end things. She was one of those rare finds—smart, beautiful, sexy, and honest. I knew she loved me with all of her being.

She was fed up and wounded by my double-life, as she referred to it. I was too. She deserved more, and I was ready to give it to her. I hoped it wasn't too late.

After months passed, her response to any job offer at SBB Capital was no longer my primary worry. It was that my people couldn't locate her. Then the call from a police officer, Lieutenant Rodriguez.

"What is your relationship with Millicent Hill? When was the last time you spoke to her?"

Thinking back on the questions, I was relieved that he didn't ask me when I last saw her. When I asked if she was OK, he only said, "That's what I want to know."

Chapter 36

Louie

I couldn't get back to Louisiana fast enough. There was something about your roots that grounded you, especially your high school years. Despite stupid senior superlatives, there was a wild innocence to those days, a carefree spirit resulting from an unawareness of real-life burdens. But, eventually life smacks you in the face: finding an apartment, making a car payment, and then spending real money on those things that you simply took for granted while living at home—furniture, pots, pans, kitchen utensils, sheets, and towels. Those things were shortly accompanied with the more serious side of life: a job with health insurance, a wife, a family, a 401K. Then, the choke hold was on, or at least that is how I viewed it.

I sped full steam into a career that I hoped would make my dad proud and would snap him out of his depression—one that would make him notice me. A career in the United States Coast Guard, just like his. No one was going to alter my course.

I sympathized with all the boys who settled for the girl instead of the dream. If I had met Millicent Jane Hill earlier in my life, I would have been one of those casualties. Instead, and ironically, I was becoming one of those casualties that my career, my calling, was trained to save. Instead of saving my dad, I was fearful that I was joining him in that downward spiral of despair.

Funny how your failures become front and center when you grow older. Those setbacks mold you. I needed a break from the hard lessons of life.

I planned to have a huge time, a one-night return to the innocent and oblivious period of youth. And, lately, my life had been far from a huge time, no exclamation marks for sure. Perhaps an exclamation mark was in store with Monica after all these years. As I fantasized, the real world quickly slapped me in the face. My flight was delayed, probably a sign of the only exclamation point for the weekend.

Anyone flying out of La Guardia understands that one "delay" often follows another delay, then another before the inevitable cancellation. Passengers then dash to the customer service kiosks, long lines form, and your day is shot.

I decided to buy a book while biding my time from the postponement to the kick-off to my weekend. On the display rack was *After the Crash & Burn*, the anticipated sequel to Francie DeVries' first novel. The sequel was dedicated to LeJeune Hollingsworth LeBlanc and Arthur Francis Hollingsworth, IV. I knew about the author; hell, I knew about the entire family.

My palms and forehead got clammy. I felt the blood drain from my face, and my heart was pounding. Pierre Trahan, the father of the man holding the book, was the last person to have held the author's uncle in his arms. I felt faint. I grabbed two waters from the store's cooler and chugged one trying to reorient myself. As I was paying for my purchases, the clerk commented about my book selection.

"This one is so good! It is the author's second book. You need to read *Crash & Burn* first. Such a sad story."

"I have read the first one. And you're right, very sad," my voice cracked.

I parked myself at my gate. I took a deep breath, then a long chug of my water to help my parching throat before beginning the sequel.

Between the information Antonio had shared, what I read in the book, and my own research, by the time I arrived in Baton Rouge, I had pieced a lot of things together. I didn't go completely "rogue" as Antonio forbade, but I had poked around the database at the office. While the Coast Guard didn't have the investigative resources of the NYPD, I knew enough to be "dangerous," as we used to say about those who just completed basic training.

Simpson Baker Baldwin graduated from the University of Georgia, owned a successful private investment firm, SBB Capital, located in Atlanta. The company's portfolio represented a range of industries from apparel, building products, alternative energy, electronics, machinery and equipment to packaging. The founder's picture, which could be on the cover of GQ, was accompanied with the company's philosophy: "We inject capital and other resources to improve efficiencies and supply chain logistics, but, more importantly, we inspire management teams by providing them with the tools to be successful. SBB Capital has a proven record of increasing equity value."

When I discovered that SBB Capital owned a private jet, it hit me that the last time I laid eyes on Millie was when she was headed to Florida on a business trip. She would be gone more than a week—the longest time that we would have been apart. We were so enthralled with her send-off that neither of us noticed the driver who had arrived to take her to the airport.

"Sorry to interrupt but are you headed to Teterboro Airport? Millicent Hill?"

"Oh yes, I am and yes, thank you," she said to the driver blushing. As the driver placed her Ghurka leather rolling bag in the car, she kissed me quickly again several more times. She rolled the window down as the driver pulled out, "God, I am going to miss you. I'll call you."

Shortly after our first night together, we shared more than each other's beds, we shared keys to our respective residences. Though it had only been three months since Millie entered my life, I couldn't remember life before her. I was quickly forced to remember because after that farewell, I never saw her again.

That week, Millie called only twice when she was on a "brief break." She had been "working like a dog." She couldn't complain, she said, because it was an exciting new acquisition, which would generate a large fee, and her accommodations weren't too shabby either—the Breakers. She gushed that we'd have to celebrate with a trip there, "It is just amazing!"

With my research in hand, I assumed that SBB Capital was the "client" whose plane had jetted her away to the Breakers. The driver's mention of Teterboro Airport glossed over me at the time, but I knew it was the airport most often used for private and corporate planes due to its proximity to Manhattan. Something definitely happened on that trip. I was betting that she had become enamored with one Simpson Baldwin.

The society page in the *Blakely Point Tribune* revealed the mother lode of information. I was hooked. I spent hours reading about the families in the quaint town where multimillion-dollar homes on Mobile Bay passed from generation to generation. It was a modern-day version of *The Great Gatsby*, one of my favorite novels.

My research didn't uncover a divorce but a movie star-like wedding between Simpson Baldwin and Bethany Fitzgerald Brooks, daughter of Mr. and Mrs. Charles Mitchell Brooks, V. There were a number of articles about the wedding at the Brooks' summer home on Blakely Point. They provided fastidious detail about Bethany's dress and her bouquet filled with an "exquisite variety of flowers from her mother's award-winning garden....The ceremony culminated with pops of the finest champagne and fireworks illuminating Mobile Bay. Simply spectacular," the society editor wrote.

The society editor provided similar detail about the celebration after the birth of Simpson and Bethany's twin daughters, Brooks Fitzgerald and Anna Baker, down to the post-christening luncheon menu. Nothing like small Southern town "news," I thought to myself.

The society editor wasn't a fan of only the Brooks' family. She provided equal coverage of the Hollingsworths. The summer homes of these two families were right next door to each other.

When my plane finally landed in Baton Rouge, I was connecting the dots. "Eve Bastian Baker" was the fictional name of "Bethany Brooks Baldwin" in Francie DeVries' sequel. Eve's successful Wall Street husband, "Richard Wells Baker," was Simpson Baker Baldwin.

If my instincts were right, Francie DeVries witnessed a murder—the drowning of the paramour of "Eve's" husband in Mobile Bay.

I began planning a little side-trip after my reunion. I was going to book a room at the Blakely Bay Inn and take a walk on the boardwalk to check out the Brooks' and Hollingworth's homes. I believed that I was not only going to find out what happened to Millie, but also where she was.

Chapter 37

Louie

Let's just say that the high wave I was riding when I started my trip continued its rapid demise as I approached the reunion registration table at the hotel. Monica PreJean was waiting for my arrival. She jumped from her seat with my name tag in her hand the moment that she saw me.

"Louie! You did make it! So great to see you!"

She peeled the backing from the adhesive sticker and placed "My Name Is Louie Trahan" on my chest. As she applied a little extra pressure to ensure it would stay in place, she leaned into me and whispered, "Not that you need a name tag, you look exactly the same. Strike that, you look better!"

Kelly Clarkson's voice was blasting "Since You've Been Gone" in the ballroom. I experienced one of those ah-ha moments. The lyrics celebrated a breakup. The committee probably hadn't looked past the title in selecting the song for the reuniting of high school friends.

Cruelly, I couldn't help thinking that since I had been gone, Monica PreJean gained at least three pounds for each passing year. As the night went on and the more alcohol I consumed, the thirty-plus pounds didn't seem to matter. She still radiated sex appeal. Maybe it wasn't just her high school figure that made us all want to "get-in-pre-jeans." Who was I kidding? Her hot bod was definitely the reason. I must have matured over the last twelve years. I noticed other qualities that were just as attractive.

My throw-it-all-to-the-wind attitude and pent-up desires landed Monica in my bed. Let's just say we made up for the "Damn it, Dean" interruption at her party. The next morning, I was feeling guilty and selfish. Thankfully, she had similar remorse.

"Last night was wonderful," she said, "but it was a mistake."

Though I was feeling the same thing, rejection twists you up. I started thinking that it wasn't a mistake at all because she said it first.

"How so?" I asked.

"You'll think I'm a horrible person, but Tristan left me for our next-door neighbor, who I thought was one of my best friends!" she said, with tears filling her eyes. "I just needed to feel desired...wanted. I've been a mess. I'm sorry."

"I'm sorry too, about Tristan, not for what happened last night. I needed it too. I'm really happy that it was with you."

It was much more than a one-night stand. It was the best of everything. A carefree hookup with an emotional connection but no expectations or guilt. Two people who wanted to feel something, with someone.

"Could I convince you to have breakfast in bed?" I asked her.

"Really?"

"Yes, really."

She relaxed, smiled, and rolled on top of me.

We proceeded to reunite one last time. It was long and strong, better than the night before. We were sober, and our respective cards were on the table. There was definitely comfort in the arms of an old friend.

"Let's keep in touch," I said after.

Then, realizing the innuendo, we both laughed and held each other for a while longer. I didn't want the therapeutic diversion to end. Monica satisfied more than my libido. She was my safe haven before being jolted back into cold reality.

My old squadron had contacts with the Mobile Coast Guard station and were arranging a boat with scuba gear. On the way to the dock, I began thinking about the loneliness I quietly endured in high school. I thought about the contrast of Monica's life then versus now. I thought about the similarities in our current situations. It made me think about Kevin Roosevelt Moore.

During those impressionable years of my youth, I spent a lot of time in my room reading and listening to all kinds of music. My evening and morning with Monica resurrected my memories of sitting in my room with my boombox with my array of CDs. In retrospect, it's no wonder I gravitated to the blues.

My favorites were Eric Clapton and The Robert Cray Band, until I discovered Kevin Roosevelt Moore, the ultimate singer of Mississippi Delta blues. In high school, I replayed my Keb' Mo' CD over and over. At the time, "Momma, Where's My Daddy?" comforted me.

But, now, heading toward Mobile Bay, thoughts of Millie, Monica, and the song "Just Like You" began echoing in my head. The soulful song reflected my life. Reuniting with an old flame and commiserating over pain from prior relationships, the lyrics were eerily fitting. My connection with Monica was strengthened through our similar heartbreaks. But, I didn't open up to her completely; I didn't tell her that I felt just like her, that I breakdown and cry, just like her.

As I made the turn onto the road that led to Mobile Bay, I did breakdown. I cried for Monica, I cried for Millie, and I cried for me.

Chapter 38

Louie

I had covered every inch of Blakely Point's shoreline on a boat but never set foot on its shore. After I checked into the Blakely Bay Inn, I realized that you can't appreciate the intrinsic beauty of the internal landscape from the water.

I settled down with my drink on the patio and quickly became immersed into the sights and sounds surrounding me. In the distance, the lights from the corporate towers in downtown Mobile outlined the skyline. On the Bay, the moon's beam outlined the boathouses. I thought about the stark contrast between the two. No hustle or bustle existed here. Instead, Blakely Point provided an instant pause to the worries of the real world. Even the humming of engines and smell of diesel from the boats returning from fishing expeditions were relaxing.

The tranquil environment, however, provided only a temporary diversion from the weight of my mission. My bourbon wasn't helping. Monica's situation resurfaced in my thoughts and made me sad. But, my empathy seemed trite. She had been with Tristan Poirrier since high school. They shared more than twelve years together; their love created children. I was only with Millie a little over three months.

I empathized with Monica's vulnerability. I knew how it felt when you believe with your whole soul that you've found your person only to have that person rip out your soul by dumping you. You are left with a broken heart, shattered confidence, and unreliable instincts.

As hard as it was losing your imagined soulmate, both of us would eventually heal. Our hearts were broken but still beating. We would live to see another day, unlike Millie.

In the morning, I would be going on a diving expedition. If my instincts hadn't totally been rocked, I said a silent prayer that I was strong enough to handle what they told me I would soon discover. Then, I began wrestling with the best way to confront Francie DeVries about withholding information about a murder.

Chapter 39

Louie

Not even noon yet, I slammed down another shot in Olie's Bar. I knew I should have listened to Antonio's warning not to get involved. But, if I hadn't, how long would it have been before there were answers? Missing persons were the lowest priority in the NYPD. Every day the department was greeted with a different crisis, an immediate threat. Antonio had done all he could. "Be patient" were the last words he said to me. But, patience wasn't in my vocabulary.

Millicent Jane Hill's disappearance was getting no attention because no one was demanding it. She'd get some now, by God. A corpse has a way of moving you to the top of the pile.

The problem was that I couldn't erase the image seared in my brain. My attempts at self-medication were not working. My head was splitting.

I stumbled out of Olie's Bar and headed to the Inn's spa for a long steam. I needed the detox and hoped the quiet setting would help organize my thoughts. My next visit was to the Hollingsworth home, as it was known to those on the boardwalk. Given my history with the family, I felt a duty to warn Francie DeVries of the forthcoming inquisition by the police.

Olie provided me with the information I needed to locate the residence.

"Walk down the boardwalk. You can't miss it. It's the only house with a purple fence."

The Hollingsworth home was not as I pictured. I imagined a large antebellum home, that part I got right. It was the atmosphere surrounding the property that I got completely wrong. I envisioned a dark, gloomy house, like the ones in the horror, mystery books I read growing up. It was far from those spooky images.

There was a collection of people on the massive porch. There was music and laughter. The yard was a collection of all kinds of things, quite the opposite of the immaculate landscapes that I passed on the way. Unlike the other homes on the boardwalk, this one was not imposing. It was inviting. It was a Blakely Point version of Bourbon Street!

I started to abort my visit, but I decided to lift the latch on the gate and crash the party. I would simply admit that I was an admirer of Francie DeVries' books, and a guest at the hotel while offering my apologies for intruding. I was halfway into my spiel when the woman with large eyes approached me. Her eyes seemed to get even bigger as she looked me up and down.

"Well, Francie's not here but sit down and have a drink!" the woman with the owl-like eyes said. "You're the best looking tour-on that I've evah seen!"

"I've been called lots of things in my life," I said laughing, "but never a tour-on. It doesn't sound good."

"Don't mind CiCi," another woman said. "She can't help that she is a boardwalk snob."

"Well, kiss my go-to-hell, Junie!" the big-eyed woman named CiCi said. "You're the one that always says tour-ons are as welcome as a skunk at a porch party!"

"Don't mind her! She could make a preacher cuss! I'm Junie LeBlanc, or now it seems I'm better known as Francie Devries' mother," as she extended her hand.

I tried not to blurt out that I knew all about her family. Junie then introduced the other participants at the mid-afternoon "tea party."

As gracious Southern hostesses do, they asked about me, and how I ended up at the Blakely Bay Inn.

"A tour-on and a Yankee on Junie's porch! This is a first!" CiCi said.

"But his roots are by way of Baton Rouge," Junie said. "Totally different! You're going to make this handsome visitor fly the coop before we show our Southern hospitality. What can we serve you to eat?" she asked, as she walked over and lifted a silver tray filled with food.

"Thank you, but I'm good, unless that is pimento cheese there."

"Yes, it is! You can't find that in New York, now can you?" CiCi asked.

"No, Ma'am. I'm as full as a tick but will make room for some "per-men-toe cheese," I replied, digging up my Cajun accent.

"You are a Southerner!" CiCi laughed.

"Yes, Ma'am, a leopard can't change its spots!"

"We like you, Louie!" Junie said. "You're welcome here anytime. Herbert, play a song."

Herbert, the only male at the tea party, was sitting on the large porch swing with a banjo. He struck up my theme song, "Louie Louie," without missing a beat.

"Dance with me," Junie requested, without really giving me a choice. She grabbed my arms and took the lead in the Southern dance, the Carolina Shag. My recent reunion had provided a little shag practice.

Monica's tutorial paid off. I was impressing them with my smooth six-count footwork and gliding Junie across the porch. It wasn't long before CiCi cut in. I was having such a good time that I forgot the reason for my visit, until Francie DeVries came walking through the gate.

Chapter 40

Simpson

The most disturbing news from my conversation with Officer Rodriguez was that I was the last person to speak to Millicent, on July 4th. I told the officer that Millicent called to inform me of a new job. After I hung up, I had my people review every personal and business call during that time period. My people informed me that I was the one placing the calls to Millicent, two of them on July 4th and then several more the next day. If I heard from Officer Rodriguez about that inconsistency, I wasn't too worried. Who could remember that type of detail months later? And I knew that I wasn't the last one who had seen her. My wife had.

Armed with the information from my people, I knew how to handle the police if they questioned me again. I would simply say that I called Millicent to wish her a happy 4th. Successful businessmen don't burn bridges. If Officer Rodriguez learned that Millicent had been at Blakely Point, I would explain that Millicent and I had crossed a professional line in our working relationship, but I had ended it because of Claire. She had not taken it well. Millicent knew we spent our holidays on the Bay. On our calls, she told me she had a surprise for me that I would discover soon. I was going to experience fireworks from my house like never before.

I thought that she was planning to show up and make a scene. I was there alone, so I left the house and checked into the Duc de Bourbon. My e-mailed receipt verified that fact. I attempted to call the next day to find out if she was in town. I was going to try and have a professional discussion, but she never answered.

Claire was going to be my cover. Claire had immediately accepted my invitation for a quick get-away to make up for missing her July 4th party. During that trip, I learned the time of Bethany's call to Claire, exactly what she told Claire about her trip to the mountain house, and what Bethany told her about my July 4th trip to Blakely Point. After our rendezvous, we certainly had numerous text messages that I knew would be now be discoverable by the NYPD. They would more than substantiate my involvement with Claire.

The picture that Claire sent me in her new outfit on July 4th, with my message about wanting to take it off her, should be enough to convince the investigators that I had moved on.

I had more than sufficient coverage; Bethany was another story. She was never in the mountains. She left the package of sparklers and the chardonnay in the boathouse. I certainly wasn't going to volunteer that information. Her absence from the mountains could easily be verified from our security cameras. She had painted herself into a corner.

Chapter 41

Louie

A head shot on the back of a book cover can portray an inaccurate image of a person, I thought. Or, on the other hand, it could be that my knowledge of the privileged background of the author's family coupled with their tragedy made me view Francie DeVries as aloof and cold. The kind of coolness where ice ran through your veins. Someone that cold could witness a murder and not tell a soul. But the woman walking up the stone steps to her family estate was quite the opposite of my heartless opinion.

I tried to avoid Southern stereotypes; her naturally highlighted hair in a side braid hanging on her tanned shoulder confirmed her origin, but her sundress looked more New York Soho than Southern preppy. Her gait was confident and regal, but there was this contrasting insecurity as she approached the party. She conveyed a reluctant wariness, a bashfulness that was totally absent from the others on the grand porch.

"There's my Francie," Junie yelled. "I was getting ready to come yank you out of the boathouse to meet Louie. He's a big fan of yours."

"I am that and now a fan of your mother as well. Louie Trahan," I said extending my hand.

Was she blushing? She looked down at the ground and extended a limp hand.

"Thank you," she said softly.

Whoever shot the photos for her book covers definitely removed the slight freckles from her nose and cheeks. They also accentuated her sharp cheekbones with some type of cosmetics. But, the woman standing in front of me didn't need any enhancements. In fact, she had no enhancements—no jewelry, no hint of perfume, no nail polish, not one tad of makeup. She was real and raw, a natural beauty to the core. Thank heavens for these boisterous, lively women. They broke the awkward silence.

"Francie, fetch this handsome man some tea!" Junie said.

"And some more pimento cheese," CiCi added. "Louie lives in New York City, of all places. Can't get pimento cheese there!"

"New York?" Francie asked. "I thought I detected a Southern accent."

"Well, I live in New York now. Was born and raised in Baton Rouge. I'm in the Coast Guard and was transferred north."

"How interesting," Francie said, with a little more inflection in her voice. "I'd love to hear more about that after I 'fetch' your pimento cheese and tea. FYI, the tea is spiked," she whispered.

After a bit, the spirit on the porch seemed to be rubbing off on Francie or, perhaps, it was the tea she consumed. Between the music and dancing, I couldn't find the appropriate time to inquire about the idea for her sequel. I was wearing out my welcome. I needed to go back to the Inn, but not before my conversation with Francie. Then Junie came to the rescue.

"Francie, why don't you take Louie to see the magnificent view of the Bay from the boathouse? While you're there, autograph him some copies of your book to take back with him."

"Great idea," CiCi said. "You could show your Yankee friends that we Southerners aren't so dumb after all!"

"That would be great. I'll pay for the books, if you can spare a couple."

"Don't let them bully you," Francie said. "Don't feel obligated, but I'm happy to share."

I thought a moment alone with Francie would provide the perfect opportunity to ask her some questions. A person in the Hollingsworth boathouse had a perfect view of the Brooks' dock. This dock now pinned a dead body beneath it.

"She's so modest," Junie said. "And timid! I assure you that she didn't get that from me. I can't write a lick but am the best Cajun cook around these parts. You won't find any Louisiana specialties on the menu at the Inn, so you must join us for dinner. Another of my faults, I don't take kindly to rejection."

As quickly as the opportunity to probe Francie's book idea extended itself, it shut just as rapidly. There was no way I could spring witnessing a murder to fragile Francie DeVries and afterward be a dinner guest.

"That's awfully nice of you, but I feel like I've intruded on your afternoon and have some things to do tonight before my flight tomorrow," I said.

"Well, skedaddle and take care of your business because we are expecting you at 7:00 sharp."

As Francie led me to the boathouse, she apologized for her mother.

"She doesn't understand what it's like to have pressing matters or a schedule, but she means well. She's hard to say no to; believe me, I know. I can be the bearer of the news that you can't join us."

As Francie was signing some books, she invited me to check out the views.

"When I was little, it felt like I was on a boat on the water. It's my writing haven, and I've sort of moved out here. Too much activity in the big house to concentrate, as you saw. I find the view very cathartic."

"I can see why."

I took in the expansive views of the Bay that were visible from every angle. I noticed tequila on the counter.

"May I?"

"Pardon?"

"I have something to talk to you about, but I really need some of this first."

I poured myself a shot and slugged it back. Not surprisingly, she appeared thrown. I took a deep breath.

"I came to Blakely Point for a reason. Let's go sit down. You may need a shot of this too."

I fixed us both a glass. As we sat down on the edge of the dock, I emptied my second shot.

"I need to know some things about your book, some factual things. OK, I'm just going to come right out and ask you. Did you witness a murder?"

"Are you a cop?" she asked nervously.

"No, I'm not, but one of my friends is, and he is investigating someone who is missing. I believe that someone is at the bottom of this Bay."

I should have been more direct and disclosed that I didn't simply believe that to be true; I knew it to be true. She knocked back the tequila and abruptly got up and went inside. She was escaping my inquisition. My job was done. I had provided more than a sufficient warning.

I started to leave. She returned with the bottle. She poured more into my glass and into hers. She threw back another shot.

"I think you're right."

She revealed everything to me. What she thought she saw, her abuse of her prescribed meds chased with her various liquid meds, the side effects, her lack of sleep, and her crazy mind. Since her childhood, she had seesawed between a world of fantasy and reality. Everyone thought she and her mother were certifiably crazy. After what she thought she saw, she couldn't accuse her neighbor's daughter of murder. CiCi was her mother's best friend. She was convinced it was all in her head when no one uttered a word. It was the spark she needed to finish her book. She thought it was all a product of her overactive imagination.

"I still talk to Luna and Becca, my imaginary friends from childhood, and my dead uncle, for goodness sake! What's going to happen? I don't care about me, but I do care about Mom. She is finally better. You saw her today. She's happy for once in her life. If I am brought into this, it will send her back into a depression that will be irreparable. This time, it will be my fault."

I knew the history, all of it. I totally understood the wave of the potential repercussions, but I had to report what I found. All of a sudden, I felt like the Trahans were going to fail the Hollingsworth family once again.

Chapter 42

Francie

I had never seen a man cry. Hell, I had never seen my mother shed one tear. I grew up thinking crying was a sign of weakness and something that was done privately.

I was sitting with a man—a strong man—in the United States Coast Guard, who appeared to have tears forming in his eyes. I didn't know what to do or think. I was instantly distracted from all the things swirling around in my head to what was going to happen to me.

When he finally spoke, he told me everything. At least, I thought it was everything. I learned about Millicent Hill, where she was from, how they met, how she ended their relationship, how he suspected something was wrong, his visit to her apartment, finding out that Simpson Baldwin was her client, and that Millie's last conversation was with him. His research into Simpson uncovered his marriage to Bethany Brooks and that the wedding took place on her family's property in Blakely Point.

He read my book on the way to his high school reunion and then confirmed his worse thoughts while scuba diving in the Bay. He was going to have to report the body to the NYPD. There would be lots of questions.

"There is more," he said, "but now is not the time." He got up to leave. "Thank Junie for the kind dinner invitation, but I need to be alone tonight."

Chapter 43

Louie

As I walked down the boardwalk back to the Inn, my entire body ached. I was spent; the kind of exhaustion one experiences after a long run, a marathon. But, I wasn't too tired for a visit to Olie's Bar; I needed a bourbon. Now was the time to follow Ernest Hemingway's advice or at least half of it. "Never delay in kissing a pretty girl or opening a bottle of whiskey."

I just left a pretty girl. In fact, I dropped a bomb on her and left her to deal with some serious baggage. She had endured enough pain in her life. Clearly, she had a delicate frame of mind. I started rethinking my abrupt exit and considered returning to check on her. Before I could act, I heard my name in the distance.

"Louie! Louie!"

I turned around. Francie was running toward me.

"I'm sorry," she said, out of breath. "I know you said you need to be alone, but I can't. I just can't. I'm scared, really scared."

"Want to join me? I'm headed to Olie's Bar."

"Yes, thank you."

After a couple of drinks, she changed my mind about dinner. She asked for my help. CiCi was her mother's very best friend from childhood, until she married Charles Brooks. He alienated them, but they finally reunited. CiCi was the primary reason that her mother was happier than Francie remembered seeing her. CiCi needed to know the truth. She couldn't and wouldn't talk to any police officer until she talked to CiCi. She couldn't possibly do it alone.

"I've never asked anyone for a favor, but there is a first for everything. I'm asking, no, I'm begging you."

Francie DeVries' big, greenish-brown eyes were expressive but mostly emitted pain, a tangible vulnerability. They were filling with tears.

"OK, but you know what happens when you extend a favor?"

She looked down. I was perplexed why this accomplished author's self-esteem seemed so brittle.

"You expect one in return?" she asked.

"Damn straight, and there is one condition."

I actually saw a glimpse of a smile.

"I guess I don't have much leverage. What's the conditional favor?"

"Haven't figured out the favor yet, but the condition is that you tell them what you told me. I'll be there for you if you need help, but this is your story to tell—no pun intended."

"Thank you."

Walking with Francie DeVries to the dinner party, I didn't think I would be able to take one bite of anything, especially spicy Cajun food. As we approached the house and opened the gate on the purple fence, a wave of tranquility washed over me. Everything about the eclectic surroundings was like a warm embrace, a welcoming of lost souls. It was as if Millie was right there with me leading me up the stairs. I heard her voice in my head, "I brought you back to your people."

Chapter 44

Francie

There was something about Louie Trahan that bolstered me up. I couldn't explain it. I felt like I was being rescued from my demons. A sense of freedom was flowing through my core. The aroma of Mom's signature gumbo drew us through the screen door.

Louie grabbed my hand and squeezed it. His skin was rough; his hands enveloped mine like a leather glove. I returned the squeeze, took a deep breath and went inside.

"Boy, I've missed that smell!" Louie said.

"Gumbo is one of her specialties. No one's is better, not even the finest restaurants in New Orleans."

The house was uncommonly quiet.

"Where is everyone?" I asked Mom, as we walked into the kitchen.

She was stirring her roux. I knew my courage was fleeting; I wanted to get this over with.

"Daphne, Farrah, and Herbert are in Fairchild. CiCi said to start without her, but not to let that 'handsome tour-on leave' before she sees you."

I glanced at Louie, and my face must have conveyed my angst. He winked at me. My insides fluttered. Other than my father during Mom's prognostications, no one had ever winked at me before. Such a simple gesture. It wasn't a flirtatious wink but more like solidarity, that he had my back—that I was going to be OK.

"It is such a lovely evening. I thought it would be nice to eat on the side porch," Mom said.

"What can I help you with?" Louie asked.

"Not a thing, except opening a bottle of wine, your choice. Everything's ready, but let's go sit a bit. Francie, please get some glasses. It's just so wonderful to have a guest."

"Francie tells me that you and CiCi have been friends since childhood. That's really cool."

"Well, we suffered a little falling out when she started dating that arrogant husband of hers, Charles Brooks, but we're all good now. He's in a nursing home and was apparently out of scotch so ordered CiCi to bring him some. He's a drunk in addition to being the biggest jackass you've ever encountered. She'll be joining us after she makes the delivery."

"In addition to Cajun food, that's another thing I miss about the South—good, solid friendships," Louie said.

"Cheers to that!" Junie said. "You know you are welcome back any time! Next time, I will treat you to my crawfish étouffée."

"One of my favorites, as well," Louie said.

Louie seemed to have lightened up, but my stomach was in knots. I wanted this evening behind me, but what I really wanted was more time with Louie Trahan before he returned to New York.

"Is Bethany home?" I found myself blurting.

"Funny question, especially from you. Bethany is CiCi's daughter," Mom said, directing her response to Louie. I think Mom was more enamored with Louie than I was.

"I saw her the other day but haven't since. I thought she may have gone back to Atlanta," I said.

"Nope, she's still here, well sort of. CiCi thinks she has someone on the side."

Mom turned her attention back to Louie.

"Louie, I don't want you to get the wrong impression of me. I couldn't give a fig about anyone's personal life, but word on the boardwalk is that Bethany's hot-shot husband is a philanderer. She's getting even."

I noticed that Louie's demeanor took a 180-degree turn. He took a big gulp of his wine.

"I'm going to serve the food now," I said getting up.

"I'll help you," Louie said.

"I'm sorry about the philandering comment about Simpson. I could tell that upset you," I said when we entered the kitchen. "There's something I haven't told you. The person that Bethany may be using to get even, the one 'on the side,' I think it's my ex-husband."

"I'm sorry for you too," he said. "You still OK to do this?"

"Yes, if you are."

Louie seemed to recover; he was at least eating. I took a couple of bites, but an unsettled feeling began churning inside of me. The blurry scene was growing clearer. Voices were returning to my memory.

"You bitch! You can't have him!"

"Who are you?"

With Louie's information, I knew that the last voice I heard was Millie Hill's. And I knew what I heard and saw wasn't a dream but a murder. In my book, it was Bethany that pushed a stranger into the water. But was it really Bethany who pushed Millie in the water? This wasn't fiction; it was real. It was important.

"You with us, Francie?" Mom asked.

I didn't have time to answer as CiCi's return interrupted us.

"Well, that took much too long! Hello there, Louie. So glad you could join us."

Louie stood up, and she gave him a big hug, like she'd known him forever.

"Isn't Junie's gumbo the best? Now, you can't get that in New York City, can you?"

"No, ma'am, not even in New Orleans."

I don't know what came over me; I guess I just couldn't wait another minute before I lost my nerve.

"CiCi, please sit down. I have something to say, and you are going to need a drink."

Chapter 45

Francie

"Well, I haven't finished your book yet, but I'm no dummy," CiCi said. "I certainly picked up on the fact that "Eve Bastian Baker" is Bethany, and "Richard Wells Baker" is Simpson. From your portrayal of Bethany in your book, she has been mean-spirited and devious for a long time. No, strike that, she's been a real bitch. I take responsibility for that. I should have stood up to Charles."

Now was not the time to ask CiCi why she silently observed Bethany's and her husband's cruel and spiteful actions against Mom and me. Why she didn't intervene in her daughter's exclusion of me? Why she didn't defend her best friend? The CiCi sitting at our table wasn't the type to shut her eyes and look the other way. She wasn't the type who would have been pushed around by a man. Blazing a trail or adding fuel to a fire was more in keeping with her personality. Even Georgia Murphey noticed the "fire in her belly."

"It's also no secret that she and Simpson are not happy," CiCi continued. "But, Bethany could never commit murder. It's not in her DNA. Junie, tell them! Tell them, Junie!"

Thank heavens, Louie stepped in. I had never seen CiCi so emotional.

"Francie isn't exactly clear on the events. The reason I'm here is that I'm looking for a missing woman. Someone who I was in a relationship with several years ago. She worked for Simpson Baldwin's company. I believe they were having an affair. The NYPD opened an investigation, but her case has been sitting. Let's just I say I am trying to help them out. I believe that she was here with Mr. Baldwin on July 4th, the last time she was in contact with anyone. After reading Francie's novel, I started piecing it together. I came here to warn Francie that she could be questioned. 'Cause you see, I've known the Hollingsworth family for many years. My father was part of the failed rescue mission."

Louie then directed his comments to Mom instead of CiCi.

"Junie, when your family's plane crashed in the Mississippi River, my father was with the Coast Guard in Baton Rouge. He was the last person to see them alive. He has never gotten over it."

With that Louie Trahan got up and walked out. For the first time in a really long time, you could have heard a pin drop in our house. Mom and CiCi appeared stupefied while processing this information. I jumped up and ran out of the kitchen after Louie.

"Was that the something 'more' you referred to?" I asked, following him out of the gate.

"Yes."

I don't know what came over me, but I grabbed his hand.

"I know I've used up my favors, but will you tell me all about it? I really need to hear it."

"Are you sure?"

"Yes, I am."

So, we went to the dock and sat on the edge and put our feet in the water. We sat motionless for a while, until he put his arm around me. I laid my head on his shoulder. I could feel his physical strength—so solid on the outside but so tender on the inside, I thought.

The sun was starting its descent into the Bay. As we sat in silence gazing at its beauty, we saw the dolphins. We pointed simultaneously. They were leaping in the air and moving back and forth in front of us. They had found an audience and were putting on an outstanding show.

I knew these magnificent creatures possessed a sixth sense. In the past, whenever the walls started to close in on me, I would head to the dock. I'd imagine drifting away in the water to a more peaceful place. At times, the urge to fling myself into the water was overpowering, but the dolphins had saved me. Their playful chirps and graceful movements settled me. Their miraculous healing never failed me.

Louie broke the silence.

"That July 4th, a heavy fog moved in rapidly. I told you my brother's account of the rescue. But, until now, I forgot about the dolphins. Due to the fog and proximity to the shore, Dad and his crew took a boat to the crash site, instead of a helicopter. When they started back to the station, the fog lifted. There were like fifty dolphins riding the wake of their boat. One after the other, springing into the air before crashing down on their sides. Instead of enjoying their playfulness, Dad was irritated by it."

I kept my head on his shoulder and didn't want to move. I didn't want to interrupt the story.

"Theo said that Dad wanted the dolphins to disappear. He yelled to cut the engines. One of the philosophical crew members said, 'They are taking that family to the afterlife. Dolphins are part of the resurrection, according to the ancient Greeks. And, according to the Romans, they deliver the dead to the Isles of the Blessed. So, no damn way I'm cutting the engines. I'm not messing around with deliverance, no way.'"

After that day, Dad would break down when he saw a pod of dolphins. After a more than sufficient pause, I looked up at Louie and saw a tear escape from his eye. I don't know what came over me, but I wiped it away and kissed his cheek. He looked down at me; I then leaned in to kiss his lips.

"I guess I no longer need my favor," he said.

"What do you mean?"

"My favor was going to be a kiss from you."

"You didn't ask," I said, as I looked into his intense, black eyes, "so you haven't used it up."

He didn't have to ask because he knew the answer as I leaned strongly into him again. He kissed me, and I wanted it to last longer. And, I wanted more than just his kiss. But, he simply fell asleep with his arm around my waist.

I awoke from fantasies with Louie as the sunlight began streaming through the windows. I always thought that the morning sun seemed so much brighter in the boathouse. Each ray bounced off the water like a pebble skipping across a pond. I lingered trying to absorb Louie's innocent touch while soaking up the happy sunbeams. I thought I could lie here like this all day. But, it wasn't too long before Louie stirred.

After what seemed like an eternity of awkward silence, he asked if I wanted to accompany him to New York to meet with the NYPD. "Better there than here," he said.

Chapter 46

CiCi

It took every ounce of self-control to refrain from telling Francie what I really thought of her new book: What goes around, comes around.

Francie's perception of life under my roof was skewed. The ironic twist was that my mother, Barbara "Boo" Fitzgerald, felt the same way about the Hollingsworth family as Francie did ours.

One of my indelible childhood memories of my mother was of her spying on the comings and goings of the house next door. I can still see her glued to the kitchen window. Weezie Hollingsworth was always entertaining. Boo never made the guest list.

Weezie Hollingsworth intimidated my mother. (Come to think of it, maybe this fear of Weezie was why she was called Boo!) The Hollingsworth family was the boardwalk's version of Great Britain's Royal Family. Weezie wore the crown well. She was the star of every show.

Mom didn't think it was funny when I told her to give Weezie a break. That was simply how they grew them in Texas, that's why it was called the Lone Star State.

"You are from Georgia, where we have Pogo, the state possum! And don't forget the peaches and peanuts! Let her be her, and you be you," I said.

Because of the promise Junie and I made, I kept these thoughts to myself. After all, Francie's book was truly fiction.

Fiction or not, her book opened my eyes to how perceptions, in fact, become reality. In Francie's "reality," the house next to hers, with its uncluttered, manicured lawn, meticulously maintained flower beds, and pristine white picket fence presented a fairy-tale picture. In my reality, my "perfect" house was hell on earth, until I met Gabe. Junie made me a believer in the forces of the cosmos because my Gabe, my Gabriel, was a reincarnation of my first love.

It was evident that Francie didn't know me. I doubted that she knew her own mother. Junie and I always commiserated over how different we were from our mothers. We rolled our eyes at their nicknames, Boo and Weezie. Our mothers tried hard to refine us, to fit us into their mold. We tried to please them because that's what Southern girls did. That's why Junie married Hugh LeBlanc. That's why I married Charles Brooks.

In reality, the DNA of Junie Hollingsworth LeBlanc and CiCi Fitzgerald Brooks didn't fit into any mold. We were daddy's girls through and through. But, unlike our fathers, we acquired a rebellious streak. We were wild horses that couldn't be tamed.

We could never be the wives our spouses wanted; truth is, we never wanted those spouses. Junie blamed the Mercury in retrograde for our abandonment of our free spirits, organic nature, and raw essence. I blamed Weezie Hollingsworth.

Whoever or whatever was to blame, we both permitted the personality traits we preferred for our mates to be substituted for predictability, which was accompanied in our mother's eyes by solid and polished, from a fine family, and good provider. Our mothers desired those qualities for us, above all else.

Junie and I talked about those things and so much more the day of our reconciliation. It was a liberating cleansing.

We took two bottles of wine up to the crow's nest, Frankie's old room. It looked nothing like my memories—the memories I missed and often revisited.

Sadly, it had become a storage room of sorts. We found a path amongst all the plastic bins and opened the windows. Instead of the cigarettes we used to sneak in this very spot, Junie pulled out one of Art's vintage pipes, stuffed with some natural herbs purchased from a shop in Fairchild and now growing in her terracotta pots.

I attributed Junie's knowledge of the euphoric effects from wild lettuce, nutmeg, mint, and even lavender to her stint in New Orleans. As we passed the "peace pipe," we gazed out across the Bay, while reflecting back on our lives, and filling in the gaps from our last communication thirty-five years ago. Junie thought our last words were precipitated by Frankie. I thought differently. In my mind, the rift started with Weezie. Perception is reality.

At first, I believed that I fell for Frankie because of Junie. She adored Frankie, and I adored Junie. Frankie always treated me like another little sister, until the July 4th parade in 1981. I was sixteen; Frankie was seventeen.

Junie and I spiked our snow cones with vodka from her father's liquor cabinet. We slurped so many snow cones that day, our lips were stained red from the syrup.

While Weezie was busy with the awards ceremony at the pavilion, we, along with Frankie, retreated to his room in the crow's nest. I loved Frankie's room. It provided a 360-degree view. Blakely Point was on one side and sweeping views of the Bay were on the other.

Junie went downstairs to find more vodka and look for mixers. Frankie opened several windows before retrieving a pack of cigarettes hidden in his room.

"I'll take one of those," I said. As I put it to my lips, I added, "Light me up," meaning for Frankie to give me a light.

"Your cigarette, or you?" he asked.

"That's funny. Just light it, hotshot."

As he flicked his lighter, he did something to make the flame huge. I was worried he was going to singe my eyebrows! I was also worried about the weird heat that was brewing between us.

There was no denying Frankie was hot; but until that moment, I thought of him as Junie's older brother. That day, there was more than a spark, there was a palpable burst of fire, and I'm not talking about the one from Frankie's Zippo chrome lighter.

"I think I could light you up too," he said, coolly while making smoke rings. "You're spending the night with Junie, aren't you?"

"That's the plan," I said, blowing smoke out the window, so he wouldn't see the grin that I couldn't seem to suppress.

Frankie got in front of my face.

"Come up after Junie falls asleep. What do you say?"

For once in my life, I was speechless. I heard Junie clomping up the stairs and thought she saved me from answering the question. Her presence would smother the embers sparking in Frankie's room.

Junie didn't appear soon enough. Frankie leaned in and kissed me. It wasn't a peck but an open mouth kiss. From the racing of my heart and the red-hot sensation between my thighs, I knew that something was getting ready to happen. It was going to be either really, really good or really, really bad.

At first, our new-found relationship was really, really good. Actually, it was really, really fantastic. We grew up together. We knew everything about each other; before long, we knew EVERYTHING about each other. I discovered the birthmark on his hip, and he discovered that my left breast was larger than my right. From our very first night together, there was no reservation and no first-time anxiety. It was natural; it was meant to be.

Junie was the only other living soul who knew about Frankie and me. If our respective parents knew we were an item, they would have kiboshed my sleepovers with Junie. Those sleepovers enabled me to sneak out of her room into the crow's nest.

My mother questioned why Junie never slept over at our house anymore. Weezie was behind that, she assumed. Mom always felt inferior to Weezie Hollingsworth. My family only owned car dealerships; they owned oil rigs. Besides the fear that our late-night hookups would be squashed, there was another reason we wanted to keep "us" under wraps. Up until now, I viewed Frankie as a brother, and he viewed me as a sister. Of course, we weren't related, but we still felt that our relationship was taboo. Weezie might tolerate me as a friend to Junie, but she would never, in a million years, view me as suitable for her precious Frankie.

Perhaps that was why the sex was mind-blowing. It was my way of sticking it to the boardwalk society, the ultimate "flip off" to the pretentious façade in Blakey Point, the phony straight and narrow path of the Boardwalkers.

Frankie lived in Houston, and I lived in Atlanta. I loved Frankie Hollingsworth with my whole being. We were scared to write to each other, so he would call me from a payphone. We were counting the days until summer before Frankie left for college.

I was prepared for college life to change him. He was anxious to turn the page for the next chapter in life, adulthood, and his first step towards his dream career, a pilot. He couldn't wait to enter the aviation program at Ohio State. At this time in our lives, our one-year age difference seemed like ten.

I was excited to be heading to my last year in high school. I wanted to be stuck in a high school time warp: Friday night football games, bonfires, sleepovers with my girlfriends telling ghost stories, week-end parties with drinking games, prank phone calls, joyrides, sneaking beer into the drive-in movie, and hanging out at The Varsity. From this point forward, I knew there was no going back.

The summer before was life changing, and I thought this one would be the same, but different. Deep down, I knew that I would be replaced with a college sorority girl, someone his mother would approve of and welcome into their summer home. But, I was not the type to give up without a fight. I was going to make this summer better than the last, one Frankie would never forget. No sorority girl in his future was going to hold a candle to the summer of '82. I planned many sleepovers.

Perhaps it was a sign that our relationship was jinxed, Weezie Hollingsworth discovered us on day freakin' one. We couldn't even hide our naked bodies under the covers. Frankie was sitting on the cushioned bench by the windows overlooking the Bay. My legs were clasped around his back, and his large, strong hands were pushing me into him. When Weezie came bursting through the door, he shot up like a cannon. I crashed onto the floor.

I thought Weezie was going to faint. She didn't scream at Frankie. She screamed at me!

"Get out! Get out, you piece of trash. Don't you ever come back here again."

Weezie's prohibition included Junie. She was absolutely forbidden from going anywhere near me. Though this ban affected Junie and my sleepovers, it didn't affect Frankie and me. We found that alternative locales around Blakely Point added to the excitement of making love. He even pulled off a room at the Blakely Bay Inn one day.

The summer of '82 flew by. As the school year started, I found those "last" high school milestones didn't mean as much to me as I thought. All I could think about was Frankie. We'd spend hours on the phone; I even experienced my first phone sex. After we talked, I counted the hours until we would talk again. He couldn't wait for me to join him at Ohio State.

"It will be here before you know it. I love you," Frankie said every time before we hung up the phone.

Everything changed that October when I called him. It was late, my parents had gone to bed. Before that call, I didn't know that the telephone company sent a monthly bill. I didn't know that the bill identified the number called, the location and the length of the phone call. I didn't know that long distance calls were so expensive. I soon learned about all those things. My father hit the roof!

He promptly removed the phone in my room. The worst part was having to come clean with who was on the other end of the line. I started wondering if my mother's nickname, Boo, originated from her dramatic meltdown. Her boo-hoo'ing lasted for hours.

"So that's why you applied to Ohio State! You cannot choose a college based on a crush. Tradition and family are more important. Does Junie know? How long has this been going on? Have you had intercourse? Have you thought about how your life could change if you became pregnant? Have you thought about how stressful life would be with a pilot? God help us all if Weezie Hollingsworth ever finds out about this!"

I certainly wasn't going to tell that Weezie found out about this five months ago—the reason there were no sleepovers at Junie's over the summer. Mom's tirade confirmed that

Weezie never reported me after all! After her discovery of Frankie and me, I walked on eggshells around my house for days. My fear of Weezie Hollingsworth grew into absolute terror. I anticipated being grounded all summer, but I never heard a peep from my parents.

At times, I thought Weezie probably communicated my ban from their property, and Mom appreciated that was punishment enough, for both of us. No doubt, she was mortified. Now, I knew it was Weezie Hollingsworth who was mortified. She didn't want a single soul to know.

I was an acceptable friend for Junie, one Weezie tolerated each summer. Her precious son was a different story; CiCi Fitzgerald wasn't in their league.

Mom felt the same inadequacy about Weezie that I experienced. She acted quickly to nip it. After all, the Fitzgeralds were a really big deal at the University of Georgia.

She promptly called Virginia Brooks, a "dear friend from a fine family." They arranged a meeting with her son, Charles Brooks, a sophomore, and "already social chairman of his fraternity." Virginia said he would be delighted to "show me around" campus during my upcoming visit.

"Charles is a business major," Mom said. "Virginia says he plans to start his own business! He has a 4.0 GPA!"

"Well, 'boo di boo,'" I said; under my breath.

Boo di boo was my version of "la di da," whenever Mom would broadcast Boo-worthy accomplishments.

Charles dutifully gave me a campus tour. Afterward, he invited me to the Chi Phi party later that evening. Fortuitously, Lizzie, my high school friend, now a freshman at Georgia, and with whom I was staying, was already planning to take me. "They are such BFMOC's—big freakin' men on campus!" she exclaimed.

I wouldn't have characterized Charles "as a BFMOC." He was cute, but not my type. He was too preppy, too clean-cut, too stiff, too milk-toast; he wasn't Frankie. Charles' do-gooder image drastically changed after he drank a couple of beers. He approached and pulled me onto the dance floor. We danced all night. He walked me back to Lizzie's dorm. He not only asked me to be his date to the football game the next day but also the tailgate before. Lizzie was beside herself.

"You definitely have to come here now! You are living every freshman's dream, a date with a Chi Phi to the Alabama game!"

Surprisingly, I had a great time. I quickly forgot about Frankie—at least at the moment—when I was kissing Charles later that evening. When I returned from that visit, for once, I thought I should listen to my mother. Athens was the place for me. I hadn't relished my last hoorah in high school because I was focused on when Frankie would call again. I obsessed over how long it would be before I could actually feel his touch instead of talking about it.

Frankie's family wouldn't be in Blakely Point that summer—too many debutante parties for Junie. I couldn't believe it! Junie abhorred that kind of thing. She even said she couldn't wait to see her mother's face when she turned down the prized invitation. Obviously, she had a change of heart, which left me heartbroken for not being able to see Frankie.

The Fitzgeralds were new money from the Atlanta 'burbs, so a debutante invitation never appeared in my mailbox. It reinforced my feelings that I wasn't good enough for Frankie Hollingsworth. I was glad that, for once, I listened to my mother and hadn't headed north to Columbus, Ohio.

My resolve seemed to turn upside down after I talked to Frankie. He understood my decision to attend my father's alma mater. He said that my independent spirit was why he loved me so much. We would plan a weekend to see each other soon.

At a Chi Phi "Welcome Freshman" party, Charles Brooks remembered me. We picked up where we left off the fall before. I was his date to the first football game. We had fun. We made out. After the third football game, he snuck me up to his room. He wasn't Frankie; but at the time, I thought he was better. I didn't feel like trash. I felt like I was good enough. In fact, Charles asked if I were related to the "Fitzgeralds," as in The Fitzgerald Center. He seemed impressed with my family's contributions to the university.

After I spent the night in Charles' dorm room, I broke up with Frankie. He understood. He still loved me. He would always love me. I cried for hours, but I thought it was the right thing. I would never be accepted by Weezie Hollingsworth. I needed to recapture my once free spirit. I needed to move on.

When I called Junie to tell her, she lost it. I broke Frankie's heart, her beloved brother.

"How could you do that to him? How could you do that to me?" she yelled into the phone.

Junie said that I would never find another man as kind and good as Frankie. She said I had changed... then the dagger.

"I thought you valued someone's soul. You are a fraud and a fool, CiCi. You have turned into Boo. You are hitching your horse to the wrong wagon. One day you will see what a terrible mistake you are making."

"Ouch! That really hurts coming from someone who has fallen for Weezie's manipulations. Hugh LeBlanc is so self-absorbed, he could be a sponge. You are a spineless hypocrite. Don't ever talk to me again!" With that, I hung up on my best friend and the sister of my first love. I wouldn't speak to her again for thirty-five long years.

Turns out, we both were right in our assessments of each other.

Weezie Hollingsworth orchestrated Junie's marriage to Hugh LeBlanc. She delved into the backgrounds of the escorts at the Debutante Gala every year to locate her future son-in-law. She single-handedly picked Hugh out of the escort line-up.

Junie catered to her mother's wishes. I went along with Boo's. Boo was planning a huge "throw-down" reception at the Inn for the future Mr. and Mrs. Charles Brooks, V.

Into our second bottle of wine, I confessed to Junie that I ran into Frankie while in Blakely Point meeting with a wedding planner.

"Let's just say Frankie and I reconnected. It was as if not a single day had passed since we were last together. We made plans to meet again. During that meeting, we planned another meeting. He apologized that he never stood up to Weezie, but he was going to now. He didn't care what she thought or what she would do. I was the only person he had ever loved, and he wasn't going to lose me again. I broke off the engagement with Charles, saying that I "was confused and needed some time to sort things out.""

"You were the surprise?" Junie asked. "Frankie told me that he was bringing a date to Blakely Point for our family's July 4th celebration! He was so excited. 'You are going to love her,' he said."

"Yes, I was. We were going to meet you here before the rest of the family arrived. Weezie blew a gasket. There was the deb party for Viv and Emi. She was the chair of the Presentation Gala. It was 'imperative' that Frankie attend his sisters' debuts. It was bad enough that you were missing it, but your pregnancy provided a legitimate excuse. But, Frankie 'would not receive a pardon for CiCi Fitzgerald.' He didn't want to get us off on the wrong foot again. He relented to go the party. I have carried the burden of that crash my entire life. If he wasn't in such a hurry to get here, he wouldn't have flown out that morning. He was so excited to get to Blakely Point to see you and announce our news. All of our news."

"What do you mean all of it?"

"I was pregnant."

"Oh my God. Oh, sweetie, you don't have to explain why you couldn't have the baby. I understand."

"I did have the baby."

"Oh my God. Bethany is..."

"Yes, she is."

"Does Charles know?"

"Yes. But not at first. I was scared to death, but it was Frankie's flesh and blood. All I could think about was how an unwed mother and her baby would be disgraced. His child deserved honor, not shame. I apologized to Charles.

The wedding was not only back on, but also grander and earlier than originally planned."

I requested a passing of the peace pipe before proceeding. I was afraid that the reunion with my very best friend, my daughter's aunt, was going to be short-lived. Before proceeding, I made her promise that she would forgive me and take my secrets to our grave.

I then told the rest of the story. You had to give Boo credit. She came up with the plan to fix things, though we both knew it was probably only a temporary fix.

Along with the Bay house, the Fitzgeralds opened a $2,000,000 account in Charles' new business, Brooks Investments. The first night of our honeymoon in Barbados, also a gift from my parents, I delivered the news that I was pregnant. I blamed my drastic hormonal fluctuations as the reason that I initially called off the engagement.

"Charles' reaction was really quite extraordinary and appeared genuine. He said he loved me; he loved the family that we were going to have, and the one we created! I thought he would be a good father and a good husband. I did care for Charles, he just wasn't Frankie. Frankie would want his child to be raised in a family, with a father figure."

"Pass me that pipe," Junie said. "I can't believe this!"

"Please let me finish before I break down!"

"Go ahead, but when did you tell Charles the truth?"

"Boo's original plan was to wait until the arrival of a sibling, one with Charles' blood. Every day when I looked at Bethany, I saw Frankie. I knew I couldn't wait. I was becoming unhinged. Charles was rapidly climbing the boardwalk ladder and was extended a membership into the Blakely Point Preservation Society. Everything seemed to be going so well for him. After Dorothy stopped by our yard one day, Mom reluctantly relented to a modification of the plan. Do you remember Dorothy? The boardwalk busy-body?"

"Yes, I know her well. A walking sack of negative energy."

"Ha. Yes. Anyway, Dorothy seemed to have a lot of intel about the Boardwalkers who had invested in Charles' new business. Mom didn't think Charles would do anything to jeopardize his boardwalk connections, but she wasn't going to take any chances. She wanted to do everything possible to make sure he didn't leave me. So even with the lowdown from Dorothy, she brought two presents to Bethany's first birthday. Basically, Boo bought his silence and commitment until Bethany was an adult. She paid him off."

"What do you mean, paid him off?"

"My parents' gift to Bethany was a $1,000,000 trust fund, which vested when she turned twenty-one. The second gift was a $5,000,000 trust, but that trust was for Charles and me. It also vested in twenty-one years but only if we were still married. After my parents left, Charles went and bought a bottle of Dom Pérignon! I knew the trust fund was the reason for the champagne, but he announced that he received another large investment from a "Boardwalker." As we celebrated his new account, I told him the truth. I tempered it as much as I could. It was a mistake. I ran into Frankie while in Blakely Point making wedding arrangements. I explained to Charles that it just happened. It could never happen again."

Junie remained calm until I said, "It could never happen again." I shouldn't have been so insensitive. It just came out. She started crying. I thought then I had said too much.

Junie and I hugged each other tightly and cried a long time. When we couldn't shed another tear, we made a toast.

"Here's to Frankie! Here's to us! Here's to family!"

I never got to the part about what Charles did after I told him that Frankie Hollingsworth was Bethany's father. I never got to tell Junie that, just like her mother, he prohibited me from ever talking to her. Before he locked himself in his study, he yelled, "It's a good thing Frankie Hollingsworth is dead, or I would kill him myself. That entire family is dead to us. You are never to talk to Junie LeBlanc again, and Bethany BROOKS WILL NEVER STEP FOOT on that property. Do you understand?"

Charles slept in his study that evening. After he left early the next morning for work, I was folding up the blankets from the sofa. I noticed the top drawer was open in the file cabinet. There was a new file labeled: The Trust. Then I saw several bottles of scotch stuffed in the back of the drawer, and an empty one under his desk.

It was the first of many bottles that I would retrieve from his office.

Chapter 47

Francie

Louie left to book me a ticket on his flight. I was headed to the big house to shower and pack. I was hoping to slip in and out quickly, but that was not to be. As I walked up the steps, CiCi was walking toward me with one of Grandpa's pipes in her hand. She was headed to the porch.

"Oh Francie, I hope you don't mind that I stayed in your room last night. I just couldn't be in my house all alone. I'm a nervous wreck. I haven't slept a wink. Bethany's ignoring my calls."

Since CiCi had reunited with Mom, I had never seen her flustered. She was consistently upbeat. I was convinced her bubbly, yet stable, aura had buoyed Mom onward and upward.

"You can stay here as long as you want, CiCi. So, you haven't been in touch with Bethany?"

"No, despite the fact that I have impressed upon her the urgency of the matter. She probably thinks Charles has demanded something, and I'm off on a trip with Gabe. You know she doesn't approve of my relationship. I think she is avoiding me. I have also called Brooks and Anna Baker, but they don't answer their phones and never listen to voicemail."

"Can you text them?" I asked.

"Oh Lawd, honey, I don't know how to do that."

"Give me your phone; I'll do it," though I really didn't have time to deal with this. I told Louie I would pick him up in thirty minutes. I pecked away as CiCi dictated her message to Bethany's daughters.

"It's Mimi. Need to talk to Bethany. She's not answering her phone. Tell her to call me ASAP. My 1st text! Let me know you got it. Love you."

Mom must have heard our chatter and stepped onto the porch. CiCi's phone immediately buzzed.

"Brooks responded," I said, explaining to Mom that CiCi sent her first text. I showed CiCi how to access it.

"I can't read that! I don't have my glasses," CiCi said.

I read the message to her.

"Mom left for a trip. You did great Mimi!"

"Oh, no! What can I do now? I sure don't want to cause Brooks any worry, and I'm not about to call Simpson."

Mom piped in.

"Do you really think that man is staying with his children? I bet not. Francie, ask her who is watching them."

I was getting panicked; I didn't know how long this exchange was going to take and didn't want to discuss my plans about New York in front of CiCi.

I quickly typed: "Who is staying with you?"

I thought that children that age were so odd. They would rapidly respond to a text but wouldn't answer their phone or listen to a voicemail message.

"The Pooles," Brooks responded immediately.

"That's their next-door neighbor," CiCi said. "Ask her for Claire's number; she's the mother."

"Can you send me Claire's number, please?"

"She is out of town too."

"Good Lord, are those children all alone?" CiCi asked. "What do I do now?"

I took her phone again and typed: "So you are at the Pooles' all alone?"

"Ha Ha. No, Mr. Poole is here. I'll send you his number. LOL!" Brooks responded.

"Thank you, Francie! I am so relieved. I'd rather talk to James than Claire any ol' day. Never cared for her. A wannabe, for sure, and a snake in the grass."

"I've got to run take a shower," trying not to exude the manner of someone pressed for time. "Let me know if you need more help."

As I headed inside, I heard Mom tell CiCi she reached Edward Bastian. She asked him for the best criminal attorney, to spare no expense, and that she needed someone pronto.

My mother was not only one tough lady but also loyal to her core. In spite of the fact that Bethany had said and done some pretty terrible things to her over the years, she sprang into action for Bethany, simply because she was her best friend's daughter. Now, I knew that Bethany was the one who had pulled up all Mom's herbs and thrown them into the Bay, and she likely placed the "KOOK" bumper sticker on Mom's station wagon. I imagine the list goes on. My mother had an amazing ability to ignore petty behavior.

I took the steps two at a time, stripped off my clothes, and turned on a hot shower. As the water was beating down on my back, I didn't know what the day held for me. But with Louie by my side, I wasn't afraid.

I quickly packed a bag. Mom was still on the back porch with CiCi. She had reached Claire's husband, James. He expected Bethany would be checking in and would give her the message to call.

"That's all I can do," CiCi said, as she started puffing on Grandpa's pipe.

While CiCi was soaking up the herbs in the pipe, I motioned Mom back inside the house.

"I'm headed to New York with Louie to meet with the NYPD. Better there than create a scene here. Let's keep that to ourselves."

She hugged me.

"Louie is a good man. I feel it in my bones. A good soul."

"I agree. I'll call you."

I was ten minutes late pulling up to the Inn. Louie was out front looking at his watch. I could tell that he was one for precision and timeliness. As he got into the car, I apologized and explained my delay.

"CiCi is a mess. I've never seen her like this but, apparently, Bethany is on a trip and not returning her calls. I had to teach her how to text her granddaughters! Needless to say, that ordeal delayed me."

"Well, she's doing all she can; that's all that can be expected of anyone."

"Yes, and Mom has been busy trying to find Bethany a lawyer. Of all people! My mother helping Bethany."

"Your mother is a good soul."

"Funny, she said the same thing about you."

"I don't know about that...about last night," he started, and I thought, oh no, here it comes. He had too much to drink and a hundred other excuses. I wasn't good at hiding my emotions. He must have picked up on the distraught look on my face.

"The tequila, bourbon, and the wine weren't the reason I stayed last night. I just really wanted to hold onto you. I wanted to get that out there."

"I'm glad you stayed."

He leaned over and kissed me on the cheek.

"I talked to Antonio, he's my contact with the NYPD, and we are meeting him right after we land. Thought it would be best to get this over with as soon as possible. He is going to meet us at the airport."

"Yes, the sooner, the better."

"I'm going to ask you something," Louie said, with a serious look in his eyes. "If you don't want to answer, just tell me it's none of my business."

I had only known Louie Trahan less than twenty-four hours, but I felt a deeper connection with him than anyone, other than my mother. I felt like I could talk to him about anything.

"You mentioned that you believe that Bethany is seeing your ex-husband. What makes you think that?"

I gave him the abridged version of my eavesdropping on Nancy and Georgia's conversation when I left Edward and Xavier's dinner party, as well as Georgia's confrontation of Henry on the phone. Surprisingly, he started laughing. He couldn't stop.

"I'm sorry," he muffled between laughs. "You've got to admit that is funny. In addition to being an author, you could be a private investigator! But I just can't picture you sitting in the bushes and spying."

"Well, I wasn't IN the bushes, per se."

Then, I began laughing too. I realized what a kooky story it was, appropriately living up to our family reputation of being the kooks of the boardwalk. Before I camped out "in his bushes" that night, Edward Bastian's advice came crashing back into my head.

"I do believe that each turn in our life path—whether good, bad, or ugly—is essential in our growth as we journey through this life. Dwelling over the 'what-ifs' or 'do-overs' of the past consumes energy that should be conserved and tapped for what lies ahead."

Without all those events, Louie Trahan wouldn't have landed in my bed last night. He wouldn't be sitting in the passenger seat of my car heading to the airport for New York.

Louie warned that our connecting flight in Atlanta was tight. In the past, tight connections and delays would set off a panic attack, making Valium an essential travel companion. With this news, I realized it never occurred to me to pack my meds. More importantly, I realized that I didn't care. There was something about Louie's mere presence that made me feel safe and secure.

When we landed in Atlanta, we hurried to the closest display screen, which revealed we had to change concourses.

"We don't have time to wait on the train."

Louie grabbed my hand and off we ran. He maneuvered through the crowd like a man on a mission. I held his hand tightly and mindlessly followed his strategic movements; we even ran on the moving sidewalk. It was a defining moment. I knew I had fallen for him. I giggled inside, realizing how silly that was.

Question: "When did you know that you were in love with Louie Trahan?"

Answer. "When he grabbed my hand in the Atlanta airport, dragged me through mobs of travelers and sprinted on the moving sidewalk for our connecting flight to New York to meet with the NYPD!"

Indeed, I was a kook, but I couldn't help what I was feeling.

We heard our names being announced over the airport intercom speaker.

"That's us!" Louie yelled at the woman at the gate, and we picked up our pace. Several passengers were on stand-by. Louie informed me that if we missed the connection, we would also miss the meeting with Antonio, who didn't have much time before reporting to duty. I sensed that Louie, like me, wanted to get this behind us as soon as possible.

As we made our way past those relaxed passengers in the first-class section, already enjoying complimentary cocktails, I saw Bethany. She was sipping on champagne. She didn't notice me because she was engrossed in my novel, *After the Crash & Burn*.

Immediately after Louie and I found our seats, the flight attendant began the recitation of flight preparation, and we were wheels up. There is something to be said about a last-minute arrival. No wasted time, I thought before I surprisingly drifted off to sleep.

I slept during the entire flight. Admittedly, I didn't think I slept at all last night, but I had never been able to sleep on a plane, even with Valium beforehand.

Louie was waiting for me when we deplaned. On the way to our seats, I had whispered to him that Bethany Baldwin was sitting in first-class.

"Ironic, isn't it?" he said. "We are all under one roof."

Louie noticed the increasing angst on my face. He put his arm around me as we headed toward the terminal. We must have seen the driver simultaneously. A man was holding up two signs, one in each hand: Bethany Baldwin and Henry DeVries.

"Wait here," Louie said to me, as he approached the driver.

I wondered what he was doing. I nervously looked around for Bethany. Louie clearly was up to something. He approached me with a big grin on his face. He obtained the driver's business card, identifying the service company along with the driver's number.

"I thought Antonio may want this. Someone's get-away just got a little more interesting!"

He grabbed my hand and gave it an especially tight squeeze.

"Keep to the facts in your book," Louie instructed, as we approached Lieutenant Antonia Rodriguez. "Don't mention anything about Henry and Bethany. Don't mention that you originally thought it was Bethany on the dock. One more thing, did you go to the Brooks' dock after that day, you know to look around?"

"No, why?"

"Just curious. You'll do great. I'm the one who may be in trouble here, but it is what it is."

As expected, Louie took control. He told Lieutenant Rodriguez about his high school reunion. He picked up my new release at the airport bookstore. He read my first book and was a fan. His flight was delayed, so he bought the sequel. Prior to that time, he researched Simpson Baldwin. When he revealed that fact, Lieutenant Rodriguez just shook his head.

"Look, Antonio, I know you told me not to meddle, but you and I both know that missing persons are the lowest priority in the department, especially when there is no one pushing the department's buttons. Anyway, here's a copy of Francie's novel. I marked the chapters that jumped out at me and prompted me to call my old squadron while I was in Baton Rouge. They arranged for scuba gear and a boat from the Mobile station. I didn't tell them why I was there. I didn't want them involved. I only got close enough to confirm there is a body in the Bay."

"Holy shit!" he said scratching his head. "OK, first things first. Can you pinpoint an area of the Bay?"

I gave him my address, and the address for Charles Brooks' home. He abruptly shot up from the bench and began making some calls. He was clearly agitated when he returned.

"I don't know what to say, Louie. I understand that your job involves search and rescue, and you did locate a body. If it is Millicent Hill's, you will get a return visit from Officer

Barrett. Let's just keep our prior exchange of information out of this."

"You got it," Louie said.

"Scuba diving is one thing, Louie; when you contacted Mrs. DeVries, well, you crossed the line."

"I understand, but can I explain?"

"Do I have a choice?" Louie said exasperated.

Louie repeated what he told Mom and CiCi about his father's failed rescue of my grandparents, aunts and uncle. It had been hard enough for me to deal with the tragedy, even though I never knew them. Who would have ever known that a complete stranger also suffered over the incident?

"I'm really sorry, but I can't say I wouldn't do it again. Whatever the consequences, I will be able to accept those more than keeping silent."

"I understand, but it's not up to me. You know that. Now the question is Mrs. DeVries, why did you keep silent?"

I explained that the crash had taken a great toll on my mother. Growing up, I was greatly affected by her withdrawals, bouts of depression, and undiagnosed issues. Everyone thought she was crazy.

"Needless to say, my childhood had its challenges. It wasn't until later that I, too, began experiencing anxiety, depression, and a host of other things. Prescribed meds helped with my writing."

I told him about the earlier incident on the dock where I observed Simpson with another woman but discounted it due to the meds. I fully disclosed that on the night of the incident, I abused my meds with alcohol. I explained the side effects I often experienced.

"I don't know if it was the same woman or not. Simpson doesn't have the best of reputations in the marital loyalty department. It was dark. I only heard one voice clearly, and I didn't recognize it. After that night, there was never any activity—no police, no investigators, no one reported missing. It seemed like a dream. So that's what I thought, and it cured my writer's block. Sir, if I truly thought that I witnessed a murder, I wouldn't have written about it. I would have gone to the police."

"I appreciate the information from both of you, but first things first. The body needs to be identified. The local authorities are already heading to the location. Mrs. DeVries, you will be contacted by them when you return."

"I understand."

"One other thing," Louie said.

"Really, Louie?" Lieutenant Rodriguez asked, clearly frustrated.

"Here," as he handed him the driver's information.

"Just so happens Bethany Baldwin was on our flight—TOTALLY coincidental—I swear to God. On our way to meet you, we passed a driver holding up a sign for one "Bethany Baldwin." Before you lose it, she wasn't there yet. I simply asked for his card in case I needed a car. I'm passing it on, just in case you need to have a little chat with her while she's in town."

"Always thinking, aren't you, Bud? Like I said, Officer Barrett will be in touch. Not that you will listen but let us take it from here."

"Aye, aye, sir," Louie said, as he saluted his friend.

After Lieutenant Rodriguez was out of sight, Louie said, "Today calls for day drinking."

I saluted him.

"Aye, aye, sir!"

I never experienced "day drinking," but I hoped this one would be the first of many firsts with Louis Gustave Trahan.

Chapter 48

Bethany

After freshening up in the restroom, I checked out the display screen on the status of Henry's flight to LaGuardia from Ann Arbor. I couldn't wait for our four-day get away to begin, but it would have to wait at least forty-five long minutes.

During our last call, Henry excitedly announced that he had an outstanding agenda for us "inside and outside the room." I was more than curious on the "outside part," but I was mostly excited about the "inside part" of the agenda. I was really looking forward to all of his surprises.

I walked into an airport bar and ordered a double martini. Simpson never planned trips just for us. Even before things began to spiral downward, our trips together were woven into his business trips, that is, before my accompaniment became "unprofessional."

While I was biding time at the bar with my drink, I pulled out Francie DeVries' new novel. Admittedly, it was quite good. I was hooked even after it became evident that her unflattering character, "Eve Bastian Baker," was me. I was saddened by how I was viewed through the eyes of Francie DeVries over the years. Her perspective was quite jaded, I thought; she obviously wouldn't see things from my viewpoint. Her family was whacko and even scary, particularly through the eyes of an insensitive teenager. But, we all grow up and change. This trip was clearly evidence of that. Perhaps, one day, she will forgive me not only for my hardened heart of the past but also for finding happiness with her ex.

I became so engrossed with the book that I lost track of time. It was already time for Henry's plane. I paid my tab and hurried to the terminal where our car service was waiting. I noticed our names on a sign and couldn't wipe the smile off my face. I felt like a giddy schoolgirl.

I informed the driver that the other passenger just landed, and I would be back momentarily. I found the nearest restroom and reapplied my lip gloss, my blush, and added a touch of perfume. I looked pretty good for a "raving lunatic." As I walked away from the restroom mirror, I said to myself, "Fuck you, Simpson."

If this weekend turned out as good as I thought it was going to be, I was ready to end things with Simpson. I was ready to surrender my 10,000-square-foot home and especially my neighbors. If Sallie and Lexie Poole were true friends to my daughters, the zip code of our new home shouldn't matter.

My happiness should matter more. I was the one who had been there for my daughters, from sunup to sundown. I ensured that every single night when they laid their heads on their pillows that they were happy, safe, and secure. It was time for their mother to lay her head on her pillow for just one night without shedding a tear.

I saw Henry approaching me at a fast clip. I beamed. He picked me up and twirled me around, then kissed me.

"Damn. You are so beautiful. I've missed you terribly! Welcome to the city that never sleeps. I sure hope you're rested."

Chapter 49

Francie

"Alrighty then. We'll start with one of my favorite spots for a Bloody Mary," Louie said.

"Is this the first course in day drinking?"

"Why, yes, it is," and he kissed me again. "But we need to get moving because I'm getting distracted."

I could feel his "distraction." I totally and completely abandoned my inhibitions and my comfort zone.

"How about a different first course?" I asked, uncharacteristically.

Without saying another word, he swooped me up and took me into his bedroom. We rapidly removed each other's clothes; he was more chiseled than I imagined. He was so strong. There was definitely something therapeutic about getting naked with someone in broad daylight—another first for me. I could literally feel the chipping away of the walls and barriers that I had erected since childhood.

"I'll postpone day drinking for that any day!" Louie said.

We showered, and by then, Louie's planned itinerary had been considerably altered. We went immediately to eat; we were both famished. We sat on the rooftop patio of a Peruvian restaurant where we shared salmon ceviche and a bottle of rosé. We hit a wine bar, followed by a locals' favorite pub to hear the world-class DJs who entertained during happy hour. Louie insisted that we try their famous tequila shot.

"I'm sorry," he said, "that was extremely inconsiderate of me to order tequila after wine. The last thing I want is for you to have a bad experience with your first outing of day drinking."

"I have an ironclad stomach after all the porch tea parties," I said, laughing. "And, I was born in New Orleans where it takes a while before the alcohol in our veins turns into blood."

"I knew you were a girl after my own heart."

The DJ started playing a song. Louie grabbed my hand.

"We have to dance to the Black-Eyed Peas," leading me to the dance floor.

Based on the name, I thought it must be a Southern beach band that I didn't know. As we were dancing, it struck me what a sheltered, bucolic life I had led. My revelries were vicarious experiences, lived through characters in the books I read and by watching Bethany and her friends.

I was really enjoying the infectious spirit from this hip-hop music genre, as Louie described it. I wasn't going to dwell on my previous secluded life. First times that come later are more spectacular, I decided. I couldn't help thinking that Louie Trahan held the key to unlock so many more.

Chapter 50

Louie

As I was holding onto Francie while we were dancing, I felt so connected to her. Growing up, she and I were affected by the withdrawals and bouts of depression and other issues that tormented our parents. The crazy thing was that the source of their pain was the same—the plane crash. Junie seemed to have shaken her demons, unlike Dad.

When I visited the house on my last trip, he was still in the recliner, but now glued to *Duck Dynasty*. I thought this was improvement from rehashing his Coast Guard days after binge watching *The Guardian*. The good news was the intense anger had vanished from his eyes. The bad news was all emotion had disappeared and was replaced with a dull, blank stare. His eyes that used to be as black as the darkest night were now a cloudy haze. I was relieved that Theo removed all of Dad's hunting rifles from the house.

Francie seemed to sense that I needed her touch. She laid her head on my shoulder. I stroked her hair and smelled her scent. I kissed her neck. She leaned her head further to the side, putting her hand on the back of my head and leading me to her shoulders. She pushed her hips into me. All I wanted was to swoop her up in my arms and carry her back to my bed. We kissed passionately right there on the dance floor, as if we were the only people within miles around.

"How far are we from your place?" she whispered in my ear.

I immediately scrapped my itinerary.

"Not close enough," I said, as I grabbed her hand and hurriedly left the bar. Those five blocks seemed more like five miles with her fingers down the back pocket of my jeans and her intermittent squeezes. We didn't speak a word; we were united in our purpose.

We didn't make it to the bedroom. We barely made it to the sofa.

Chapter 51

Bethany

I was not oblivious to the fact that most would view my life as easy and privileged. I didn't have to work, that is, for a paycheck. I didn't have to fret over one financial obligation. When the bills came in the mail, I left them in a stack on Simpson's desk. I never opened one of them, much less anguished over how they would be paid.

Neither I nor my girls ever experienced the decline of a credit card purchase from the exclusive boutiques where we shopped. Other than those credit card receipts and my receipts from the grocery store, I didn't have a clue about the cost of anything. I never spent one second clipping coupons, searching for specials, or flinching at the total on any register. I never mowed a lawn or chipped or dirtied my spa manicured nails on the flower beds surrounding our award-winning landscapes at my primary, secondary, or third residences.

Admittedly, I used to think that all material things made you happy and feel special. I certainly indulged in that theory with my designer wardrobe, jewelry, weekly spa treatments, trainer, hairdresser, our yard and maid service, our club memberships, and the most sought-after address in Buckhead. In pursuit of all things pretty and grand, my budget was unlimited. However, the only thing I really understood about the word budget was how to spell it, and that was due to getting one of the best educations money could buy. Imagine what I could have learned had I not ditched my private college after two years. I had a fabulous wedding to plan and wanted to start a family immediately.

As a former straight-A student, I was now failing in matters of life. I didn't appreciate or enjoy any of the luxuries in my life because I was empty on the inside. I was miserable.

My outlook changed when Henry DeVries became my lover. After the first time in his hotel room on July 4th, my perspective of happiness was significantly altered. He made me feel incredible in bed, but it was more about how he made me feel outside the bedroom.

On this trip alone, Henry spoiled me with a Broadway play, dinner at a Michelin-starred restaurant, a carousel ride in Central Park, and an exquisite hotel accommodation. Despite those niceties, it was the way he held my hand, squeezed my thigh, affectionately placed his arm around my shoulder, and passionately kissed me that made me feel like a princess. I was motivated, inspired, and prepared to leave my depressing, lonely, and suffocating marriage to Simpson Baldwin, the marriage that my father "arranged."

"Simpson Baldwin is from a fine, successful family in Buckhead. And, he's a Chi Phi at Georgia. I've extended an invitation for him to join us for the July 4th festivities. Trust me, he has much more potential than those hoodlums you hang out with on the Bay, like your mother used to do."

Admittedly, I was more than intrigued because of Dad's animation when discussing the newest intern at Brooks Investments. This Simpson Baldwin converted Dad's indifferent detachment in our family to passionate enthusiasm.

After meeting him, I knew why. I fell for him that July 4th. We were engaged three months later. A job offer at Brooks Investments immediately followed. As it turned out, Simpson was the hoodlum, not Henry DeVries.

I was ready to begin living life to the fullest, until the knock on our hotel room interrupted the best love-making I had ever experienced.

Chapter 52

Francie

My phone woke me up. The ring was muffled inside my purse. I was curious because I rarely received calls.

Louie was still napping, and I didn't want to disturb him. I was content to stay put with my head on his rock-hard chest, feeling it rise and fall with each breath. I was in a zen-like state and could have spent the rest of the evening just like this. I didn't know what time it was or how much time had passed before I heard my phone buzzing again.

The day's events must have really zapped Louie. His breathing remained steady. After two more missed calls, I wondered if it was someone with the NYPD.

I delicately moved Louie's arm from around me without waking him. I took my purse into his bedroom, retrieved my phone, and shut the door. It was Mom. She had been calling continuously for the last five hours. It hit me that I never called her after our arrival. Of course, she didn't leave any message. She detested talking on the phone with a live person, so talking into a recording was completely out of the question.

She picked up on the first ring.

"I have been worried sick, sick about you!" she immediately said, skipping any type of greeting.

"I am so sorry; it was so hectic at the airport. Our connection was tight, and then Louie's friend from the NYPD was waiting for us," I whispered, trying not wake Louie.

"Well things got crazy here pretty quickly. There are divers in the Bay and all kinds of activity on CiCi's dock. CiCi was hiding out here while she was trying to reach Bethany, but Bethany won't answer her phone! CiCi couldn't take any more, so she left!"

Louie must have heard Mom's agitated voice echoing off the walls. He tapped gently on the door. I put Mom on speaker. We sat on the edge of Louie's bed listening to her rants about the nerve of Bethany to ignore CiCi's calls and her description of the scene outside her window. Florescent police tape was wrapped around CiCi's dock, blocking access to the boardwalk. Swarms of Po-Pos in rubber gloves were collecting evidence, and onlookers were nosing about our house. When she finally paused, Louie took my phone.

"Junie, this is Louie. I know this is unsettling, but the police have all the information from Francie and me, so you don't need to worry about anything."

"Thank you, Louie. I also want you to thank your father for trying to help my family. I want you to tell him that they are still here; they led you to us. I am so thankful you are there with my baby."

Louie put his arm around me and squeezed my shoulder. I was thankful that he was with me. His presence alone comforted me more than any tonic, legal or homegrown. I could use a healthy addiction for once.

"You won't believe this," I interjected. "Bethany is in New York. We had a connection in Atlanta, and she was on our plane!"

"Well, we knew she was on a trip somewhere. I told CiCi that she had done everything she could to warn her of this shit show."

I didn't mention that Bethany was with Henry. If the NYPD was interested in speaking to her, they knew where to find her.

"I'm glad you didn't mention seeing Henry," Louie said, after we hung up.

"Why is that?" I asked, thinking that Louie may have thought it was a sign that I still had feelings for him. I wasn't prepared for his response.

"I just don't want you to get dragged into this any more than you are."

"What do you mean?"

"Well, I know how these guys think. I don't want to upset you or cause any unnecessary worry, but one theory could be that you wanted revenge. The police might say that you thought Millie was Bethany."

"Oh, Louie!" was all I could muster. I felt a sharp pain in my chest. I felt dizzy. I collapsed on the bed.

Louie jumped up and ran into the bathroom. I heard water running. When he returned, he placed a cold cloth on my forehead. He wiped my face, which was now covered with beads of sweat. I understood now why Louie instructed me to stick to the facts in my book and not to mention Henry and Bethany to Antonio.

"I shouldn't have said anything. Are you OK?"

"It depends," I said, regaining my composure. "You don't think I did it, do you?"

"Given the facts that we know, it's clear that Millie wasn't in Blakely Point by happenstance. She was there with Simpson Baldwin. Bethany will be the prime suspect, but I don't want them to get any other ideas."

"Well if I was capable of murdering someone, it would be Henry. He received a nice chunk of change when we separated, despite his cheating on me. He even proposed to me after spending a weekend with Georgia. I learned about that in the bushes as well!"

"I don't need to know anything else. I don't want to upset you any further. You feeling any better?"

He padded my face again with the wet cloth.

"Yes, thanks," but there was still a knot in my stomach. I wished I had never written that stupid sequel. I wanted to burn every copy.

"Good, because you scared the shit out of me," Louie said, as he wrapped his arms around me.

As Louie held me, I was reminded of Edward's wise words.

"We can't think about all the things we should have done along the way because we can't retrace our steps. We can only move forward."

If not for my book, Louie Trahan would never have entered my life, and I sure hoped that we would move forward together.

Chapter 53

Bethany

Henry wrapped himself in a towel and cracked the door to shoo away housekeeping. I knew something was terribly wrong when I heard their voices.

"NYPD, Henry DeVries?"

"Yes, sir. Is something wrong?"

"We're here to speak to a Bethany Baldwin. Is she with you?"

A million things ran through my head, as I jumped up and retrieved my clothes strewn across the floor. This must be Simpson's doing somehow, I thought. Documenting an affair so that he could use it against me when I left his ass.

"Yes, but can you give us a minute?"

"One minute," the gruff voice responded.

"I wonder if something happened to Dad?" I asked, not wanting to disclose my real thoughts.

"I sure hope not," Henry said, pulling on his pants and then straightening the bed covers. He hugged me. "You ready?"

I sat down on a chair. My legs were visibly trembling. I thought this really may be about Dad. Mom had been blowing up my phone since we arrived. I should have answered at least one call, I thought, as Henry opened the door.

Two uniformed officers waltzed into the room. From their demeanor and glares, if they were going to deliver some tragic news about Dad, their bedside manner sure needed some work.

"Bethany Baldwin?"

"Yes, that's me."

"We have some questions for you," as the silent officer whipped out some type of recording device.

"Where were you on July 4th?"

I looked at Henry in disbelief. Was this really happening? I knew Simpson's power was far-reaching, but extensive enough to subject me to an interrogation about an affair by two New York police officers?

"I don't mean any disrespect, but I'm more than a little curious as to the basis of the question."

"This can go one of two ways. We can return with a warrant for your arrest and take you down to the station to answer questions, or you can cooperate with us here."

"Arrest warrant? Are you serious? Is Simpson behind this?"

"Ma'am, we just need you to answer the question."

"Well, for your recording there, this is bullshit and a violation of my rights, but in the spirit of cooperation, on July 4th, I was at a picnic in Mobile, Alabama."

"What time was this picnic?"

"I drove from Atlanta to Mobile, so it was from the time I arrived, I don't know, around noon."

"How long did the picnic last?"

"All afternoon and actually into the evening. I stayed at a hotel in Mobile. I assume you've asked my husband what he was doing as well. Did he tell you about his mistress and his room at the Duc de Bourbon? So, you can tell him to stick it. I am not scared of him or his tactics. Are we done here?"

"No, we are not. I need to understand the timeline. You drove from Atlanta to Mobile for your picnic. Are you saying you didn't leave the hotel at any point on July 4th?" the speaking officer said, as he raised his eyebrows. "No stop for gas, wine, or a firework stand?"

"Interesting. So, he's following me too. You tell him that he can follow me all he wants. I am not going to roll over on this. I didn't get your names."

"I'm Lieutenant Rodriguez, and this is Officer Barrett."

"How much is he paying you?"

"We don't know or work for your husband, Mrs. Baldwin. We are investigating a murder."

"Murder? That's a good one. How is it that I am supposed to have information about a murder?"

"That's why we are here. It's in your best interest to cooperate."

"Who was allegedly murdered?"

"Millicent Hill."

"Who the hell is Millicent Hill?"

"Are you saying you don't know her?"

"Yes, that's exactly what I'm saying. I've never heard of anyone with that name."

"Do you call strangers, Mrs. Baldwin?"

"Excuse me?"

"Our records verify that you once called Miss Hill."

"I'd like to see that. This is bullshit! I need to call my lawyer and have him lodge a complaint against your department for interfering with my vacation."

"A vacation? Would that be with Mr. DeVries?"

"Yes, it would be. Tell Simpson that he is not the only one with someone on the side. Unlike him, I only have one, not hundreds, and I am in love with mine."

Henry had remained silent the entire time. I was worried that he was going to bolt. I mean, I would. This was more than crazy. Simpson's fingerprints were all over it, and his attempt to scare away a chance of true happiness for me. My admission that I was in love must have moved Henry.

"I think you need to leave," Henry said, emphatically.

"Sir, I must ask you, is Francie DeVries your wife?"

"Ex-wife. Am I going to be interrogated now too?"

The lieutenant ignored Henry and turned to his sidekick.

"Read Mrs. Baldwin her rights." He pulled out handcuffs as his partner started the recitation, "You have the right to remain silent..."

"Seriously??" I yelled. "What is it you want from me? An admission of an affair. Yes, I am having an affair," I stated firmly into the recording device. "I am damned proud of it. My husband has numerous affairs, so I am going to be crucified for one? There, is that what you're here for? If so, you got it."

"We aren't here about your extramarital activities, ma'am. A body was discovered at the bottom of Mobile Bay under your family's dock. We believe you are responsible for that body. If you want to call your lawyer, you are advised to do so, or you can tell us exactly what you were doing on July 4th right now or down at the station with your lawyer present. It's up to you."

I decided now was not the time for obstinance. I didn't have anything to hide. I admitted my affair. I was in New York, after all, on a fortuitous stage. I was the star of the show. It was time for me to highlight Simpson's despicable behavior. If these were his henchmen, I was going to give them a dramatic earful.

I laid out my entire day, starting with the avoidance of Claire Poole's party, one of my husband's mistresses. I communicated that Simpson had to miss her party due to a business conflict, the so-called conflict that landed him in Blakely Point.

"You need to check the passenger log that day on his private jet. My hunch is that this Millicent Hill was identified as "Pat Miller," a reoccurring traveler, who was racking up more than frequent flyer miles. When I was preparing for my evening with Henry in the boathouse, I saw a stranger on our dock, obviously another mistress. I overheard a conversation between them on the phone. He was likely with another one of his mistresses at the Duc de Bourbon, where he had a reservation. I was only upset because the house of cards he was playing with his lovers was interfering with my plans to spend the evening with Henry at the boathouse. I left and met Henry at his hotel instead."

I must have appeased them for the time being, as I wasn't being carted away in handcuffs. They said they would be in touch and instructed me not to think about going anywhere other than a return home. They were watching my every move.

After they left, I called my mother. She obviously knew something from all her phone calls. She didn't answer.

The next call was to my father's lawyer. If there was a body under our dock, I was sure that my husband, the father of our children, was either responsible or even possibly trying to frame me. I was no longer going to keep my mouth shut.

Chapter 54

Louie

"If you're sure you are okay, I'm going to hit the shower. I can't remember the last time I took a mid-afternoon nap."

"I am, but I do have one question," Francie said, as she was nervously wringing her hands.

I sat back down on the bed beside her.

"What is it?"

"Do you believe me?"

"What are you talking about?"

"What you said about Henry and Bethany and that I could be viewed as having a motive. Until I saw the driver's sign at the airport, I didn't actually know anything was going on. I just overheard a conversation, and it was from a very unreliable person. I need to tell you everything. I want to get this off my mind."

"Francie, you've had a lot thrown at you in the last twenty-four hours, including me. I can assure you that you don't need to relive any of the painful history between you and Henry or anything for that matter."

"It's important to me. I need to talk it out with someone, so I don't feel like I am completely crazy."

"OK, but don't pass out on me again."

Francie explained her association to Georgia Murphey. She never really knew her. She discovered that Georgia and Henry hooked up during their vacation summers at the Inn. They continued their hookups while Henry and Francie were dating and possibly even during their marriage. He had even been with Georgia in New York earlier on the night that he proposed to Francie.

Georgia and Henry had recently reconnected at the Bay. During a dinner that Henry arranged, Francie believed that Georgia seemed delighted to tell her, outside of Henry's presence, that he only introduced himself to her because of a dare. She told me about catching Henry and Georgia together. When she was leaving Edward's dinner party, she heard Georgia accusing Henry of seeing Bethany.

Francie highlighted some of Georgia's scenes, like the discovery of CiCi and Captain Gabe and divulging it to Bethany. She said that Georgia seemed to always be causing some type of drama. I knew girls just like Georgia in Baton Rouge.

"Sounds like Blakely Point is more like Peyton Place," I remarked. Who would have thought so much debauchery could take place on the pristine boardwalk?"

Despite the involvement of this disloyal busybody, the reality was that Bethany was seeing Henry, and that Francie, on her own admission, thought it was Bethany sitting on the dock. Her book portrayed an unfavorable image of Bethany, or Bethany's character, over the years. Some could argue that Bethany's nasty treatment of Francie since childhood coupled with the fact that Bethany was in a relationship with her ex established a motive.

Francie's memory of the events and her highly medicated state could have altered her thinking. She may have snapped and pushed Millie into the Bay, having mistaken her for Bethany.

I tried to bury this alternative. I knew that she was not capable of hurting anyone...intentionally. But, perhaps her medicated alter ego was.

Chapter 55

Francie

While Louie was in the shower, I laid back on the bed and tried to block my spinning thoughts. Was my depiction of the events of that evening accurate? It was all such a blur. Was the reality of the situation different from what I had written?

I wasn't certain of anything, and I was growing more anxious over Louie's comments about Bethany and Henry. No one would believe me that I didn't care one iota about any relationship between them. That was the truth. I didn't care. Sure, I resented Bethany over the years, her superiority and spiteful exclusion of me. However, she was no different from Nancy Summerville or any of the others just like them in New Orleans. One thing I was certain about myself: revenge wasn't in my DNA.

My mother preached against retaliation. "There is simply no room for negative energy," she consistently said, and it wasn't just talk. She definitely walked the walk. However, the "kooky" practices she employed to ward away negative

346

forces had alienated her. Nevertheless, she held her head high, remained true to herself, and now relished in the benefits. Her circle of friends adored her. Herbert more than adored her. Looney or not, her friends knew she had their backs. She was as reliable as the beautiful sunsets in the Bay. I needed to hear her voice.

"Two calls in one day, now that's a first! Are you OK?" Mom answered, foregoing, hello.

"Yes, I was just missing my mother; is that a crime?"

"No, but that is probably a first too!" she said, laughing. "How's Louie?"

Mom didn't like to chit chat, and she was never one to beat around the bush. I was wrong about her motives with Edward Bastian. Matchmaking was not her thing, but her comment that Louie was a good soul was all she needed to say. She wasn't one for dispensing gratuitous compliments.

"All is well here. I just wanted to give you my flight information for tomorrow and check on things there. Have things quietened down?"

"A little but Po-Pos are still scouring CiCi's dock and even ours."

"Ours? Whatever for?"

"Who knows. But, I am not going to stop them, especially since they know we didn't have anything to do with it."

"So, the police have talked to you?"

"Oh yes, I told them that everyone in this house, including CiCi, was on a cruise the week of the 4th, except you, of course. They've spent most of the day in our boathouse and on our dock. Complete waste of time!"

"I don't understand. Why are they on our property?"

"Well, Charles Brooks would be my guess. He has probably been burning their ears off about the unstable family next door."

"Were there any questions about Henry?"

"Henry? What in the world does he have to do with anything?"

"I'll explain later. Do you know if CiCi ever talked to Bethany?"

"I don't. I haven't heard one word from CiCi, poor thing. These nosy boardwalkers have started rumors about me rubbing off on her and that she's gone completely nuts!"

"Why do you think that?"

"Edward told me. The society convened an emergency meeting to discuss the repercussions of all the police tape on the boardwalk. It has created quite the stir. If CiCi has caught wind of that, she may never come back. There must be rumors about her skipping town, too, because there are already people asking about the house."

"What do you mean?"

"Well, Farrah said a real estate agent was asking all kinds of questions about CiCi, where she was and when she was coming home—that someone was interested in the house. Edward says the word is that CiCi's gone off the deep end. Speaking of Edward, Herbert and I are headed there soon. Xavier is cooking dinner."

"I don't know what to say about CiCi, other than I don't blame her for getting away for a bit. As for the chatter on the boardwalk, as my wise mother would say, 'that is nonsense generating negative energy.' Give my regards to Edward and Xavier."

"You're right. And, I will. They want to meet Louie! So, tell him that he has a standing invitation for the best French food ever."

"I will. See you tomorrow. One more thing, I love you."

She didn't respond. No "I love you too," "good-bye," "talk to you later," "thanks for calling," or "see you soon." I smiled because my mother had this justifiable reputation of hanging up the phone when she finished talking or listening.

Louie came walking out of the bathroom with a towel around his hips and his body still wet from the shower.

"Did you say something?" he asked.

"I was talking to Mom," I said.

I wanted to tell him that I loved him too. I couldn't help but think that my feelings for Louie were likely bat shit crazy, looney, and weirdo, all the names that Mom and I had been called over the years. I recognized that it was crazy to have such strong feelings after less than twenty-four hours together. It seemed like we had been together much longer, like he was part of our family.

My thoughts about Louie dropping his towel fizzled when he asked if I needed to freshen up. It had been a long day, and I had an early flight in the morning. We needed to leave shortly for dinner to avoid a long wait. I hoped that I wasn't imagining things, but something was different about him. Louie Trahan, a decorated Coast Guard officer, was suddenly nervous in my presence.

Chapter 56

Francie

While our dinner conversation was rather subdued, the locals' favorite steak house was full of activity and energy. The quaint restaurant was on the East River and offered views of both the Brooklyn and Manhattan bridges. There was no other word for it but mesmerizing.

The menu's front cover not only displayed both bridges but also provided their history. It was hard to believe that the Brooklyn Bridge was built in 1883 and the Manhattan Bridge, in 1909. I was amazed at the technical and engineering acumen that could have existed then to construct these exquisite, architectural marvels. And they were still functional, providing transportation for the hundreds of cars that crossed them every day. Lights beamed from the bridges, but their lights paled in comparison to the lights from the bridges' ultimate destination—New York City.

At that moment, I remembered the playlist that Millie made on her trip from West Virginia to New York. Louie put it on as we collapsed on his sofa. The songs described the opportunity offered by the majestic lights from the skyscrapers reflecting on the East River and the fear of their splendor. I wondered if he was grieving while the songs played. Since then, his distance between us was palpable. Was it due to Millie, Georgia, Henry, Bethany or me?

I tried to convince myself that my worries were a product of my shaky self-esteem. However, when he remained cold after we returned from dinner, I knew my instincts were real. What were my instincts telling me? I begged Uncle Frankie to help me with clarity. I lay wide awake in bed, as Louie was lightly snoring, and I prayed for my dead uncle to talk to me, but he didn't say a word all night long.

I must have dosed off at some point; the smell of coffee woke me up in an empty bed. I walked into the kitchen. Louie was already dressed.

"There's sleeping beauty!"

I suddenly felt better hearing those words; but with every rise, there is a fall.

"I was afraid the shower would wake you; I've been called into the station. I've arranged a driver to take you to the airport, but I have time to fix you breakfast."

He poured me a cup of coffee, then turned to his cooktop and flipped on his gas stove. He placed bacon in the pan, cracked several eggs in a bowl, and whisked them rapidly while placing bread in the toaster. I could have watched him all day, but I had a breakfast to eat alone and a plane to catch.

From the minute that Louie walked out the door, I could feel symptoms of my panic attack setting in: sweating, dizziness, and pounding heart. I wanted Valium, but I didn't have any. My meds hadn't crossed my mind when packing, despite being headed to the airport for not one, but two flights, coupled with an interrogation by the NYPD about a murder. I had been amazingly relaxed. I knew that was due to Louie's presence.

But, Louie wasn't here. The atmosphere that I initially found so exciting—the views of the Manhattan skyline, the traffic across the bridge, the people, and the horns—now formed a vice grip around my throat. I wanted to snap my fingers and be back on the Bay. I grabbed a bottle of bourbon from Louie's bar and took a big gulp and then another. "You can do this," I told myself, as I left for my ride to the airport.

I texted Louie while en route: "On the way to the airport. Thanks for arranging the driver, the meeting with Antonio, the day drinking, dinner… thanks for everything." I really wanted to add: "See you soon! Love, Francie," but I didn't. That would be something someone said in a relationship. I hit send and then spent the rest of the ride staring at my phone waiting for a response.

I checked my signal about thirty times. After each instance, I reminded myself that I was in New York, not Fairchild. You have a strong signal, you kook, I said to myself. I wanted to talk to Uncle Frankie. I even wanted to talk to Becca and Luna. They could help me. They would assure me that he wasn't thinking of Millie during the wild sex on his sofa. They would assure me that Louie wasn't questioning my innocence. Most importantly, they would assure me that I was innocent.

I checked my phone immediately after passing through security. My heart skipped a beat when I saw there was a message from Louie.

"You're welcome. Safe travels. Talk soon."

Six simple words that evoked no emotion compared to my twenty plus. Thank heavens I omitted "See you soon!" and "Love, Francie."

I plopped down at the first bar I passed and ordered a double bourbon. I couldn't get home fast enough.

Chapter 57

Junie

I was so relieved that Francie was not around to see all the news trucks, reporters, and the stories about the discovery of a body in the Bay. If Francie had been here to witness just a smidgeon of the circus around CiCi's dock and boathouse as well as our own, I knew it would have precipitated a meltdown.

It appeared that all the "at the scene" photos had been taken and evidence collected. I was hopeful that by the time Francie arrived from New York, things would be back to normal, except for the police tape around CiCi's dock. Apparently, that was going to be there for a while.

My calls to CiCi continued to go straight into that voice mailbox, and I wasn't about to be recorded. I really wanted to tell her about the realtor's car that kept stopping at her house. According to Farrah, there was someone interested in her home. Was she really considering selling her family estate? If she was, I couldn't believe she hadn't told me. She probably knew that I would have my own meltdown with that news. Having CiCi back in my life had saved me. I was with Herbert now, and he did make me happy, but there was nothing like a marvelous next-door neighbor who was also a forever friend. That is what CiCi was to me and had been since we could walk and talk.

I decided that the next time I saw that tacky realtor's car drive by, I would find out what was going on. It turned out to be sooner rather than later. When I was watering the flowers in CiCi's window boxes, I saw the wrapped car. I marched right out into the middle of the street and began waving my arms.

When the car stopped, I walked over to the driver's window. The woman rolled her window down. I couldn't see her eyes because of her large sunglasses, but I didn't have to see them to know she was unhappy with me.

"Are you drunk or high?" the woman asked me with disdain. "What's your problem?"

"My problem is you! Why do you keep riding down my street and pulling into my neighbor's driveway?"

"I am a friend of the family."

"How so?" I asked.

"I spent many summers in their home. I have just been sick about the news and wanted to send my regards."

"What news is that?" I asked.

"You're joking, right? I know who you are."

By now I figured out who she was too. It was hard for her to hide from the advertisement plastered all over her car. This was the woman who broke up my daughter's marriage, caught CiCi and Gabe, and ratted to Bethany. This Georgia Murphey was up to no good.

"CiCi seems to have disappeared. It must be difficult for her to stay in that house," she continued.

"Are you going to sell it?"

"Given that I am a friend of the family and all, I thought it is the least I could do."

"Has she asked you to sell it?"

"That is what I am hoping to speak with her about. I can't imagine what she is going through. Have you heard anything about who drowned?"

"No, I haven't. But, I'll let her know you came when she returns. Until then, don't drive by our street anymore."

She rolled her window up and sped off.

I couldn't wait for Francie to get home and tell her about my encounter with that sleaze bag. It seemed like Francie had been gone for weeks. I wanted to hear all about her trip with that sweet, handsome Cajun. Secretly, I hoped she thought the same thing. I knew the trip was about serious business, but hoped it included a little time for some pleasure. My Francie deserved a good man, one just like Herbert.

The minute she walked in through the door, I suspected my romantic wishes for my daughter were in vain. She was withdrawn, more than usual. Something happened in New York, and she didn't want to talk about it. She asked if CiCi was still gone, and the only other words out of her mouth were "good." She wanted her bedroom back and marched straight up the stairs and shut the door.

Now was not the time to pry or ask questions. She definitely had been through a lot. But something told me her mood had nothing to do with the NYPD or the panic attacks she got when flying alone. I sensed it had something to do with Louie Trahan.

Chapter 58

Francie

I was encouraged that the last two days proved that I could give up my meds. I wanted to get stronger not only for myself but also for Mom. But, as soon as I walked through the front door, I knew one thing for certain. I couldn't go near the boathouse. The uncertain question was would one Valium be enough?

To avoid the answer, I locked myself in my old room in the big house. I made it through the night; but the next morning, my optimism waned. I knew the boathouse was off limits. I even contemplated telling Mom where I kept my Valium and asking her to throw them all in the Bay. But I didn't. I knew why.

In the past, after every bad episode, I vowed to take action, to consider alternative therapies or less addictive meds. But then, like now, I made excuses. There was my agent to appease; there were deadlines to meet, or there were Mom's nuisances to overcome.

None of those excuses were available to me now. Mom was doing great. New deadlines for another novel wouldn't be scheduled for several months.

"My heart isn't in it," I told my agent when she was already offering an advance on the next one. I withheld the primary reason. I felt like a fraud. Neither of my two novels were original ideas. They simply summarized my life.

Yes, the first was hugely successful, and the sequel was on track to do even better. But, there was nothing else to write about. The thought of cranking out another novel exhausted me.

My agent thought that I merely needed a little break. "Take three months," she said. "The next one will be even better."

This time my excuse wasn't Mom or deadlines, it was the investigation. There was too much going on right now for me to ditch my Valium completely. I may need them.

Mom sensed my agitated state. I was still eating breakfast when she suggested a walk and then a trip to the spa. Both were firsts in my life with her. I thought she wanted to get me out of the house, keep me active, and avoid any down time. Activity would prevent my mind from ruminating over negative thoughts and depression from kicking in.

I couldn't help but laugh.

"Walk? Spa?" I asked. "Who stole my mother while I was away?"

"The Po-Po did, that's who. I have been holed up in this house, watching the shit show. I am going stir crazy. We need some cool cucumbers on our eyelids!"

How had Louie described the boardwalk? Pristine? As I was walking with Mom, I no longer felt provincial, I felt lucky. The comparison between this view and New York City's was dramatic. They were polar opposites. I chose this one, bucolic simplicity and all.

Edward and Xavier were pruning the hydrangea shrubs in their back yard.

"We were just talking about you two!" Edward said, as he approached his white picket fence.

He gave us both his patented kiss on both of our cheeks.

"Some of our babies are still blooming. We made a divine arrangement for you. With all that's been going on, we thought you may need some fresh flowers around."

"I think it's time for a break!" Xavier said. "How about a glass of rosé?"

"See why I love him so much?' Edward said. "That's a fantastic idea! After you, my lovely ladies," he extended his arm toward the slate steppingstones, leading the way to his bungalow.

"I guess we're skipping cool cucumbers on our eyelids," I said to Mom, as we sat down on the porch.

"Edward's is better than any old spa. There's always tomorrow for that."

I saw that Mom was going to attempt to keep me and my mind occupied. She was amazingly present. Perhaps, it was her way of trying to make up for all the times in the past when she had been absent, not physically but emotionally. She didn't understand that I didn't blame her anymore for anything. She'd probably not believe me if I told her I wouldn't change one thing about her.

As we settled in on the porch with our wine and our effusive hosts, I was reminded of Mom's comment about Farrah— that she could make a killing if she learned how to bottle her "soothing spirit." I thought it was Mom's spirit that should be preserved. It was more than soothing, it was uplifting. It was like an infusion of positivity and authenticity. She was the real deal. She had Xavier and Edward in stitches relaying the story about Georgia salivating over CiCi's house and waving her down in the street.

"How is CiCi holding up?" Edward asked.

"Well, I hate to say that there is something to the boardwalk gossip. She has skipped town. When couldn't get Bethany to answer her phone, she just left. I suspect that she is somewhere with Gabe, but she won't answer her phone either."

"It is also interesting that Bethany hasn't contacted the lawyer I referred. He's been waiting for the call but not a peep. It's too bad because he is absolutely the best," Edward said.

"As they say, you can lead a horse to water, but you can't make them drink," Mom said. "Or either, Bethany hasn't talked to CiCi. She's been in New York; she was on Francie's plane."

Edward moved to the edge of his chair.

"New York?"

I gave Mom "the look." Mom recognized "the look" because she often gave it to CiCi, Aurora from Daphne, and Farrah when they slipped information that wasn't appropriate to be shared.

"Francie is giving me the look," she said, mocking my glare. "Honey, Edward and Xavier are brothers from another mother. You can trust them completely. Right now, I trust one of you handsome men to fetch me some more wine!"

Xavier stood up to fulfill Mom's request.

"Edward, I would like your attorney's contact information. If Bethany is not going to hire him, I would like to," I offered.

Mom gave me a look, not—THE look—but one of bewilderment. Before she could say anything, I decided to put my cards on the table because Edward was like family. I laid it all out. He didn't attempt to placate me. He immediately reached for his phone and called his friend, the best criminal defense attorney in Birmingham.

Chapter 59

Simpson

When I returned home from another trip with Claire, her husband, James, filled me in on the girls' activities in great detail, down to their meals. Did he not notice that they were going through puberty and didn't require hands-on involvement with daily necessities? They just needed to be supervised.

There always seemed to be a hoard of teenage boys at the Pooles' house. Worse yet, his girls and mine had probably snookered James all weekend. I seriously doubted that they were currently at the mall. My daughters abhorred shopping mall groupies.

"Oh, and one more thing, CiCi called looking for Bethany," James said. "I told her I would relay her message when Bethany checked in, but Bethany must be having a ball. She hasn't called, not once. CiCi didn't say it was urgent, and I didn't want to interrupt her trip. I know that Claire doesn't like for me to bother her when she gets time away."

I chuckled to myself. James was such a moron. He never questioned Claire's increased time away. He was clueless that she had been all over me the last three days. "I can't get enough," she repeatedly told me. Claire obviously needed a strong man, not a weak putz like James Poole.

Claire had been the perfect distraction after Millicent's abrupt disappearance. Plus, while we were away, my people identified who was on Bethany's girls' trip. She was shacked up with that pencil-pusher accountant, Henry DeVries. I put my people on her the second I discovered the sparklers and chilled chardonnay that she was planning to share with the nerd. My people nailed Bethany. The only better evidence would be finding the geek's pocket protector in the boathouse.

I was unpacking when the doorbell rang. I assumed it was James again; he must have remembered another unimportant detail that he failed to communicate the first time. I actually laughed as I headed to the door. I knew why Claire was at my beck and call. A little bit of James sure went a long way.

It wasn't James at the door but a police officer. My brain began rapidly playing through scenarios. Maybe the girls were in trouble. Maybe something happened to Charles—thus the reason for CiCi trying to locate Bethany. I didn't consider that it would be Lieutenant Rodriguez. I was relieved that the girls were still out because the officer cut directly to the chase.

"You haven't been truthful about your relationship with Millicent Hill," Lieutenant Rodriguez accused. "Would you care to change your statement about July 4th?"

The stakes were higher; she was no longer missing, but dead, he revealed. Her body was discovered at the bottom of the Bay. I could cooperate with him now; or if I preferred an arrest warrant, he could make that happen quickly.

He obviously had obtained my cell phone records. My people had told me that I had placed two calls to Millicent on July 4th and several the next day.

I was proud of myself having the forethought to check those out as well as for the so-called reason that Millicent could have been in Blakely Point. I was also reassured by the numerous trips and sexting with Claire since July 4th— this evidence should more than substantiate that I had ended things with Millicent.

"I will certainly cooperate, sir, but not because of your false threat about an arrest warrant. You know as well as I that you don't have anything close to probable cause. If I recall our initial conversation correctly, you certainly didn't disclose a murder investigation."

"Well, I have now and expect a truthful account this time."

"The facts are that Millicent Hill and I worked together closely. Regrettably, we crossed a professional line. I broke it off because of a relationship with another woman, Claire Poole. Before you pass any judgement on me, my wife and

I simply co-exist for the sake of our children. We turn a blind eye to our extramarital activities. Anyway, Millicent did not take it well. I attempted to remain friends. Successful businessmen don't burn bridges. I called her to wish her a happy 4th. On that call, she told me she had a surprise for me—one that I would find out soon. I was going to experience fireworks like never before or something to that effect. When she said that, I thought that she was planning to show up and make a scene. Millicent knew we spent our holidays on the Bay. So, I checked in at a nearby hotel, the Duc de Bourbon."

Lieutenant Rodriguez asked me to spell the name of the hotel and its location. I was thankful that I had checked in there, and my e-mailed receipt verified the fact. I was well prepared to counter this decorated cop.

"Claire told me that my wife was going out of town and begged me to come back to Atlanta so we could be together. Claire is our next-door neighbor, by the way. It was too late to return to Atlanta, so I went to the hotel instead to avoid a scene by Millicent."

I was pleased with my performance. He didn't seem impressed.

"Who's Pat Miller, Mr. Baldwin?"

"Pat Miller is the name I use for my various lady friends, sir," without skipping a beat.

"Who was the real Pat Miller on your plane to Fairchild on July 3rd?"

I didn't think about that detail. I was confident that was an easy fix. I mean my pilots were indebted to me.

"That is a mistake. I hoped that Claire would join me, but she couldn't get away. The travel logs must not have been updated."

"Do you know where your wife is?" the Lieutenant asked.

Was I imagining a smirk in his otherwise stoic expression?

"She's out of town, and, frankly, I don't know her schedule. Like I said, we co-exist. I don't ask questions."

"I'll be in touch."

I poured a scotch. I kept my emotions intact during the questioning. But Millicent, dead? My mourning for Millicent was quickly replaced with thoughts about Bethany, who must have seen Millicent and snapped. Was Bethany really capable of murder? Why would she have snapped? She has her own boy toy. Had she and Millicent argued? Could it have been an accident? She clearly planned an evening with Henry at the house—the sparklers, the chilled wine, and her lie to Claire about being in the mountains.

I was dealt the most powerful hand in poker. I was sitting on a royal flush. My people established Bethany was having an affair, disqualifying her for alimony. She could no longer sue me for divorce on grounds of adultery. She was also likely facing a murder charge. If there was a time to leave the marriage, now was the time.

Still, I needed to be careful in my disclosures. I didn't tell Lieutenant Rodriguez that Bethany never went to the mountains but had been at the Bay house. She didn't come home that evening; she was likely shacked up with Henry somewhere. I was analyzing various scenarios when the girls finally showed up.

I didn't cross-examine them about where they had been. There were larger issues looming, like the possibility of news accounts of Simpson Baldwin's wife arrested for the murder of his mistress. This scandal could be detrimental to my business. It was time to start damage control. Bethany needed a lawyer—a damn good one.

Chapter 60

Francie

Only a week had passed since being in New York, but it seemed like a lifetime. I convinced myself that the romantic and intense interlude on Louie's sofa was attributed to the day drinking and to his need for consolation over Millie. After that, he was extremely distant, or that was my interpretation of his behavior. The last communication with him was the lukewarm text that he could have sent to his mother.

"You're welcome. Safe travels. Talk soon."

I mean, seriously? What kind of response was that after I completely and totally abandoned all of my inhibitions and, for once, tried to live in the moment? I had given myself to him unconditionally. I had been spontaneous and fun, or, at least, I thought so.

On the bright side, I remained strong in my commitment to resist Valium despite the battle raging in my brain. On the other hand, I was overcompensating with other cure-alls, like the rosé at Edward's.

When Mom and I returned home from the impromptu visit with Edward and Xavier, I continued to overserve myself but, now, my poison was her tea. I couldn't shake Edward's obvious concern about my potential legal issues.

I wanted to try the herbs Mom constantly stuffed in Grandpa's pipes. I wanted to escape to my world of numbness, to feel no pain. I wanted to be happy; I wanted to be like Mom. How crazy was that? I would never, ever have predicted in a million years that I would have wanted to be like her when I grew up.

I knew that having her best friend back in her life was a big part of her happiness, so I was more than worried about CiCi's AWOL status, as Bethany referred to her mother's disappearances with Captain Gabe.

Selfishly, her AWOL status meant that my bedroom was available. There was no question in my mind that the minute I entered the boathouse, I would head straight for my Valium. I was more than loopy. I hadn't eaten, but I knew I couldn't stomach food. My insides were beyond queasy.

I must have passed out. When I woke up four hours later, I noticed that I had missed two calls from Louie. I made sure I wasn't dreaming. I got up, splashed water on my face before looking at my phone again.

He left a message after his second call. Here it comes. I was anticipating the big blow-off, likely pending in my voicemail. He probably thought his silence this week laid the groundwork. The time would have dulled the pain. I would be prepared.

The cooler fall temperatures had arrived, so I slipped on some sweatpants and a jacket. I grabbed my phone. I tiptoed down the stairs, exited the house, and headed to the boathouse ignoring the off-limit warnings in my brain. The full moon highlighted the neon yellow "POLICE LINE DO NOT CROSS" markings wrapped around CiCi's dock.

Other than the sound and sight of the police tape flapping in the breeze, the stillness of the darkness was interrupted by that ol' hoot owl. The deep throated stuttering "Hoo, hoo...hoo, hohooo." Tonight, the owl's hoots sounded like a muffled foghorn warning of a hazard. I heeded his warning.

Before listening to the message from Louie, I poured a shot of tequila with my Valium on standby. I felt my uncle's hand on my shoulder, and he led me to the dock. Uncle Frankie reminded me that many believed the great horned owl was a good omen when it came to love, and he added, "They have exceptional senses. Listen carefully to the wise bird. It's not a danger call; it's a mating call," he said.

Mating call? What was Uncle Frankie thinking?? And where had he been lately? What was he thinking about all the turmoil beating down on me? Was he angry at Louie? Did he associate him with his father's failed rescue? Over the past week, I needed Uncle Frankie to give me strength and clarity. I begged for him to talk to me, but he didn't. So why now?

But now was not the time to question him. I trusted him. Like the wise ol' hoot owl, he had exceptional senses.

I retrieved my phone from my pocket. My hands were shaking as I hit play on Louie's message. The owl began to sound encouraging—"Hoo, hoo...hoo, hooooo."

"I'm sorry I haven't checked in before now. A lot going on here. A crude oil tanker accident. I'll spare you the details. I've also been doing a lot of thinking and trying to sort things out. I'm due some time off and will be heading south. Lots to talk about."

While his message exceeded the number of words in our last communication, it was cryptic at best. "...Heading south." Was that to Alabama or Louisiana? What had he sorted out? Was I simply a substitute for his feelings for Millie? It wasn't a clear message of rejection, but it wasn't a clear overture to see me.

"...Lots to talk about." Did he mean in person? Louie didn't seem like the kind of guy who would end things over the phone. But then, I felt incredibly stupid for even thinking that we had something to end. Our time together obviously meant more to me than to him.

"What does it mean?" I asked Uncle Frankie. He didn't answer. The only sound was the owl's "hoo, hoo... hoo, hohooo." Was I just tired of hearing the owl, or was my uncle leading me? I left the dock and went back to the big house.

Surprisingly, I fell asleep once again and didn't wake until I heard music blasting from the porch the next morning. Still in my clothes from the night before, I made my way down the stairs. There were several open champagne bottles on the kitchen counter. I peered through the window and saw that the whole gang was already assembled, including CiCi and Gabe. Mom was throwing confetti all over the porch.

Mom had been troubled by CiCi's disappearance, her lack of contact, and the continued visual of her dock as a crime scene. But, the worst anxiety stemmed from the fear that CiCi was selling her house. Mom was definitely excited with CiCi's return but celebrating with champagne, music, and confetti seemed a little much, if not full-on inappropriate, even for Mom. This gathering was over the top, especially with a murder scene within eyesight.

I knew Mom didn't care about the judgments that were likely already circulating from the Boardwalk Po-Po about this spectacle. Wasn't she listening as I was bearing my soul to Edward about the fact that I could be a suspect? Didn't she hear Edward call his friend, the best criminal defense attorney in Birmingham, and retain him, not for Bethany, but for me? This was beyond crazy!

I wanted to run right past them to the boathouse and hide away from everything. I jumped as the door opened.

"There you are!" Mom said. "I was coming in to wake you. You are missing the celebration! What on earth are you wearing? You need to hurry and change; I have a surprise for you!"

I wanted to scream at her. I wanted to march out onto the porch and yell at all of them!

"Hurry! You don't have much time," Mom insisted.

I was still stunned. Before I could form any expletives, I heard Uncle Frankie.

"Listen to your mother. Chop, chop!"

I was trembling. What was going on?

"You heard him. Now, chop, chop!" Mom said, as she clapped her hands to emphasize her point and then went flitting back outside.

What the hell! Mom heard her brother too. I suppressed my anger, pushed aside my bafflement, and took a hot shower with a generous application of Mom's homemade soaps and oils. They seemed to work their magic. I felt cleansed.

When I finally arrived at the party scene, it didn't take long to see that CiCi was well down the road to being plastered.

She had substituted her champagne glass for an entire bottle.

"You are NOT going to believe this, Francie darling!" she said, as she stumbled over to give me a hug.

Was her news related to the investigation? Given the mood on the porch, I wondered if Millie's drowning was ruled an accident and the case closed. Was this Mom's surprise?

"Seems Charles has gotten word about the police tape around our dock and has gone absolutely bonkers! He says that my association with Junie has disgraced our family name. And I must choose—Junie or him. I told that bag of hot air that was the easiest choice I was ever going to make. I chose Junie!"

Any other time, this would have been excellent news. No wonder Mom was beside herself! Charles Brooks was not going to come between CiCi and her ever again.

"It gets even better! He said that I would be hearing from his lawyer, Willard. I told him to make sure that Willard calls me at Junie's; that is where I will be staying. He told me that he would have me committed—committed, is what he said!"

Farrah was filling up glasses with more champagne and was laughing. Farrah thought CiCi was a hoot on a normal day; she was belly laughing today.

"Tell Francie what else you told Charles," Farrah said, laughing.

"I told him if I weren't staying at Junie's, I would voluntarily commit my own damn self. I also told him that our house was the talk of the boardwalk. His precious Preservation Society has been meeting secretly about us. Now you know, Francie, I don't give a rat's ass about any of that, but Charles sure does."

I wanted to ask if she talked to Bethany; more so, if Charles knew that his daughter was a suspect in the murder of the mistress of his cherished son-in-law, his long-time protégé. I wanted to ask a lot of things.

"Someone fetch Francie a glass so we can all have a toast!" CiCi said.

I didn't want a glass. I didn't want to toast anything to do with Charles Brooks. I wanted to interrupt Mom and ask her if CiCi's return was her surprise. I was too late for that. Herbert hoisted her up around the waist so she could clang the wind chimes with a spoon.

I slipped back inside for a glass of water. A panic attack was coming on. I splashed water on my face at the kitchen sink. Then, I heard everyone yell, "Surprise!!"

"Where'd she go?" I heard Mom ask.

I looked out the window...standing on the porch was Louie.

I thought I may faint, vomit, or both.

Chapter 61

Louie

When I was making my way down the boardwalk, I was still several houses away from the Hollingsworth's when I heard the clatter from the porch. I lifted the latch to the gate on the purple fence. I was getting nervous. I didn't see Francie. I hated surprises, but Junie talked me into it.

After hanging up with her on the phone, I recalled Junie's dinner invitation on my first visit and Francie's warning that Junie was hard to refuse. Boy, that was the truth.

I was able to get an earlier flight than anticipated. When Francie neither answered nor returned my calls, I called their land line. Junie informed me that Francie was already asleep, that she had not been feeling well since her return from New York.

I surmised the origin of Francie's infirmity. I intended to call her to ensure that she made it home safely, but the tanker accident consumed every minute. I had barely slept in seventy-two hours, then got distracted with new information that I wanted to share with Antonio. After I met with Antonio, I headed to Fairchild as quickly as possible.

"Look who's here!" Junie said.

"Louie, meet my Gabe!" CiCi yelled. "I warned Gabe that he better be good to me because I was smitten with a tour-on, a Yankee, no less!"

So, this was the Captain Gabe that Georgia Murphey outed. With CiCi's husband confined to the nursing home, they obviously weren't hiding anymore.

Captain Gabe's handshake was possibly the strongest I ever felt. His grip was so commanding, it gave me pause like I don't ever recall. The size of the hands in the Trahan family were legendary; but this Gabe, his hands were larger and rougher than mine. Undeniably, he could take me down quickly in an arm-wrestling match. But for our age difference, I'd think he was marking his territory—sending me a message not to mess with his woman. After all, Blakely Point was like Peyton Place. But, CiCi's unsubtle affection for Gabe, coupled with his contagious smile and confident presence, convinced me that my first impression was off-base. And, I was confident that CiCi Brooks was quite capable of taking care of herself.

"Where'd Francie go?" Junie asked. "She was just here. I told her to get ready for a surprise! I'll let you go get her," she said winking, "and darlin, while you're inside, be an angel and get a couple more bottles of champagne from the kitchen. Chop, chop!"

I entered the large foyer and from my previous dinner here, I knew the kitchen was to the right. I went to retrieve the champagne and saw Francie standing by the kitchen sink with a dish towel in her hand.

I was stupid to think that Francie would come running into my arms. Her reaction upon seeing me was just the opposite. She made no move toward me at all. She was frozen in place, motionless. Water was dripping onto the floor from the rag in her hand. Her puzzled expression was as if she was looking at a ghost. She was the one, however, who looked like a ghost. She was so pale; her skin was translucent.

"This was a bad idea showing up without talking to you first. I called twice, but never heard back from you. I wanted to make sure you were available to meet in person. I didn't want to tell you over the phone."

I didn't even have a chance to explain that things were over. She dropped the rag and gripped the kitchen island with both hands.

"Are you OK? Sit down, I'll get you some water."

I got water, retrieved the dish towel, soaked it with cold water, and wiped her sweating forehead.

"So, it's over?" Francie asked.

"Yes."

She seemed dizzy like in New York; but this time, she was standing on a tile floor, not on a soft bed. I instinctively moved toward her to break her fall if she fainted. I reached her before she toppled; she went limp with her head on my shoulder.

"What's wrong? I thought you would be relieved."

"Relieved?" she asked, with barely the energy to speak.

"Well that is probably the wrong word. I should have never said the things I did in New York."

She still looked dazed.

"I got the impression that you didn't appreciate my feedback, or you didn't see where I was coming from."

"What feedback?"

"My comment about keeping Henry and Bethany to yourself. I just know how investigators think. They examine every angle."

"Are you talking about the investigation?"

"Yes, what did you think I was talking about?"

Francie started laughing. She laughed so hard that her color returned but was fluctuating from one extreme to the other. The blood that previously drained from her face came rushing back.

"God, I need some champagne! And Louie," she said, as she squeezed me closely, "it's great to see you!"

She kissed me. It was better than the kiss that delayed our day drinking or the one on the dance floor that landed us on the sofa.

The fragile and detached Francie LeBlanc transformed back into the wild, free, and very sensual woman who I had experienced in New York. I carried her up the stairs to her bedroom. We were completely blocking out the party on the porch until we were interrupted by Junie.

"Francie? Louie?"

Junie's voice echoed throughout the house. We heard her stomp up the stairs. When noticing that Francie's door was shut, she started knocking.

"Francie, Francie, you must come out! Louie is here!"

I winked at Francie.

"We'll be right down," I said.

"Oh goodness me! Take your time. No hurry. Take all the time you want, sweet Louie!"

Francie and I laughed, kissed, touched, and repeated; and with Junie's permission, I took a long time.

Chapter 62

Francie

"Now, I'm ready to hear about how it's over!" I said, kissing Louie's neck.

I really only cared about one thing: to lie beside him for the rest of the day and night and then the next day and the next night. Was this really happening?

"Let's grab a bottle of champagne and slip to the dock. I'll tell you everything there," Louie said.

We didn't make it to the dock. We didn't even make it to the gate. The minute we stepped onto the porch, Mom grabbed Louie for a dance. Herbert was like a one-man band, blowing into a harmonica attached to some type of brace around his neck so he could strum his banjo simultaneously. Aurora was shaking a tambourine. Farrah began singing, "When the Saints Come Marching In."

I knew the words. Aurora did too. The hymn was a staple in New Orleans. It was the anthem of our birthplaces. So, when Farrah belted out, "O, when the saints," Aurora and I joined her. "O when the saints," we echoed. "Go marching in," she sang. We responded, "go marching in," before singing in unison: "O when the saints go marching in, O Lord, I want to be in the number, when the saints go marching in."

Though there were different meanings attributed to this gospel song, I thought it represented salvation, a deliverance from harm. I was certain Farrah agreed. That was why she started singing it.

The more champagne we drank, and the more we sang and danced, the less I cared about hearing the details of the investigation. I sure didn't want to dampen Louie's spirit rehashing things about Millie. I wanted the police tape to disappear, so he wouldn't be reminded of her.

Curiously, the yellow neon reflections didn't seem to be having any impact on CiCi's mood, or any of the others. I was quickly getting the sense that everyone knew the investigation was over. As I originally thought, this celebration was too early in the morning and too raucous for a simple welcome home party for CiCi. My thoughts were confirmed when Mom whispered that she wanted to tell me but waited for Louie.

"It's nothing but craziness, and for once, it isn't our crazy!" Mom said.

I wondered what she meant by that. Her comment made me question if Millie's drowning was ruled an accident.

Bethany couldn't have been guilty. The spirit on the porch, especially CiCi's, certainly didn't support that outcome.

"I want to dance with my hero," CiCi said, as she grabbed Louie. I was now more than curious. After enough twirls by Louie, I cut in. It was time for us to retreat to the dock.

Chapter 63

Louie

"Antonio indicated that the investigation was stalled. The Fairchild Police Department reported that Bethany's and Simpson's accounts of the evening of July 4th were supported by the evidence. Millie may have simply fallen in the water and drowned. I wasn't buying that. The body I saw was attached to an anchor. Antonio agreed, but the theory by the local PD was that Millie slipped and grabbed a rope attached to an anchor on the dock. Unfortunately, it wasn't secured to any mooring. There were some chards of broken glass from a wine bottle on the dock. The locals say she was probably drunk. It was, after all, July 4th."

Antonio's words began echoing in my head. "I'm sorry, Louie; I really am, but let it go. It's out of my hands. The local guys have closed the case."

"So, they concluded it was an accident?" Francie asked.

"Well, the message to me was to 'let it go,' so it was pretty clear they weren't investing any more time or resources. I couldn't let it go. Perhaps it was my sleep-deprived state or the influence of too many mystery novels I'd read over the years, but I didn't believe it was an accident. I don't know what triggered my curiosity about Georgia Murphey. I think it was something you said about her causing drama. It didn't take long to uncover more than a little drama."

I told Francie about the breaking and entering and theft charge reported by Cannon Summerville that I discovered searching police records. When he returned from a fishing trip, his apartment had been cleaned out. According to the report, Georgia caught him cheating on her, hired some movers, and used her key to remove all his belongings. The breaking and entering charges didn't stick because Cannon had given her a key. The authorities weren't interested in a lover's spat. Plus, all the items were donated to charity. The Summervilles filed a civil action against her, which was settled out of court.

Georgia's subsequent relationships ended as badly. Property damage claims ranged from slit tires to spray-painted graffiti. She also has an extensive record of stalking charges.

Francie had never heard of the movie *Fatal Attraction*, but one of the lawsuits portrayed Georgia in an eerily similar fashion to the character played by Glenn Close with her Michael Douglas obsession. I omitted the details of the movie because I didn't want to remind Francie of Georgia's seduction of Henry. The actions detailed about Georgia in the complaint made that psychological thriller look like a Disney movie. The woman was demented.

"As a favor to me, Antonio agreed to pay Georgia Murphey a visit. He thought my hunch had merit. But, based on her numerous counter allegations against law enforcement in all her previous cases, Antonio knew he had to tread lightly. He followed her for a couple of hours. It didn't take long for him to move from hunch to presumption. She was preoccupied with activity at CiCi's house. The cigarettes that she tossed out her window were the smoking gun, to be precise. They were Virginia Slims. A butt of the brand was discovered on the Brooks' dock, wedged between the slats of the pier. That was enough for him to get clearance to have a little chat with her."

"Oh my gosh! It was her," Francie seemed incredulous. "The voice that I heard on the dock...I guess it was the shrieks of anger mixed with madness that threw me off."

"Yes, it was. When Antonio went to her house, he noticed a floppy straw hat on her coat rack, with the initials BBB monogrammed on it. He remembered the reference in your book. A search of her vehicle found chards of the same glass found on the dock, and a pair of shoes in her trunk with blood stains. The same blood type as Millie's."

"So, she thought Millie was Bethany."

"Yep. A follow-up interview with Bethany revealed that Georgia followed her that day. She had forgotten that detail before. Bethany was with Henry at his hotel in

Mobile. She noticed Georgia's car following her on her way back to Blakely Point. When Bethany got home, she saw a woman sitting on their dock on her beach towel, wearing her hat with one of her father's antique anchors beside her. She overheard a phone conversation between this stranger and Simpson; the woman was obviously Millie. Bethany left and went back to Henry's hotel. Simpson's story changed a couple of times, but he finally admitted that Millie was there with him. When he returned from running errands, she was gone. He could tell Bethany had been there. He thought there must have been some type of confrontation, and Millie freaked out and left."

"Is Georgia claiming innocence? I mean is it really over?"

"Yes, babe. It's over. She confessed. She thought Millie was Bethany. Bethany was cheating with her boyfriend. She suffered a breakdown—her words. She believed that she couldn't be held responsible for her actions; she didn't know a Millicent Hill. But, I believe, law enforcement may view the matter a little differently."

Part VII

Chapter 64

Francie

Since the birth of her grandson, Mom's outlook on the July 4th holiday had totally changed.

Mom decided that it was time to fill Grandma Weezie's shoes as chair of the Boardwalk Independence Day parade. Unlike Grandma Weezie, Mom didn't want or need "any daggum committee."

"After all, I do throw the best parties," she said. "I learned that from my momma!"

She was absolutely right about that! Weezie's celebrations were clearly documented in all the scrapbooks that were now removed from storage. In addition to the scrapbooks, Mom also removed Grandma Weezie's red bins filled with Independence Day decorations. She displayed the timeless pieces of American flags, banners, patriotic wreaths, garlands, and streamers from the bin, but with her own unique flair.

The best part of the now-welcomed traditions was that Mom began sharing memories about her parents, Weezie and Art, and her siblings, Frankie, Viv, and Emi. Frank Gustave Trahan would spend hours beside his "Nana Junie" on the porch swing listening to stories about his namesake, Mom's brother and my guardian angel. Louie and I couldn't hear enough of them either.

Mom declared herself in charge of decorating Frank's stroller, then wagon, then scooter, and then bike for the parade. While creative patriotic clothing and embellishments on the various transportation modes had been the standard from the first parade, Mom eliminated all prizes for "the best" of anything, especially costumes. Mom and CiCi always dreaded the annual parade due to those "damned, patriotic outfits."

"When I was Betsy Ross, my dress was hot and itchy. It made me break out in hives," Mom said. "I was miserable and couldn't stop crying. CiCi told me to take it off. But, Momma worked so hard at putting it together and was so proud of it, that I couldn't. Weezie always loved a competition. Anyway, it must have been ninety degrees. The only way I survived was because CiCi kept dumping shaved ice that she snuck from the snow cone vendor down my back and under my big Betsy Ross blue bonnet."

When Mom's tenure as the parade organizer began, she was tempted to ban costumes all together. "Costumes are for Halloween," she said, but she wasn't one to declare rules or restrictions for anything, much less a parade. "Anything goes," she expounded, but CiCi thought differently.

"Costumes must go!" CiCi commanded.

Based on what I now knew about Grandma Weezie's interference with CiCi and Mom, not to mention CiCi and Uncle Frankie, I wondered if it was CiCi's way of telling Grandma Weezie to shove it! I didn't share my opinion with Mom because I agreed with CiCi. Mom finally relented to CiCi mentioning the abolition of costumes to Collier Duval and Priscilla Hodges, leaders of the Boardwalk Po-Po.

"Children hate them, and it's become too competitive. Everyone is trying to outdo everyone else. And it's the poor mothers who bear the brunt. Independence Day has only one 'c' and it stands for celebrating, not costumes or competitions!" CiCi decreed.

Mom implemented other changes too. The parade route would begin at the Trahan House, formerly known as the "Yellow Awning House." I silently thought this was the only modification that Grandma Weezie would have accepted to her parade guidelines.

The parade no longer ended at the Blakely Bay Inn pavilion but at the "Hollingsworth" house. Mom provided the refreshments, not the Inn. After her very first year, everyone agreed that everything was much improved. The game changers, in my opinion, were the heavily spiked red-and-blue snow cones for the parents!

After the parade participants departed, we would assemble in front of the purple fence for our annual July 4th picture. Herbert would patiently snap our family photo, which for the first two years, was comprised of Mom, me, Louie, and Frank. Then the family was expanded to include our twin daughters named after Mom's sisters, Vivian Louise and Charlotte Emerson. Herbert was added after a small wedding on the Trahan lawn. I started my own scrapbooks—and like Grandma Weezie—I dedicated one solely to July 4th.

I added captions documenting the date and event, similar to Weezie's scrapbooks. Louie teased me that Becca and Luna were jealous of my scrapbooking obsession. Admittedly, it probably was an obsession because I knew that life was precious and could be turned upside down in a New York minute. I needed to preserve the memories.

Teasing aside, I gave Becca and Luna enough of my time. My last novel was *After the Crash & Burn*. I returned to writing about my first friends in my children's book series, *The Adventures of Becca & Luna*. My real-life children and their second cousins provided me lots of great material.

Hidden within all the adventures, I incorporated lessons from my life: A perfect family doesn't exist, and what constitutes "normal" is in the eyes of the beholder. Beautiful things can be behind even a garish, purple fence. Of course, numerous odes to Junie warned of the perils of "negative energy." And, I couldn't omit CiCi's wisdoms about being true to yourself and avoiding "wannabes." I included Edward Bastian's mantra: "Dwelling over the 'what-ifs' or 'do-overs' of the past consumes energy that should be conserved and tapped for what lies ahead. We can't think about all the things we should have done along the way because we can't retrace our steps. Only move forward." I even paid tribute to Ass-Crack Miller's, "Things aren't always as they seem," and Nancy Summerville's, "All is not 'sparkles and picnics.'"

CiCi changed her opinion about Henry DeVries, despite that he finally attained his "wannabe" boardwalk status. Henry adored Bethany, and Bethany loved being adored.

"They act like lovey-dovey teenagers. They are worse than Gabe and me," CiCi told Mom.

It didn't matter to anyone, especially me, that my ex-husband was the source of Bethany's happiness. I certainly wasn't going to disappoint Uncle Frankie with any ill-feelings against his daughter. I now understood Frankie's repeated instructions to "focus on me." At the time, I interpreted them as "Quit focusing on the perfect, perfect, perfect life of Bethany Brooks Baldwin."

Frankie knew Bethany's life wasn't perfect; in fact, it was far from it. My tainted impressions of Bethany likely tormented Frankie, in addition to CiCi's silence over the years. Something in CiCi cracked when Bethany was suspected of murder of her husband's mistress.

The truth shall set you free.

It was as if Millie Hill's death exposed more than an affair. Ironically, she exposed a host of human frailties amongst the boardwalk society. She influenced CiCi, though CiCi never knew her. Millicent Hill gave CiCi the strength to unload her burden.

I was genuinely happy for CiCi and Bethany. I was even happier that Frankie's legacy was still alive for Mom. There was enough happiness to be shared by all. I struck gold with my Cajun lover and was beyond happy. I was immensely content.

As a result of the disclosure of previously guarded secrets, the celebration of Independence Day changed rather radically. New traditions were forged. After the parade, photographs, and family picnic in "Nana Junie's" boathouse, Louie took us all on a boat ride around Mobile Bay, which eventually involved tubing. Vivi never fell off, Charlotte did. Just like Luna, my imaginary friend, had prodded my dad, Vivi would yell at Louie, "Faster, faster!"

Speaking of Dad, Mom relented to the return of the tradition that he started, the reading of the Declaration of Independence. After Herbert finished the delivery, we would light sparklers on the dock before watching the fireworks launched from the Blakely Bay Inn. We celebrated not only our country's liberation but also our own. And, the people on that dock represented a lot of liberation!

After the fireworks, Mom, Herbert, and CiCi would entertain their respective grandchildren at the Hollingsworth house, along with Captain Gabe. Who knows what time the children eventually fell asleep, but they were all united in the crow's nest, Frankie's old room. After removal of all the bins, Herbert built bunk beds to accommodate Frank, Vivi, Charlotte, and their second cousins—Henry Arthur ("Hank") and Cecilia Pritchard DeVries. Even Bethany's twin daughters, Brooks and Anna Baker, didn't want to miss out on the fun. Buckhead, with friends, no longer trumped time with family. Everyone loved spending July 4th at Blakely Point, but what was not to love about spending time with Mom and CiCi?

Louie and I had endured such lonely childhoods that our philosophy was the more children, the merrier, especially with family. Hank always clutched an airplane, like the grandfather he never met, and followed my Frank everywhere he went. Cecilia, though younger than my twins, tried to run the show, but Vivi set her straight every time. I hid my smile.

After the fireworks display, the parents were not invited back to the big house. Like Mom used to "shoo" away Dorothy Reynolds from our property, she and CiCi "shooed" Louie and me and Bethany and Henry.

Louie and I would walk hand-in-hand down the boardwalk with the accompaniment of the "hoo, hoo...hoo, hohooo" from the ol' hoot owl. We'd pour a glass of champagne, sit on our big porch swing, and listen to the July 4th playlist that Louie assembled.

The songs weren't patriotic to anyone but us; they represented our respective journeys. We declared our independence and shouldered "the powers of the earth, the separate and equal station to which the Laws of Nature and of Nature's God entitle [us]...." Though I couldn't sing a lick, when Don Henley's "New York Minute" and Tom Petty's "Learning to Fly" played through our speakers, I'd join in at the top of my lungs.

The Bay Inn's fireworks grand finale didn't hold a candle to the grand finale on our porch. Turns out, Louie was a "natural," Herbert said, bragging about his favorite new banjo student.

Without fail, when Louie began picking his banjo and singing and playing his favorite Keb' Mo' song, "Life is Beautiful," the dolphins would appear in the Bay and put on a grand performance. In another otherworldly sense, the Hollingsworth family and the Trahans were reunited every July 4th by the music from the living connection to the Mississippi Delta. And it was a blessed reunion indeed!

For us, things had changed in a New York minute, and we both learned to fly. Life was beautiful.

Acknowledgements

Most importantly, I salute my three sons, who inspire me every day, and my three sisters, whose love and loyalty are precious gifts (and they also laugh at my jokes, unlike my sons).

Hugs are extended to the multitude of friends who read my manuscript (or listened to me read) and have been a rock of support and encouragement for many, many years. I have to call out several: Tammy Hill who helped create Junie, and my forever friends from Wake Forest University: Becky, Jane, Lisa, Pam, Sylvia and last, but certainly not least, Laura Cavagnaro, my real-life CiCi, who pushed this book into the "red zone."

A huge debt of gratitude to my published author friends: Susan Sparks, my law school compadre, and Steven Norton, hairdresser extraordinaire, who generously offered their time, resources, and encouragement.

There are not enough words to express my appreciation and admiration to the talented women on my creative team: to Grace Casey, Marrow Design, not only for the cover design but also her incredible responsiveness, flexibility, "can-do" attitude, and professionalism, to Erica Levy Photography, her smile is as beautiful as her amazing photography, and to Pam Saunders, SweetP.Design, LLC, whose illustration of the "purple fence" captures the authentic, whimsical essence of Junie Hollingsworth.

Finally, a gigantic thank you to the expert team of editors, and formatters, especially Rachael Cox (whose tolerance and patience is boundless) and Susan Lower, for their invaluable contributions!

Made in the USA
Monee, IL
11 May 2021